PROCEEDS OF CRIME

D. J. Harrison

Published in Great Britain by Open Circle
Publishing in 2013

ISBN 978-1-909607-06-4

Open Circle Publishing
49-51 St Thomas's Road
Chorley
Lancashire
PR7 1JE
www.opencirclebooks.com

For Emma and Tina

Also by D J Harrison

The Jenny Parker Novels

Due Diligence

Limited Liability

1

'This isn't the No 1 Ladies' Detective Agency.' I glower at Big Mick as the distraught woman with two dishevelled children is shepherded out of my office.

He looks down at his feet and his big bald head reddens in its entirety.

'Sorry, Jenny. I didn't know what else to do with her,' he mumbles in apology but I'm in no mood to let it go.

'There are agencies out there funded by taxpayers' money just waiting to help unfortunate people like her. Let them deal with her problems. For heaven's sake, Mick, I don't need this sort of thing. We don't need it. We're supposed to be running a business.' I'm trying hard to look stern but I know Mick can see straight through me.

'But you saw how desperate she is. There's nobody out there willing to help her.'

'So you expect me to suddenly sprout angel wings and set up in competition to Social Services?' Now I can barely hide my smile. Mick knows that even if I weren't willing to do anything for the poor woman's sake, I'll do it because it's Mick that's asking.

I owe him a lot. He saved my life and, although he never reminds me about it, he has no need to. Every night I re-live the horrible moments before his arrival, the dreadful feelings of abandonment and violation. Then he came with his massive strength and laid waste to the evildoers.

'I have wages to find, mouths to feed, I have no resources for this kind of crusade.' My protest sounds weak even to my own ears now. I look at him as sternly as I can manage with his little boy eyes staring back at me from his moonscape face.

The woman had told me that she was a single mother living on benefits in a Salford City Council flat. Four men had broken in while she was there and ejected her onto the street. Her protests to the police and the council had proved ineffective. The authorities seemed powerless, relying on the slow progress of the law. Notices had to be served, court orders obtained, the process would take weeks or even months. Meanwhile, they had her home, her belongings, everything.

2

It beggars belief that someone built these monstrosities in the name of slum clearance. They deemed terraced back-to-back houses to be unsatisfactory, they demolished them, displaced whole communities into these anonymous high rise blocks. When I say they, I really mean us, society. I can't absolve myself from blame, even though I wasn't born when it happened.

Mrs Mather's flat is reached by breathlessly climbing countless flights of concrete steps until I reach a walkway with a half-height wall between me and the dizzying abyss. There is a lift, it even works, doors sliding obediently when summoned. I decided on the stairs because I didn't like the pile of something in the far corner, nor the way it smelled. Instead, I improved my fitness levels with a vigorous work out. The man squatting in the lift has no idea what benefits his presence brought to my wellbeing.

Mick was insistent that he should accompany me. As usual, he wittered on about my safety, how it was a rough area.

'It's Salford and it's the middle of the day – are you implying I can't look after myself?' Mick had to back down. 'Anyway,' I said, 'you'll only start kicking down doors and chucking people around.' Now I'm here, I have the feeling that I'm the one who should have backed down.

Number 614 comes into view, a bottle green door with a small square of armoured glass at eye level. I knock, press the bell, knock again. Then I bang on the door with both fists. A tired child in a badly smudged dress eventually hauls open the door and stares blank-eyed at me.

'Can I speak to an adult?' I ask. 'Your mother, perhaps?' She continues to stare. I notice her feet are bare and although she is small she might be approaching teenage years. 'Your mother,' I repeat. 'Can I speak to your mother?' Her eyes show no reaction or hint of understanding. The short hallway has an open door at the end which emits the glow of a television. I can see a man's head and shoulders poking above an armchair but he shows no signs of being at all interested in a visitor.

I push gently past the child and stand in the doorway. Three men are sitting in armchairs watching a porn film. The one nearest to me has another child kneeling by his feet, holding his penis. She is handling it mechanically and expertly. When she sees me enter she looks up but continues with her masturbatory duties. What she's doing shocks and disgusts me, but it's the look in her eyes that reaches deep into my soul. She has the body of a young girl, but with the hardened gaze of hope long abandoned.

She kneels amid wreckage and detritus, broken toys, smashed dolls, beer cans and pizza boxes. The television flickers pink scenes of depravation. My presence has no effect. The three men continue to stroke themselves or be stroked. It occurs to me that these men are customers, with no interest in anything other than receiving the services they paid for.

'Stop that,' I yell at the girl. She looks up at me and hesitates. The man grunts in complaint. I walk over and take her hand, drag her away. She reluctantly releases her grip. The man shouts words I can't understand. There's no plan in my mind, only an instinct to take these girls away from this horror. My other hand grabs the girl in the hall and I try to lead them to the door.

The girls are shouting, again in a language I can't comprehend. I respond in soothing English. A large man dressed only in a soiled vest and grey underpants emerges from a side door and blocks my escape. The girls cower and bleat louder.

'Get out of my way,' I shout. One of the girls detaches and runs back to the television room. The man swipes at me. I release the other girl in an attempt to defend myself, the heavy blow hits the side of my head and I'm thrown against the wall. For a moment I can't move or stand, my legs are giving way. Then I gather myself in time to swat away his grabbing hands and kick his knee.

4

The girls have run away. My only objective now is to escape. My blow to his knee has only served to enrage him. There's no room to dodge in this narrow hallway. Behind me the television room offers no respite. Backing away, disengaging, gaining five steps' distance then head down, I thrust forward quickly, butt the abdomen, and, as he leans forward, smash the back of my head into his face. The pain is intense, testimony to the success of my attack. I barge past him, fending him away with my fists, kicking his legs from under him, leaving him littering the floor.

Outside, I sprint down the walkway and begin bolting down the stairwell, holding the handrail and swinging myself down each flight. The force of each landing hurts my knees. My left ankle is sore. My right leg is taking all the pounding. This is the only way to escape. This has to be the fastest way down these stairs. If he is pursuing me, he has no chance of catching me up, as long as my legs can take the punishment.

I emerge from the stairwell, breathless and staggering. Four men, one talking excitedly on a mobile phone, are waiting for me.

'Hold on.' The guy with the phone grabs me. They all look and sound Eastern European and crowd around me.

'Let me go,' I demand. The man speaks gibberish into his phone but keeps hold. There seems no way out. The men are thin and stringy, but look fit and athletic. The man holding me is a brute, he towers over me while one big hand has me by the arm.

'What do you want?' he asks.

'Social Services,' I say. 'Looking for Mrs Mather and her family.'

He repeats this into the phone. 'Wrong flat,' he relays. 'No Miss Martha, wrong flat. Why take girl? Boyfriend very upset, not nice.'

'Sorry,' I say. 'My mistake, wrong flat.'

He speaks again at some length then I feel his grip relax. 'Bad mistake,' he says, but indicates to the others to let me through.

I walk quickly away, stiff-legged, knees hurting from the percussion of my hasty descent. The Range Rover is thankfully intact. I drive to the police station in the precinct and confront the duty sergeant. I give him the address, the details, a description of the man who struck me. He writes slowly and painstakingly. It's taking an age. All he needs to do is send some policemen round there, get the poor abused girls and take them into care. I tell him this. Then I tell him again. He looks up from his form-filling and puts down his chewed biro.

'Look, Mrs er...' he glances down, '...Parker. These are serious allegations. If there are minors at risk we need Social Services present. I understand your concern. We will do everything we can. Now please take a seat over there while I get on with it.'

I sit and fidget, and consider giving Mick a ring – perhaps it might be quicker to send him around with a few of the lads. A feeling of anger and helplessness grips me. How can this be happening? Mrs Mather's flat has been trashed and used as a vice den and nobody seems to be able to do anything about it. My mobile stirs, it's Mick asking where I am.

'I'm at the police station reporting the people in the flat. There's child abuse going on, the police seem totally unconcerned, maybe you should go.'

'Better not, especially if the police are involved. Have patience, they'll sort it out.'

'Thanks, Mick,' I say with thick sarcasm. 'Maybe your original idea would have been best. I'll let you know what happens.'

Nothing happens. I sit in frustrated fury while the sergeant makes a series of unhurried phone calls. He sees me rise as he puts down the phone, but waves an admonishing hand to set me back in my seat. The policeman who arrives to take my statement looks about fifteen years old. He knows nothing about what's going on, only that I have to write it all down myself and sign it several times. I look at my phone. Over an hour has passed. The sergeant deigns to speak to me at last.

'Okay you can go now, Mrs Parker, leave it with us.'

'Have you been round and rescued the girls?' I ask.

'Not yet, soon; we're waiting for Social Services to get back to us.' I decide to leave while I still have my liberty and the sergeant still has his teeth.

3

Mick squeezes into the chair opposite my desk. It's been a busy few days, we've been short staffed. Several of the lads have had to work double shifts. When a single shift is twelve hours, I can see their point when they object to working two shifts in a row.

'Well?' I ask.

'All except Trafford Trailers are covered for tonight. I'm still phoning round trying to get a casual in. Otherwise I'll do it myself.'

'Thanks,' I say. 'If it comes to that, see how much overtime Alan can stand before you relieve him. I need you during the day, not sitting around watching trucks all night. Anyway, you've got Joan to think about, she needs you more than anyone while she's not feeling well.'

At times like this I realise how much I miss Gary. Okay, it was a different world when he was alive. He was the boss and I was scared half to death and preoccupied with getting Toby back. I remember that familiar figure perched on the corner of my desk and a deep hurt is resurrected. It's my fault he died. I feel as guilty about it today as I did that horrible night. Big Mick is the nearest thing I have to a manager. He is a huge, amiable ex-wrestler whose mere presence tends to diffuse any potentially violent situation. Although violence is something we try to avoid, it does form part of our business. GOD Security protects things that criminal elements covet, and sometimes they resort to brute force to try to get them. We have to be prepared to match that or preferably deter its use. No guns though. Gary was always adamant. No guns, not under any circumstances. Even though he was shot dead the general good sense of this policy stays with me – no guns. This is twenty-first century Manchester and there's a lot of bad people around who don't feel the same. When they turn up it's a matter for the police alone. My lads are told to walk away.

Emma comes in with a broad grin on her face, not that this is unusual for her. This time she seems even more enthusiastic than usual.

'Look,' she says, 'it's come, I told you it would.'

'What's come?'

'The tender. Remember you said it was pointless filling in all that paperwork? Well, now it's come. We're on the tender list.'

I look at this thick sheath of documents. She's right. I didn't think we had a chance with this one. A huge local government contract for Stretford Borough Council. Contracts like these are normally the exclusive province of the giant outsourcing firms that dominate the market. Now we've got a chance to compete with them. My heart leaps at the prospect.

'Well done you,' I say. 'When does it have to be in?'

'End of the month,' Emma replies.

'What? Three weeks to price it all up? That's a bit tight, isn't it?'

'I'll help,' Emma says. 'I can do costings, you know I can.'

'Thanks, you've got yourself a job then.'

Emma grabs the tender documents and clasps them to her chest as if they were guinea pigs. I recruited her from Landers Hoffman, the accountancy practice that I once worked for. She used to sit opposite me and never failed to raise my spirits even during those dark times. Now she keeps up the good optimistic vibrations and keeps GOD Security's accounts in order. A bit like I used to do for Gary but without the edge that a spell in prison brings. I've no doubt she'll do a good job, but I know that we'll have to do something very special if we're to have a chance of landing this contract.

There is something about being leered at by a man that brings out the worst in me. Across the restaurant table, Stuart Donaldson's eyes are tracing the outline of my breasts under my blouse rather than looking me in the eye. With difficulty, I repress the urge to embarrass him with a sharp comment or to hit him with a polite enquiry about the health of his wife and children. Instead I lean forward to give him a better look and press home the proposition I came to make. Security Group is the company who runs the Stretford contract this year. Stuart's company is their accountancy firm, and he's the man with the information I need if GOD are going to be running it next.

'Look Stuart, I really need you to do me a favour. I know you're bound by client confidentiality and I wouldn't dream of compromising that. It's just that I don't have the time to put all the numbers together before the tender date. As for your clients, they've had the contract for five years now. They know everything about it. GOD Security has no chance of competing with such a massive business. All I want to do is make a credible bid, something that will keep me on the tender list, maybe get a chance to pick up some crumbs later.'

'Oh. Look Jenny, I'd hoped you'd asked me out to lunch for a different reason.'

I laugh, flashing my eyes, pretending to be embarrassed. 'Oh I see.' His turn to look awkward.

'No, not that. GOD Security, I'd hoped you wanted new auditors and that's why you invited me here.'

'Well, that's always a possibility,' I lie. Things are complicated enough without the likes of Stuart Donaldson getting his eyes on the kind of business I'm conducting.

'Look, Stuart, here's the details of my Dropbox account.' I push across an envelope containing a single piece of white paper with a list of the information I want typed on it and two hundred and fifty others, purple with a portrait of the queen printed on them. 'Bear in mind that everything I'm asking for is public information, it's only that it'll take me too long to derive it myself.'

We enjoy our meal, talking pleasantries, and I leave him to pay the bill. He's the man after all, and not short of cash either. Mick is laughing when he picks me up on Deansgate.

'You'll never guess who called while you were out.'

'The queen?'

'No. Jim Almond from Security Group. Now what would he want that we might be prepared to give him?'

'The Stretford contract, and you know darn well that's what it's about. At least he's got the decency to come to me, rather than offer inducements to you.'

'He knows how close you keep things.' Mick smiles sideways at me as he negotiates Blackfriars Bridge.

'How does he know that?' I wonder.

'I told him,' Mick says. 'I said I knew nothing about the tender and that he should speak to you.'

'When was this?' I ask.

'Oh, about an hour ago.' My breathing steadies, that's much too early for Stuart to have rung Jim with the substance of our lunchtime chat. Now that would have been upsetting, Stuart doing the right thing by his client.

'Good.' I dial the number and accept Jim's invitation for a cup of coffee tomorrow morning at his office. There's no inconvenience involved. It's half a mile away from my own Trafford Park base.

4

Now that the Stretford tender has arrived I'm feeling more and more convinced that GOD Security needs to win this job. It may even be a matter of survival. Since Gary's death, new work has been hard to find. I have to face it, my talents do not include sales and marketing. Our client list is confined to O'Brian and other friends of Gary. O'Brian, now there's another reason we need to get in more work. Lately he's been busier than ever.

Jim Almond greets me with a smile and a firm handshake. I sit at a neat round table opposite his desk while he pours coffee into SG emblazoned mugs. The walls are adorned with framed certificates, proclaiming company successes and personal qualifications. He is a small man, busy, robust and charming. Having dispensed the drinks he sits down and begins to speak.

'I'll be brief,' he says. 'I know how busy you must be.' The phone rings on his desk. He tries to ignore it at first but the compulsion is too great. 'Hello, ah, yes. Look I'll have to get back to you on that. No. Well that's not good. No. Look, I'll ring him and find out what he's playing at. No. Actually I'm in a meeting. I'll call you back.'

He replaces the phone and sits back down. 'Sorry, Jenny.' The phone starts ringing again. He visibly winces. His mobile sets off and he retrieves it from his pocket, looks at it, answers. 'Good morning, how are you? Oh sorry. It's a bit awkward, I've got someone with me. No not late. Of course I do. I will. Okay, talk to you later.'

He apologises again. 'Sorry.' The desk phone stops then starts again.

'We should get out of here before one of us is driven mad,' I stand up.

'No, no.' He waves me back to my seat. 'All I want is to discuss the Stretford contract. You're on the select tender list.'

'Yes, I know we are. We got the documentation yesterday. I was surprised that we pre-qualified.'

'Do you know why you were put on the list while half a dozen more established businesses were excluded?'

'I presume they wanted us because we're local, we operate in the borough.'

He smiles. 'You're on the list because I had you put on.'

'Why would you do that?'

'Because you're someone I know I can do business with, Jenny.' The damned phone pipes up again. I feel like screaming, I also feel mortified by his patronising tone. Gary once told me that Jim Almond wouldn't give you the time of day unless he'd finished with it. My stomach churns as I anticipate what is to come.

'Times are hard for all of us,' Jim continues above the shrill ringing. I have an urgent need to unplug the bloody thing, but I also need to hear what he's about to say.

'We've done all the hard work on this one. Stretford are a bugger to deal with. Their offices were very antagonistic to begin with. They accused us of taking local government jobs, that sort of thing. You would think a Tory authority would be all for private enterprise, but not these guys. Every penalty clause is invoked, every invoice dissected and scrutinised. Quite frankly, it's a complete pain in the arse.'

'But a four million pound a year pain in the arse,' I say.

'Another reason you're well out of it. What's your turnover now, Jenny, two million?'

'Oh, considerably more than that,' I say.

'It would more than double your size. I doubt your management team would cope.' He emphasises the words 'management team' as if he's speaking about some mythological beast. He isn't far wrong, he's looking at the whole team right now.

'Anyway.' He pauses. The phone is mercifully quiet. 'There's no chance they would award it to you, believe me.'

I look into his eyes and I think I detect a miniscule of doubt but I'm not certain.

'It would be best for us all if you put in a covering price. I'll let you have a detailed bid; all you have to do is to submit it. Stretford will see you as a professional outfit and we might get to recoup some of the losses we made on the first contract.'

'What about the others?' I ask.

He smiles and winks. 'All sorted, no worries.'

'And why should I pass up this chance? What's in it for me?' At this point I half expect some personal inducement rather like the one I recently handed his accountant.

'We'll leave you alone, let you keep the business you already have. We won't go after your work. If anyone asks us to quote I'll let you decide what price I put in. Quid pro quo.' His use of Latin irritates me in a way that even the nagging phone couldn't. I know what he's saying is complete bullshit. His reps are in and out of every one of our clients all the time. What damage he can do to our business he already has. All his efforts so far have failed to make a dent in our customer base, but he has made sure that our margins are cut to the bone. Getting price increases through with SG sniffing around has proved difficult. What Jim doesn't know is that profit margins are not a concern for me. Gary and O'Brian have seen to that aspect.

The urge to shout defiance and storm out pleading mortification at such corrupt practices quickly subsides.

'Sounds like a contract we wouldn't be able to swallow,' I say. 'The forms were submitted in a burst of enthusiasm by one of my staff. I never seriously considered competing with you for it. Let me have your price, Jim, I'll make sure we avoid any embarrassment. Mind you, I'll be expecting some big favours in return, you'll owe me big style after this, Jim.'

'Don't worry.' He looks relieved. 'I'm a man of my word, I'll make sure it's worth your while.'

No he's not, no he won't are the echoes in my thoughts as I take my leave.

5

I badger the police every day about the horrible situation I discovered at Mrs Mather's flat. 'Enquiries are ongoing,' is all I ever get out of them. 'We'll ring you and let you know the outcome,' they say and none of them ever does, until now.

A young voice is on the phone asking me to visit the police station at a time convenient to me.

'What's going on?' I ask. 'Did you arrest those men, are those poor girls safe?'

'I'm not at liberty to comment,' he replies coldly.

'Why do I have to come then, is it to identify the man who attacked me?'

'No, madam, we need a statement from you.'

'But I already gave one.'

'Yes I know, but we need to take one under caution now.'

'Under caution? Are you arresting me?'

'No, not at this stage. As I say, you are invited to make a statement at your own convenience. You're entitled to have a lawyer present if that's what you want.'

My heart is almost stopped. My breath certainly is. Almost mechanically I agree to attend at 3 p.m. tomorrow, a time not convenient to me, but entirely determined by him. I telephone Stephen right away. Stephen is my solicitor, the third one I have had.

The first one lost me my liberty. The second lost me custody of my son Toby. I'm hoping that Stephen is going to be third time lucky. One thing I have learned from my bitter experience is that solicitors are only as good as the instruction you give them. And sometimes they're not much good at all. Every time I put my trust in them I seem to come out badly. The criminal justice system hasn't been kind to me in the past.

'The police want me to give another statement, this time under caution,' I explain. 'Three o'clock tomorrow, at Salford.'

'What have you been up to, Jenny?' he asks.

'Nothing. I interrupted a child prostitution racket, reported it to the police, now they seem to think I'm the guilty party.' I quickly run through the situation I discovered at Mrs Mather's flat.

'Okay,' Stephen says, 'leave it with me, I'll see what I can find out.'

I put down the phone to discover O'Brian, he with the wispy grey hair and twinkling eyes, perched on the corner of my desk. This is not a good time to be dealing with O'Brian. There's actually never a good time, but this particular one is marginally worse than most. My heart sinks further when I see the fat briefcase he's brought with him. He indicates it with a nod.

'There's a hundred in there, business has been brisk.' He smirks as if he's doing me a favour. I suppose most people might be over the moon to receive a hundred thousand pounds in cash: not me. It's too much, following on too quickly from the fifty thousand he brought in only two weeks ago.

Before Gary was killed, he persuaded me to devise a scheme to accommodate O'Brian's illegitimate cash dealings. Small amounts of cash, like the five grand I recently pressed into Stuart Donaldson's palm, are easy enough to hide. Money like that can be put in a drawer, used in small amounts over the course of a year. Nobody is any the wiser. A bit of shopping here, some holiday currency there, not a problem. Nothing to alert the authorities. Anything bigger though and HM Revenue and Customs are very alert, in fact they have teams of specialists scrutinising businesses as well as personal transactions.

There is this draconian piece of legislation called the Proceeds of Crime Act, designed to confiscate the ill-gotten gains of drug dealers, terrorists and organised criminals. To please Gary and to repay some unknown obligations to O'Brian I devised the caravan park business. In simple terms, we buy a residential caravan park where people pay five hundred pounds per month for their vans and gradually convert it to a holiday park where they pay five hundred pounds a week, at least on paper. It's all to do with the way it's accounted, after all that's what I am, an accountant.

The result is that the residential element continues to break even while O'Brian's money, ostensibly from holiday lets, passes through unscathed to end up as legitimate profit. My problem is that it only works if the amounts of money being laundered are proportionate to the size of the business. As soon as these become unbalanced, HMRC will be on to us like a shot. I didn't much like prison the first time and I expect a much longer sentence if they ever get me again.

'It's too much,' I say. 'We did five hundred last year, that was stretching it almost to breaking point. Now you've brought me two fifty in less than three months. I can't do it.'

O'Brian prods the bag with his foot, sliding it barely an inch in my direction. 'You'll think of something.' He flashes a smile then leaves.

Truth is I need O'Brian's money. Jim Almond is right when he says that margins are down. Without the contribution I'm able to channel back in from the caravan business, Mick and all the lads would be out of work. Worse, Gary's family would lose their home. I won't let that happen because of my failings.

We do all the security for O'Brian's companies, that's how he gets his money back. Instead of charging him, I invoice the caravan company. This way, we both get what we want. O'Brian's work accounts for almost half our turnover and it's very profitable. That's O'Brian's contribution to the wellbeing of all at GOD Security. Now he's getting greedy. He thinks I can absorb unlimited amounts of cash and he's wrong.

6

Stephen Bailey meets me at the entrance to the police station. 'I've been making a few enquiries, I'm afraid it doesn't look all that good.'

'What do you mean?' My heart starts to race. I begin to wonder if they brought me here because of laundering O'Brian's money.

'Well, that family you reported have hired a prominent Human Rights lawyer. The two girls you said were being abused were taken away by Social Services and given a medical examination. No evidence of sexual or any other abuse was found. Now the family are screaming blue murder, saying their poor innocent daughters have been subjected to a degrading invasion of their privacy, that it will affect their marriage prospects, all sorts of things.'

'How does that involve me? I only told the truth, reported what I saw.'

'A complaint has been made about you. They say that you assaulted the father and tried to abduct his daughters. They're accusing you of running a protection racket.'

'Listen, those bastards occupied Mrs Mather's flat. That's got to be a crime.'

'It's not as simple as that. They have Bulgarian passports, as EU citizens they have every right to live in this country. Apparently they showed the police a lease they say was given to them by Mrs Mather. They're accusing you of demanding additional rent, of extortion.'

My frustration at hearing all these lies is almost too much to bear. I breathe slowly, holding onto the handrail on the police station steps.

'It's important that you compose yourself,' Stephen says.

He's right. God only knows how I would react if I got all this directly from the police during a PACE interview. I have to admit my temper sometimes gets the better of me and has been known to land me deep in trouble.

It takes a full five minutes of breathing and standing before I can speak reasonably again. 'These smartarse lawyers, who's paying for them? They can't really be a poor Bulgarian family, can they?'

'Legal Aid,' Stephen says. 'The British taxpayer is footing the bill.'

Inside, we're kept waiting for almost half an hour before being taken to an interview room. A young earnest policeman and an older plain-clothed policewoman begin the familiar ritual; saying the words, starting the tape, recording who is present. In reply I give them my name, address and date of birth.

Stephen leans forward. 'Are you making any charges against my client?' he asks.

'No,' the woman answers. 'She's here of her own free will, any charges will depend on the outcome of this interview and our further enquiries.'

'So no charges have been formulated against my client?'

'Not as yet.'

'In that case, we will point out for the record that my client reported an incident of serious sexual abuse to the authorities. She acted in good faith, as an honest citizen. She made a statement at the time and stands by that statement in its entirety.'

'Why did you go to 614 Rutherford Towers?' the policewoman asks.

'Mrs Mather told me her flat had been occupied by squatters. I went to look at the situation.'

'Why did she ask you to go?'

'She didn't ask me to go. She only asked for help.'

'What is your occupation, Mrs Parker?'

'I'm an accountant. I work for GOD Security.'

'Does your work include debt collection?'

'Yes, sometimes. We do offer a debt recovery service to our clients.'

'Thank you. When you went to the flat, what were your intentions?'

'Only to look at the situation.'

'When you saw the situation, did you feel angry?'

'Wouldn't you? Those poor girls and those disgusting men.'

'So you were angry?'

'More upset than angry.'

'But still angry?'

'Yes.' I don't like the way this is going, I look sideways at Stephen who is calmly making notes. The policewoman, DC Whitehouse, continues her questioning, glancing down at her own notes.

'Your record shows that you get violent when you are angry. You assaulted your room-mate in prison and left her badly injured. You attacked a doctor at Hope Hospital, and even struck a barrister in court. Your anger's got you into trouble before, hasn't it?'

'Are you implying I went alone to the flat and attacked someone because I was angry?'

'We are not implying anything, only asking questions, Mrs Parker. You confirmed that you were angry, your record states that you have a history of violence.'

'Look, I was acting in self-defence. Dawn nearly killed me.'

'Dawn?'

'My cellmate.'

'And the doctor, did she attack you first?'

'No, that was a misunderstanding, I never touched her.'

'And the barrister, did he attack you in open court?'

'No, again a misunderstanding.'

'A misunderstanding that left him needing stitches and a head wound.'

'He stumbled and fell when I pushed him, that's all.'

Stephen remains silent. I wish he would do his job and start looking after me.

'Do I have to put up with these insinuations?' I ask him.

He looks up and doesn't answer me directly but addresses DC Whitehouse instead.

'My client is trying to do her civic duty here. She has seen offences being committed and reported them.'

'We are investigating allegations of assault against your client.' The young policeman speaks for the first time. 'We need to establish the facts.'

'I already told you the facts.' I half rise, a result of the seething resentment building up in me. In time I see Stephen's arm move across to restrain me. I slump back into my seat.

'He assaulted me,' I finish, feeling weak and desperate.

'What were your intentions with regard to the two daughters?'

'What two daughters?'

'The two females in the flat.'

'They were children being used for sex, one of them was wanking one of the men off, it was disgusting.'

'So what were your intentions?'

'To get them away, to take them out of there.'

'So you grabbed them and dragged them out?'

'I held their hands and led them away.'

'And the father prevented you?'

'The father? It was a man in grubby underwear, he hit me and I let go of the girls. Then I managed to get past him and escape.'

'Did you strike him?'

'He was blocking my way.'

'Did you hit him?'

'Yes, I kicked his leg and maybe hit him once or twice with my fists. I was in fear for my life.'

Whitehouse looks at her colleague, raises her eyebrows and then says, 'We'll leave it at that, Mrs Parker. Unless you want to say anything else?'

I shake my head.

'For the benefit of the tape Mrs Parker has shaken her head in reply.' She leans over and stops the tape.

'Clausewitz.' Stephen speaks as we exit the police station.

'Who?'

'Some Prussian general, I think. He came up with the tactic that the best form of defence is attack. That's what your brothel-keeping Bulgarians are doing, probably not for the first time either.'

'They've accused me of assault and kidnap! With my record I could be in trouble.'

'I doubt it.' Stephen stops walking and faces me. 'Judging by the junior team we faced in there all the police are doing is going through the motions. Don't worry, you've probably heard the last of this.'

I let out a breath in relief then anger begins to grip me again. 'What about those poor girls, who's looking after them?'

'Well, Social Services will be scared stiff of going near them now. Getting them off their backs is the Bulgarians' main concern. That's if they are Bulgarians.'

'Someone needs to do something then.'

'Not you. I strongly advise you to keep well away. If you turn up there again the least you could expect is serious trouble with the police. These are dangerous gangs of organised criminals, you might not get out alive. I'm serious. Leave it alone. Let the authorities deal with it.'

'How? The police aren't interested. Social Services are running scared and the council can't even give Mrs Mather her flat back. How will they deal with it?'

Stephen shrugs and bids me a good day.

7

Emma is showing me the results of her hard work. 'Look.' She points to the printout of a large spread-sheet thickly populated with numbers which are too small to read easily. 'I've been through the tender information, these are all the jobs, itemised with numbers of men and hours of cover.'

A pang of guilt hits me as I look at the effort she's put in. The information I bought from Stewart Donaldson arrived several days ago. What with the police interview and everything else, I've not been through it in any detail. Now, Emma has come up with her own estimates.

Emma doesn't know about my little arrangement. The last thing I want to do is disillusion her. As far as she's concerned, everything I do is squeaky clean and it's best to keep it like that, especially for her sake. If there's a problem I want it to be my problem and not involve her in any blame.

'So what's the overall cost?' I ask.

'Altogether nearly two million pounds. That's not including overheads and management. We have to take on more admin staff so they need to be added in. When I factor in office costs and profit margin, it all comes to two point four million.'

'Good job, Emma. That looks great. Leave it with me.' Right now I need to leave early to attend Toby's birthday party. My ex-husband, Tim, has been even more difficult lately when it comes to me having time with Toby. I am amazed that he has invited me to the party. I presume his new wife is preoccupied with the new baby.

The party is in a pub, an odd place for a fifth birthday at first glance, but it's one of those appalling establishments that caters for families by having a ball pool and adventure playground tacked on. Toby is glad to see me, Tim less happy. She is sitting morose and sullen in a corner, nursing the baby. She must have decided to come after all, keep an eye on Tim, make sure he's not being in any way pleasant to me. I almost feel sorry for the man, but not quite; he's made his bed and she is lying in it. Not that I was a good wife to him, he's better off enduring her kind of pain than mine.

All I care about is Toby. His excitement at having all his school friends sitting around the pub table, wearing hats and blowing things that unroll and hoot, shows in his laughing face and shining eyes. I can see he's proud to see his mother here as well. As he voraciously devours the proffered parcels, ripping them apart to spill out their contents onto the floor, I suddenly feel a pang of pain. The vision inside Mrs Mather's flat haunts me. The toys that her children loved lying mutilated on her floor.

'Hi Tim.'

'Hello Jenny.'

'You've put on a good do for him, he looks happy.'

'Yes, he likes coming here. We sometimes bring him on a Sunday.'

'Can I have him next weekend?'

Tim looks suddenly uncomfortable. Getting time with Toby is not easy after my custody application failed so disastrously. He darts a glance over to the glum-faced woman in the corner.

'I'll have to check what we're doing.'

'Whatever you're doing surely I can have Toby? It'll give you a bit of time together with the baby.'

'I'll have to check.' This is very frustrating.

'He's your son, Tim. You decide what's best for him. He needs to see his mother. She's not his mother; you should have the balls to stand up to her.'

I regret my outburst as soon as I make it. I just can't help myself when it comes to dealing with Tim. The idea that she controls when and if I get to see my own son is almost too much to bear.

'She might not be his biological mother but she's the only real mother he has. She's there for him every day, looks after him.' Tim is red in the face. It doesn't help that he's been guzzling beer, it's a five-year-old's party and he's drinking as if he was out with his mates.

'You shouldn't drink so much,' I add automatically. This triggers another adverse reaction and Tim huffs off and sits next to her, pint glass in hand looking like a whipped dog.

A man in a threadbare clown costume and badly drawn make-up begins to perform less than magic tricks and blows up long balloons which he fashions into impossible dogs. The children are held spellbound. Toby glows with pride as he is chosen to assist in the performance, holding on to props, waving the magic wand, having money extracted from behind his ears. The fake clown retires to the sound of genuine appreciation and rapturous applause. The children break ranks to clamber and swing and run and jump. Parents begin to arrive, extracting unwilling offspring from the tumult. Tim sidles over.

'We've decided it's best for Toby that he has a bit more of a settled life now he has a sister. We feel he needs to be at home for the sake of stability. It'll only confuse him if he spends time away and there's his sister to think of. How will she feel if Toby keeps going away and she doesn't?'

Undigested bitterness rises up my throat. This is her talking. Tim is only the messenger. Nevertheless, shooting is too kind for him, he needs to be punished.

'He's my son,' I splutter weakly, ashamed at the sound of my own pathetic voice.

'We are a family, a proper family, that's what's best for Toby. You can keep in touch, but we're not letting him spend weekends with you from now on.'

I'm devastated. What Tim is saying is so unfair, so cruel. How can it be better for a child not to see his own mother?

'You can't do this to me, Tim, to me and to Toby, it's not right.'

'I'm sorry, the decision is made, it's what we know is best. Anyway, you're the one who abandoned him in the first place.'

It's true, I did, but not willingly. I was cruelly imprisoned, kept away from Toby when he needed me most. I stomp across and stand in front of her. She holds the baby protectively as if worried I might tear her away.

'The court decided Toby belongs to us,' she says. 'If you hadn't tried to take him away things might have been different.'

'You can't deny me access to my own son.'

'Oh yes we can and the courts say we can. We got sole custody; all you have is visitation rights when we decide it's convenient. No more weekends away for him, it's confusing and upsetting. He's happier here with us.'

Before I can reply Toby runs towards us, shouting, 'Mum, Mum, I've hurt my knee.' I turn to console him, but he's with her, showing her the graze, receiving her comforting hug. She looks over his shoulder in triumph and my blood turns to iced water.

8

'We can make an application to the courts.' Stephen's voice is tinny over the hands-free loudspeaker. 'Other than that, there's nothing you can do except try to be nice to them – butter them up, that sort of thing.'

'I just called her an evil bitch, does that count?' I laugh at myself despite the anguish I am feeling. Not a good start.

'Look, things like this have a habit of working themselves out. Your ex probably just wants to make a point. Leave it a few weeks then try again. They might be more receptive.'

'Meanwhile I don't get to see Toby.'

'Look, I understand it's tough, but you need to play this for the long game, slow and cautious, don't keep reacting like you do. It doesn't help matters.'

'How long before we can go to court?'

'Oh, the application can be done quite quickly, a week or two. The hearing might take six months to arrange.'

'I want you to do it, then.'

'I have to advise you that it's unlikely to succeed, particularly as there's been no material change in circumstances since the previous one. Look, Jenny, before we do anything, pop in for a proper chat.'

I arrange a meeting and then hang up. He's not much help, but at least he's telling me what he thinks is the truth. His predecessor seduced me with promises that I would be awarded joint custody, then failed to deliver. This is bad, but that was worse.

As I drive, I think about taking Toby and a big chunk of O'Brian's money and leaving the country.

The Dropbox files hold everything I asked for, detailed accounts of the first four years of the Stretford contract, including a list of employees and their remuneration. The basic rates of pay at Security Group are similar to ours, but they have sickness entitlement, pension contributions, holiday pay, travel allowances and subsistence payments. We don't bother with things like that. The lads get paid when they work and not when they don't.

When I allow for their higher establishment costs and overheads, the numbers show that we are easily twenty per cent cheaper than they are. No wonder Jim Almond is so anxious to persuade me not to compete with him. All that talk about how he had us put on the tender list was total bullshit. I bet he spent a lot of time and effort trying to get us excluded. The fact that he failed shows me that Stretford are more interested in saving money than protecting the status quo. Times are tough for everyone and local authorities are having as bad a time financially as anyone else. My sadness and anxiety over the Toby situation recedes slightly as a feeling of genuine opportunity takes hold. We might be in with a good chance of this business after all.

Carefully, I compare Emma's estimates with my purloined data. She has been very thorough. I can't see anything missing and she has made only one or two minor assumptions that I disagree with. It all boils down to a few simple numbers. Security Group's costs are at least three million pounds a year. On top of this they need to make a profit of at least ten per cent, three hundred thousand pounds. Using our own men, using Emma's figures, our equivalent price would be two and a half million. So far so good. Unfortunately, the terms of the tender require that any employees transferring to a new contractor do so with protected terms and conditions. This means that I will be saddled with the same wages as SG.

In practice, I expect everyone to transfer over to us. SG won't want to keep them. They will have no work for them. I'll be glad to have personnel that already know the work, having been doing it for several years, so there's good and bad on that requirement, but mainly good as far as I am concerned. I don't want to have to recruit sixty men and train them from scratch. To be honest, I couldn't do it. So adding in the extra labour costs, I'd have to increase our bid to about three million. Still, it's probably cheaper than SG and we make a decent profit.

There's another snag that hits me. More than half of GOD Security's workforce will be on the better pay and conditions inherited with the contract. If we're successful, I have to allow for the extra costs I'll inevitably need to apply to my existing workforce. This makes it very tight; if I'm going to succeed I'm going to have to take some big risks, including an assumption that we hit the ground running with no teething problems.

My initial optimism dulls. I push away my laptop and return to brooding about Toby. I am desperate, unhappy, unloved, unappreciated and dog-tired. Even so I sleep only fitfully, waking frequently from visions of being stalked in the dark by men with knives and evil intent.

9

'Tell Mrs Mather I can't get involved. I'm sorry, Mick, I've done my best. There's a chance the police will charge me with assault and kidnap, so I can't risk any of you going round there either. We would all be in a lot of trouble.'

Mick perches glumly in Gary's favourite spot, my desk groans at the excess strain.

'Those bastards need teaching a lesson. They can't waltz into our country and do as they please. They stole her flat, threw her out and nobody seems to care.'

'It's what they're doing in there that sickens me most, Mick. I know it's tough on Mrs Mather but she can get another flat, even if it takes time. Meanwhile, there're little girls being sexually exploited. The police and Social Services are running scared. These Bulgarians are a cunning lot. They're obviously well practised.'

'I don't get it,' Mick sighs. 'How come they didn't just round up the lot of them and send them back where they came from?'

'Listen, Mick, by the time they went to the flat all they would have found was Mum, Dad and two daughters. All nice as pie, place cleaned up, innocent smiles all round. Paperwork all in order, European Union citizens, every right to stay here. Nobody seems able to do anything about it.'

'I can,' Mick says. 'I don't care about any of that stuff. I never voted for the EU in the first place. If I went to their country and threw my weight about they'd be sure to take a dim view and they wouldn't be put off by any EU legislation. I'll sort them out, nothing to do with you or the firm, personal-like. I promised the poor lady in any case.'

'No, please Mick, leave it for both our sakes. Bashing a few heads won't help, you'd only get into real trouble and what for? The guys you hit wouldn't be worth the bother. Even if you threw them out, another lot could easily turn up the next day.'

I can see by his face that he's determined. 'Let me make this clear, I understand your anger and I'm angry too. I'm even more upset than you are, I saw with my own eyes what was happening in there. I spoke to those little girls. Believe me, if I thought it would help in the least I would have sent the whole team round there long ago. Don't do it, Mick, I'd hate to lose you, I rely on you, you know that.'

'I can look after myself,' Mick mutters.

'I didn't mean that. Let me spell it out. If you or anyone else from GOD Security goes anywhere near that flat you are out, fired, sacked, finished. That's it. I can't make it clearer.'

Mick stands up and leaves without reply. I hope he sees I'm serious and I hope even more that he keeps away. Without his help this job would become almost impossible. There's no-one else I trust like I trust him.

Jim Almond appears at the doorway to my office. It's a shock. The head of our fiercest competitor allowed to wander around freely.

'Ah, Jim,' I compose myself quickly.

'Here.' He puts an envelope on my desk. 'It's all filled in. All you need to do is put in your company details and sign it. If you want to do that now, I'll make sure it gets there with ours, before the twelve o'clock deadline tomorrow.'

I smile outwardly and wince inwardly. Nice try.

'Oh that,' I say. 'Forgot all about it. Tomorrow you say? Okay, leave it with me.'

'It'll take five minutes, that's all,' he tries again. 'I'll wait while you sign it, best to get it out of the way, you being so busy. I know what it's like.'

'Don't worry, Jim, I won't forget.'

I am dying to look inside the envelope to see what price he wants me to bid, but if I do that I'll have no excuse for not signing it. He might also detect from the look on my face that I'm going to go back on my promise and put in a competitive bid. It's a fair bet that he already suspects as much, but I'd rather keep him guessing anyway. I ignore him and the document long enough for the atmosphere to become uncomfortable and force him to leave. As soon as I see him drive away I telephone O'Brian. He agrees to meet me at his house.

As I negotiate the long winding drive, I remember the first time I visited O'Brian's house. Then I had been trapped in the rain by his huge Rottweiler while knocking on the wrong door. It was only later that I learned that my discomfiture had been observed on camera by the security guard. Gary and the rest of the lads were in stitches when it was replayed to them. Now I realise that O'Brian's appearance out of the rain, carrying a pet duck, had been carefully choreographed to put me at a disadvantage.

I was there to reject his original money-laundering proposal. Now I'm here to put a new, improved version forward for his consideration. The back door of the huge mansion is unlocked, the dog securely tethered, and I enter the kitchen unscathed and dry this time.

O'Brian is awkwardly making tea. He looks up. 'She's shopping in town with her mother, so she is.' He carries the drinks to the table and waves me to sit. He pushes a white mug towards me with a giant yellow OBC logo. Underneath written in bold green letters is *Friends of the Environment.* I have no idea what that means, nor do I intend asking.

'How are you, Jenny?' he asks.

'Been better, still can't get to see enough of little Toby.'

'Ah that's a shame, he'll be missing his mum, so he will.'

'How's business?' I ask.

'Hard. Harder than usual. There's no margin in the job at all now. I'm barely keeping my head above water. The construction industry is in big trouble, people going bust on us all the time.'

'But the cash payments have increased.'

'Ah yes, thank God, that's the only thing that's keeping us going.'

'I don't understand how you can afford to take out big lumps of cash from the business, especially now when as you say times are hard.'

He gives me a withering look as if I'm encroaching on dangerous ground. When he says nothing for a good three or four minutes, which feel like an hour, I have to break the silence.

'I don't mean to pry into your affairs, Peter. I have to understand more about the cash. Now you're bringing more and more, it's getting impossible to deal with safely.'

He keeps on staring at me, so I carry on. 'If I'm to handle more cash I need to expand the business. There's a big job for Stretford we're up for. The tender's due in tomorrow. Before I put in a bid, I need to know how long you're going to be needing me.'

'Oh, don't you worry. The cash side is doing okay. We only need to up our present arrangement a touch, buy a new caravan site or some such, it'll be fine.'

'There are no more on the market at present. Anyway, I'm reluctant to add another one. That might be pushing it too far. No. This Stretford job might be the answer. It's five years, so I need a commitment for that length of time and for at least as much money as we're doing now.'

'Things have picked up lately, I have no reason to suppose it won't continue.'

'Look, Peter, if I get the Stretford job it will have to be subsidised by the caravan contracts and your cash. If the cash stops, GOD Security will go to the wall, I'll be risking the whole business.'

'How would that work then, with the Stretford contract?'

'It'll more than double the size of the business. It gives me a lot more scope for introducing cash and paying you back. More plant and equipment hire, more van hire, that sort of thing. But if I do this, if I take this risk, I need you to underwrite its profitability. If I start losing money on the contract, I'll have to use your cash to prop it up. You have to agree to that, otherwise I can't put the business on the line like this.'

'There's no use getting a loss-making contract. That's only a waste of money. No good for either of us.'

'It's not my intention to lose money, but if we're to win it I'm going to have to price it very tight.'

'Show me the figures then,' he says.

I spread the papers out on the table. One of them lies in a wet patch which makes the ink run.

'This is the covering price I was given by Security Group. They want me to bid three million, seven hundred and fifty-seven thousand.'

'Who else is in for it?'

'Three more, but I'm pretty sure that SG have made a similar arrangement with them. I'm certain they'll all do what SG ask them to, and make sure their bids are considerably higher than SG's.'

'And how does that price compare with what you can do it for?'

I show him all the information, including the printouts provided by SG's accountants.

'How did you get hold of all this?' O'Brian is clearly impressed by my thoroughness. The warmth is starting to return to his voice.

'Oh, us accountants have our ways,' I smile.

'My bloody accountants better not be giving out my secrets like this.' He looks thoughtful. 'I hope not, anyway. Maybe we should check them out?'

'What, ask them?'

'Not me asking them, you. See if you can't garner some nice titbits about O'Brian Construction. What do you say, worth a try just for peace of mind's sake?'

'What if I get the info, what then?'

'Then I'll confront the beggars, that's what I'll do. Heads will roll. I'll show them they can't mess me about.' He has the look of a man beginning to enjoy himself. 'What about the Stretford contract, what do you reckon you can do it for?'

'About three million.'

'Have you allowed for TUPE in that?'

'TUPE?'

'Transfer of Undertakings Regulations. It means that you have to take on the men already doing the job at protected pay and conditions.'

'Oh yes, I've even allowed for having to bring our existing workforce up to the same standard.'

'Good girl.' His enthusiasm is enough to prevent him sounding at all patronising. 'If SG's costs are already three million, they won't want to do it for less than ten per cent profit. A big group like that might look for a fifteen per cent rate of return, but that would be greedy. Unless they were sure of being covered. Interesting.'

'What do you think then, three million should get it?'

'If you think that their guy trusts you, you put in a couple of hundred thousand more and still get it. Three one, maybe three point two.'

'Thanks, Peter, but before I do I really need you to tell me where the cash comes from.'

He looks hurt, as if I'm doubting his integrity and trustworthiness, but his eyes still have a sparkle.

'Look, it's very sensitive.' He looks around his kitchen. I'm certain he is doing this purely for effect. 'The cash is coming from the building jobs, usually residential. New houses, big ones, or refurbishments of old property, like this.' He waves an arm. 'A lot of the clients like to pay cash so we do them a deal. Invoice them for half, which they pay to show everything is above board, the rest in cash which I give to you.'

'Why don't you just invoice the whole lot, put the cash element through your business?'

'No can do. The client would get investigated, we would have to say who we got it from. Clients don't want that. Our way, they get to use cash that's getting harder and harder to spend. Word has got around. We're getting more and more work on this basis.'

'So these clients, they have cash they don't want anyone to find out about?'

'That's right. A bit like you and me really,' he smiles.

10

The plump, balding man sits opposite Stephen. He wears a frayed, blue, pin-striped suit with a waistcoat that barely meets in the middle.

'This is Anthony, I've asked him for advice regarding your custody application. He has kindly agreed to provide it.'

Anthony smiles a thin smile as if indicating what a great privilege I'm receiving.

'Ah yes, Anthony is the barrister you told me about.'

'Actually he's a judge, sits in the family court a great deal, very experienced in your sort of case.'

My heart takes a skip. A judge! For a moment I wonder if this is some highly questionable tactic on Stephen's part, a clandestine meeting with the judge before he hears my case.

'So Anthony will be hearing my case then?'

'No, that would be improper,' Stephen quickly answers. 'Anthony has reviewed the case notes I sent to him, in the unlikely event that the case were listed before him, he couldn't hear it. No, he's here on your behalf to tell you his opinion on the likely outcome, there's nobody better than him to do that.'

I feel uncomfortable and bewildered. What am I supposed to do or say? Stephen keeps addressing him as Anthony, is that what I should call him or does it have to be your honour? I don't like it. Stephen should have warned me, briefed me in advance.

'Okay,' I say, 'what chance do I have of getting custody of my child?'

'Given the circumstances you can now demonstrate that you have a steady job, a good income and a genuine desire to be a mother to your son. All these positives weigh heavily in your favour. The courts recognise the importance of the child's relationship with his mother.'

'So I've got a good chance then?'

Anthony, his honour or however I should refer to him looks mildly offended as if I'm interrupting a much longer speech.

'As I say, there are positives, good positives,' he continues without answering my question. 'There are also other factors that the court needs to consider. Unfortunately one of these is character. Your record has not been exemplary. The fact that you served a prison term is no good reason for denying you custody of your son. It does however raise issues of fitness, which the other side will make great play of. They may claim that you have a violent streak and that your record attests to that. They may even suggest that this may put your son at risk.'

'That's not true, I've never hit Toby, I never would.' I'm on my feet shaking with frustration. 'How dare anyone suggest such a thing?'

'I understand the reasons for your outburst, Mrs Parker, quite understandable, not something that would be looked kindly upon in court however.' He fixes me with a look and I subside into my chair. 'As I was saying, you must be prepared for a thorough examination of your character and your criminal record if your ex-husband is going to resist the application.'

I open my mouth to speak and then stop myself, realising that he's not engaging in a conversation with me, rather delivering a judgement that he's already reached. Anything I say or do will have no effect on the outcome. I feel like an admonished child.

'Although your character as a mother can be brought into question and important evidence can be presented which attests to your previous offending, I don't consider this to be compelling. On the one hand, you were imprisoned for money-laundering offences, while in prison you were convicted of grievous bodily harm and there have been two subsequent occasions when you have exhibited violent behaviour. One of these was in the hospital, where you had to be restrained, the other in open court.

'To set against this, we have an intelligent, able young lady with a good job and more than adequate income. You have no drug addictions or alcohol dependence. Since those regrettable incidents, you have led a blameless life, you are obviously devoted to your son, you place his wellbeing above everything else and have demonstrated this by taking the opportunity on every occasion access has been granted to you. Furthermore, while your son has been in your care, no harm has befallen him and you have scrupulously adhered to the custody arrangements and returned him to his father at the allotted time. On the whole, I would say that the character question is one with points on both sides, but that there is insufficient weight there to deny you custody of your son.'

I feel ecstatic. This judge has been through everything the real judge will and is giving me my son.

'So I'll get him?' I ask.

'On balance I doubt that your character would preclude it. However, I now have to consider the child's welfare. The court has to put this on the top of its priority list. You can show that you can provide him with a good home and are a loving mother. The question of the father's access would have to be decided, but that can be a matter for agreement or direction by the court.'

I like this but I'm learning not to interrupt. Anthony is obviously used to delivering these long-winded deliberations in court without any interruption.

'I now turn to the paramount question of the child's welfare. Whereas the court would be in possession of long and detailed reports, I am, for the sake of reaching a considered opinion, assuming that these reports provide no negative indications for either party. Under the circumstances, I think this is a reasonable approach. Young Toby has a stable home life. He lives with his father, his stepmother and a baby sister. He is settled, in a good school, and enjoys the company of his friends as evidenced by the recent birthday celebrations. His health is good, his academic progress satisfactory and he shows no signs of upset or distress. There is a natural bond, an important fundamental relationship between mother and son. The courts recognise this and place due emphasis upon it. The balance has to be struck, however, between the needs of the mother and those of the child. Where an infant is concerned, the presence of the mother can be of paramount importance.'

I'm beginning to feel sick to my stomach. It's as if I'm hearing the sentence of death handed down. There suddenly appears to be only one outcome.

'On balance therefore, I would advise you that the court would be unlikely to uphold your appeal for custody. It would almost certainly decide that uprooting the child at this stage in his life would not be in the overall best interest of the child. I'm sorry I can't be more positive.'

He looks up. I can't stop my tears.

'However, the arrangement you have currently, access only at the whim or discretion of his father, influenced no doubt by his new wife, is both unsatisfactory and unfair. I strongly advise you to set aside a custody appeal, at least for the time being. Apply instead for formal access arrangements. If I were sitting I would find it hard to resist a plea for alternate weekends and two or three weeks during school holidays.'

11

It is a mistake arranging this meeting directly after seeing Stephen and the judge. This should be light relief, at least for me. The tapas bar fronts onto Deansgate, but I reach it by simply walking out of the solicitor's office, down a short passage and in through a rear door.

Simon Constable, O'Brian's accountant, is already half way through a bottle of red wine. It's a while since I last saw him, back in the days when any new set of accountancy rules spawned a series of discussion meetings that ended in boozy lunches. The interest he showed in me then, although firmly rebuffed, is obviously still there to the extent that he jumped at the chance to have lunch with me.

Looking at his perfect haircut, clean-shaven face and immaculate white shirt and tie, it is hard to believe this man is anything other than perfectly law-abiding. Anyway, that's what O'Brian wants me to find out, at least to the limited degree that involves O'Brian's interests.

'Ah, Jenny, lovely as ever, you are looking well.'

'Thank you, Simon, I could say the same about you,' I smile. No packet of money this time, at least not yet. This is about his salacious ambitions and seeing how far I get with those to begin with. We order food, then I ask, 'Anyway, how's business?'

'Business is good, at least the insolvency side is. We've got more work than we can handle.'

'Don't you feel a bit guilty about the way you take over struggling businesses, sell their assets, pay yourselves enormous fees from the proceeds and send out a report telling the poor creditors that they're getting nothing?'

'That pretty well sums it up.' He smirks. 'What about you, how are you getting on?' His face suddenly clouds over as if he's had a disturbing thought. 'You're not in need of a job, are you?'

'Relax, Simon, I've no intention of coming back into accountancy, even if they'd have me, which I doubt.'

He visibly brightens. 'How about your personal life, has that settled down now?'

'Not really. I'm divorced, my son is living with his father.'

He looks happy at this news. 'So, footloose and fancy free?' he smirks again.

A deep well of nothing opens inside me. I am swallowed up by overwhelming sadness. I feel a longing for warmth, love, friendship, fond laughter, honesty and compassion. A relationship that offers all of these and one more thing, safety. Until I feel safe I'm unable to even consider it. This man is pleasant, good-looking and rich. He's also married, unfaithful and devious. Looking at him now makes me feel very unsafe and I struggle not to lose myself in the emotional turmoil boiling inside me.

This should have been a half-serious enquiry, to put O'Brian's mind at rest. Instead there's something very upsetting about the situation. This man is a prominent business man, husband, father, pillar of society. Yet he's meeting me in this back room of a quiet restaurant in the obvious hope of getting his hands and more into my knickers. My stomach churns. I push away the plate of patatas bravas and sip some water.

Simon calls for anther bottle of wine.

Excusing myself, I stand for a few minutes in the sparsely appointed ladies' toilets. There is a feeling of unease that I'm unable to breathe away. It would be simple for me to walk out of here, turn left up the stairs and away from Simon, and intrigue and pain. I could tell O'Brian his man is trustworthy; he'd be pleased about that.

The thought of that smug look makes me shudder. I doubt I can pass muster under that piercing gaze if he asks me how hard I tried.

'I went to bed with him, Peter, let him do what he wanted, still he wouldn't betray you,' I imagine the conversation and Peter's reply: 'Only the once? Couldn't you have tried a bit harder? Maybe he's weakening. Go back and have another go.'

I walk out of the toilets and turn right down the steps to where Simon waits patiently, fiddling with his Blackberry.

'It's delicate.' I get to the point before his fantasies about me lusting after his body get too set in his mind. 'It's about O'Brian, Peter O'Brian. You'll be aware my business does a lot of work for him. That's not a problem. Things are going well. It's just that I'm worried that we're getting too dependent on him, that we'll get into what my business studies tutor used to call the Marks & Spencer Syndrome, where we're totally dependent on one customer.'

'So you're concerned he'll start squeezing your prices, exploit his position?'

'No, not that. I'm aware he drives a hard bargain, that's not my worry. It's the financial security of the business that bothers me. Construction is having an even harder time than other sectors.'

'Ah.' He looks relieved. 'Then you shouldn't worry, O'Brian is in good shape, even in these parlous times. Amazing shape really, considering the plight of his competitors. He seems to be able to pull work out of nothing.' Simon tops up my glass even though I've not yet taken a single sip of the wine.

'Thanks, I'm grateful for your reassurance, though I do need to find more work outside O'Brian's, become less dependent.' I try to look like I've been struck by a good idea all of a sudden. Judging by his flushed expression I'm wasting my acting skills. 'Maybe you could help.'

'We already have security included in the service charges we pay for the office,' he says.

'I was thinking about some of O'Brian's customers, you know the ones he builds the big houses for, maybe that would be a lucrative market for us.'

'Quite possibly, you should ask Peter for a list, I'm sure he'd be happy to help.'

'At a price,' I say. 'He'd make sure he got his share of anything we did. No, I need to find another way. I'd rather pay a one-off commission to you than a continuous one to O'Brian.'

He shows no reaction to this suggestion, positive or negative.

'I tell you what,' I say. 'Give me the list, I'd be happy to contribute a year's university fees for your lad, whether we get any work or not.'

'O'Brian wouldn't be happy.'

'O'Brian need never know. My lads can knock on plenty of doors, it's knowing where to start them off.'

'I see, so it wouldn't be anything direct or overt?'

'No, if I get the business then as far as O'Brian is concerned we got it through a direct marketing campaign. The fact that some of his ex-clients came to us is pure coincidence.'

'Ten grand, you say, in cash,' he whispers.

'No, six. Yes in cash.'

12

Twelve noon on a Friday is the traditional deadline for tenders, especially local authority ones. Also customary is that these are delivered by hand, as close to the time as possible. It's five minutes to when I hand my envelope in at reception, have it stamped and receive my receipt. As I turn away from the desk, I become aware of Jim Almond at my side.

'Nearly forgot.' I smile at him, hoping he feels the innocence that I am trying to radiate. He is holding two envelopes.

'Everything okay, Jenny?' he says.

The foyer of Stretford Town Hall is no place for me to confirm or deny my complicity in his attempt to pervert the local authority procurement process. I point to his documents.

'Having two goes then, Jim?' I keep smiling, exuding what I hope is casual bonhomie. Inside I wish I'd sent Emma to make the delivery.

Jim is looking intently at me as if unsure about something. He is holding one envelope in each hand now, as if weighing one against the other. The giant clock behind the desk indicates one minute to twelve. With a sigh, as if the weight of the world is on his shoulders, he selects an envelope and passes it over. As the clock tower begins to strike he is handed his chit of paper.

'Do you fancy lunch, Jenny?' he asks. I pretend to consider it while thinking about all the awkwardness and evasion that would be involved.

'Thanks Jim, that's kind of you. I have to be getting on though.'

Jim walks out of the building with me, still clutching the remaining envelope.

'What's with the other document?' I ask. 'Shouldn't you have delivered that as well?'

'Ah, no. I had two bids prepared, one a bit higher than the other. I wanted to see if yours went in or not before I decided which one.'

13

'They got in through here,' Mick explains. 'It's an old brick wall, they pushed it with the lorry until it fell over.'

The man standing in the rubble is unhappy and he has every right to be. He winces as if in pain as we approach, his huge chest heaving in frustration.

'Morning, George.' He looks at me and nods. 'Bit of a mess here.'

'It's a bloody disaster, that's what it is. I pay you good money to protect against this sort of thing, don't know why I bother.'

I refrain from pointing out that it's his wall they knocked down and that I have a man in hospital. 'What did they take, George? Anything special?'

He freezes at the question, stops breathing entirely then lets out a gush of despondence.

'What do you mean, special?' He looks at me intently.

'Mick says they took a trailer. Seems a lot of trouble to go to, there's lots of them parked up on the side of the road.'

'They took a fully loaded trailer, hooked up a unit to it and drove it out through here. Nobody stopped them.' George looks unhappier by the minute.

'Alan tried,' I say, 'and now he's in Hope Hospital. He raised the alarm, called the police and called Mick. Then he went out to confront them, which he shouldn't have done, he did his best, George. They only got one trailer.' I look around the crowded yard. 'It could have been much worse, do you know what the trailer was carrying?'

George's face transforms from angry red to pale white in an instant. 'No,' he replies much too quickly. 'I'll need to check the consignment notes.'

'Look, George, I'll make sure you get what you need from us for your insurance claim. I'll also let you know how

Alan is recovering. Meanwhile do you need me to arrange some temporary fencing and put some extra men on tonight?'

He nods glum acceptance.

'And I'm going to find out who's responsible. I'll be making my own enquiries, see what we have in the way of CCTV records, that kind of thing. Believe me, George, I'll not rest until I get to the bottom of this.'

We leave him, still looking very glum. Mick grimaces as we get into the car. 'Something wrong there, don't you think?' he asks.

'What do you mean?'

'George seems very cagey all of a sudden, normally he's right as rain is George,' Mick frowns.

'He's upset, it's understandable,' I say.

'Yes, but he's too upset for my liking.'

'You were the first here, weren't you?'

'Yes, Jenny, I jumped in a van as soon as Alan called me. By the time I got here they were gone. I took Alan to hospital, they'd given him a bad beating.'

'How long did you take to get here?'

'Not more than twenty minutes.'

'And there was no sign of them?'

'No.'

'So they knock down a wall, get into a yard with dozens of loaded vehicles and steal only one?'

'Not only that, they had to do a bit of shunting.'

'What?'

'The trailer they nicked was blocked in, they had to move at least two others to get at it.'

'And they did all this and left within twenty minutes?'

'Yes, Jenny, do you see what I mean?'

'I do. I wonder what was in that trailer?'

'George already knows, I could see it in his face.' Mick's mobile purrs and he answers it with a wave of apology. 'Yes, oh God, I'll tell her.'

He turns to me. 'Alan's dead, those bastard thieves killed him.'

My flat on Salford Quays was the second one Gary provided me with. The first, much nearer the city centre, turned out to be a very ad hoc arrangement but this one has provided me with a safe haven for almost two years now. At least there's been no repeat of the attempts on my life. I still sleep in the same bedroom in which I was once attacked.

After Gary's death I discovered that my apartment was rented from a property speculator friend of his. This guy went bankrupt in spectacular fashion and I was able to buy my home from the receivers. My landlord had paid one hundred and twenty thousand pounds for it, I managed to persuade the receiver that as sitting tenant it would save them a lot of time and legal expense if they sold it to me for sixty-two thousand pounds. I'm not sure it's a great investment in these troubled times, but it'll do until I buy a nice house for Toby and me. Meanwhile, it represents the bonus I got when the caravan sites began to pay off.

The stack of toys in the corner of the lounge remind me with a pang of anxiety that Toby hasn't been here for months. The sooner Stephen sorts out some proper access the better. Meanwhile, he's told me to avoid any confrontation with Tim and especially with his wife.

There's nothing in the fridge worth eating. I promise myself I'll do a big shop tomorrow and fill it with wholesomeness. Meanwhile, I settle for a late supper of toast and marmite and then go to bed, head full of Toby and remorse and anxiety.

The telephone clamours for attention, dragging me from my bed. The flat phone almost never rings. The lads know I'm available for them at any time but they know I prefer a text message, if it's really urgent then they ring my mobile. Nobody even knows the number here, I'm not sure of it myself. It's 2 a.m. I pick up and expect some apologetic wrong number.

'Jenny Parker?'

'Yes, who is this?'

'You are messing with us.'

'What are you talking about, who are you?'

'You think you're smart, that you can interfere with our business. We're going to get you, we're going to make you suffer, we're going to destroy you.'

The phone goes dead. I ring 1471 but the number is blocked. Whoever it was sounded really upset.

14

'Good news.' Stephen's voice on my hands-free.

'I could do with some,' I reply. I'm feeling deep despair as my mind turns to Toby.

'I've spoken to the police,' Stephen says. 'There will be no charges brought against you regarding the incident at Mrs Mather's flat.'

'Is that it? Is that the good news?'

'I thought I'd let you know.' Stephen sounds sheepish.

'Sorry. I've got a lot on my plate at the moment. What about the girls, did they get taken into care?'

'They wouldn't say. All they told me was that the Crown Prosecution Service decided there was insufficient evidence to obtain a conviction against you.'

'So a woman sees atrocious acts of sexual depravity involving under-age girls and all the police can do is reluctantly drop charges against her? What kind of society is this? Someone needs to do something about these men. If the police won't then I will.'

'I strongly advise you to let it lie. The police are doing everything the law allows them to.'

'Then the law is wrong.'

My dark mood is not helped by the greeting I get at the office. Emma, eyes red with crying, introduces two be-suited men with leather brief cases.

It's much later before I can speak to Mick about Trafford Trailers.

'I'm sorry, look, I've not had a minute. I've had all afternoon with two men from the Health & Safety Executive, would you believe. They wanted everything. All our procedures, our contracts of employment, asked for risk assessments, all sorts of gobbledegook. Apparently unless I can show them we have a safe system of work they're going to prosecute over Alan's death.'

'That's bollocks,' Mick says. 'They should be prosecuting the bastards that killed him, how can that be right?'

'It's not, it stinks. It's not as if we haven't better things to do than talk to these clipboard-wielding jobsworths.'

Mick asks, 'Can you go to see Alan's widow? She's been asking me about death in service benefits and pensions and such like, I've no idea about that sort of thing. I said you would deal with it.'

A sudden panic swells up inside me. What can I tell her? As far as I know there's nothing. I pay the lads a wage, that's all. I never thought to take any provision for situations like this. There must be special insurance you can buy, but it's too late now.

It's all become too much, I realise. There aren't enough hours in the day when things are going well. Now I have a death on my hands, a grieving widow, the Health & Safety Executive and the police to deal with over Trafford Trailers. The whole business is going to the wall over this one incident and it's my fault. There should have been better protection for Alan when he was alive and money for his widow now he's dead. The responsibility lies with me, there's no-one else to blame.

I promise to see Alan's widow in the morning, a prospect that does little to improve my fitful sleep. The flat phone rings again, this time at 3 a.m. The voice is hard and menacing.

'Jenny Parker, we're coming to get you, we're going to make you wish you had never been born.'

'Join the queue,' I say, as I yank out the wire.

15

The parking meters in Byrom Street are voracious beasts, their huge tariffs mirroring those charged by the lawyers' offices that front onto it. Despite the exorbitant cost, all bays are full and I have to cruise around waiting for someone to run out of time and money. The alternative is the cramped Spinningfields multi-storey or the waste ground by the river; both are almost as costly and also involve a walk in the rain.

Stephen greets me with a white insulated jug of instant coffee, made the way only he likes it, thick and bitter. One sip has me doubting I'll sleep for week.

'I hope you're giving me a discount, all I hired you for was Toby and now there's all these other things.' I slap a thick sheath of documents onto his polished table.

He sits behind a neat pile of folders. 'Where do you want to begin, Jenny?

'Let's start with the one positive, shall we? The Stretford contract, have you had a chance to look at it?'

'Yes I have. I've had some notes typed up to help take you through it.'

'I don't understand, surely it's the same one that SG had, isn't it? Can't I just sign it and get on with the job?'

'You can, but I wouldn't advise it.' He flips open his copy and begins to explain it all. After half an hour we are not a quarter of the way through and I am losing the will to live. Some of the things Stretford want from us are ludicrous, I can't believe SG agreed to all this.

'Is there any point?' I ask. 'Isn't it a question of me agreeing or not being given the contract?'

'Certainly not, it's fairly standard practice. As preferred bidder you have the chance to negotiate the terms and conditions. Only if you fail to agree will anyone else be considered. If you like I can send the council an amended contract to start the ball rolling.'

'Okay, better do that.'

'When they come back with their position, we can narrow down the points of disagreement.'

I nod my assent, anything to stop this painstaking process. 'Okay, now the Health & Safety Executive prosecution, what can you do about that?'

'Not much I'm afraid.'

'What do you mean?'

'I mean that you will be found guilty.'

'Guilty! Some bastard's killed my man and I'm the guilty one?'

'Not you, GOD Security. They've only prosecuted the company, they could easily have done you personally as well. Listen, Jenny, the law requires employers to have a safe system of work in place. If someone gets killed or injured, as far as the court's concerned, your system wasn't safe. It's always an automatic conviction, that's the way the legislation is framed.'

'It's a very stupid law,' I gasp.

'A lot of them are,' he replies. 'Expect a sizeable fine on this one, fifty thousand pounds wouldn't surprise me.'

'That'll put us out of business.'

'Then we could plead mitigation on the grounds of hardship.'

'What about Alan's widow, doesn't she get some of that money?'

'No, it goes to the Treasury.'

'But surely if I was to give it to her to look after his kids, wouldn't that be better?'

'Better yes, much better. But that's not how it works, I'm afraid.'

This is a nightmare. I'm not cut out for this sort of thing, it makes me feel so angry and bitter. Every time I come up against the law of this land, I am treated with the utmost injustice. It started when I unwisely accepted a bribe and went to prison for money-laundering. Then Dawn, my crazed cellmate, almost killed me and my sentence was extended for defending myself. Toby was denied me and I'm left powerless to even have him visit. I witness child prostitution and am threatened by prosecution myself. Always the same, the law is set against me. Now I face this.

'How do you sleep at night, Stephen?' I ask. 'All this nonsense you have to administer, all this injustice, all this bad law, how do you stand it?'

'I don't make the laws, Jenny, that's the politicians' job. All I can do is help as much as I can when they're applied to my clients.'

'It's not fair,' I say on the point of collapse into self-pity. 'It's just not fair.'

16

George Bottomley leans back in his frayed maroon chair, swivels towards me and slurps his tea unsteadily.

'Mick says you wanted to see me.' He looks much more composed than at our last meeting by the demolished wall.

'I wanted to make sure you had the cover you need, that you're happy with the arrangement.'

'Yes, yes it's okay for now, but I'll not be wanting to pay for two men on nights for very long. I know it's sensitive for you but you have to realise the extra cover's for your benefit, not something I asked for.'

'Bear with me, George, I'll review it in a couple of weeks' time. Maybe then we can go back to normal. How's the police investigation going? What about the CCTV recording, have they been able to identify anyone from that?'

'Well there's the thing, there isn't one. It wasn't working, it seems your man hadn't activated the system properly. Of all the nights to mess up, that was the worst.'

'I don't get it, George, the system records automatically. Alan didn't have to do anything. He couldn't have messed it up.'

'Well whatever he did or didn't do, the recordings for the night of the break-in are all blank. Nothing to go on, the police say.'

'Oh.' I'm pretending to be surprised even though Mick has warned me already about the CCTV footage. 'You should have told me, George. We'll have them on our office server. There's an automatic upload to our system from all the premises we look after. It's simple to do. We don't charge you any extra for it.'

George's demeanour changes. His look tells me what I might see on those fictional recordings, if they existed. Before he can recover his composure I ask, 'What was on the trailer, George?'

'I told you, I don't know.'

'You told me you would have to check. You must have told the police something.'

'It was detergent from P & G, a load of detergent.'

'So you're telling me that someone went to the trouble of breaking down a wall, shunting trailers around, killing my security guard and wiping the CCTV all for a few packets of washing powder?'

'Seems that way.' He looks at his feet.

'Okay, George, I'll go through the uploads and have a look if there's anything useful. If there is, I'll make sure the police get a copy. Do you want me to send you one as well?'

I watch him staring into space for a moment then leave without waiting for his reply.

17

'It's not too late for you to pull out.' Jim Almond appears more sanguine in person than over the phone. 'There's too much work for you to swallow all at once, save yourself a lot of grief.' At least he's stopped ranting on about how I shafted him and broke my promise to cover his price.

'I didn't agree to meet in order to give up the job. It takes GOD Security to the next level. All that guaranteed work for the next five years, it's important to us, I'm sure you can understand that.'

'Then why did you bother coming? If you're expecting me to make the transition a smooth one, then think again. I'll make sure you only get the men I'm glad to see the back of. The awkwardist, laziest and most militant I get to transfer over to you. I may have lost the contract but I can dump all my rubbish on you.'

'I get the picture. I'm sure we'll cope. With the Stretford contract, GOD Security is a nice size, able to bid for other big contracts, not as hand to mouth as we were. We've got some credibility now, we're a business with good prospects. I need someone to manage it.'

His eyebrows arch. He doesn't look as if he saw this one coming. A smile begins to play around his lips. 'You're offering me a job?'

'Yes.'

'You couldn't afford me.'

'So you are interested?'

'Well.' He looks straight at me. 'I'd consider it if the money was right.'

'Assume the money's right, Jim. Can you see yourself putting GOD Security on the map? Giving the likes of SG a run for their money, growing the business and sharing in the rewards?'

'I have to admit there's scope for rapid expansion in your business. I also have the feeling that we would work well together.'

'Okay, here's the deal. I reckon you're on fifty-five now, plus car, plus pension.'

'Fifty-seven.'

'Okay, fifty-seven. I'm offering sixty-five, sort out your own car and pension. There's a bonus of ten thousand pounds if the Stretford contract makes a profit in the first year, plus I'll give you a profit share in the whole business.'

His eyes dart around his office, as if taking in all the paraphernalia he's piled up in here, letting it all go, bidding it all farewell.

'I'll have to give three months' notice.'

'Give as much notice as you need to, Jim.' I stand up and shake his hand. 'I'll start paying you from today anyway.'

He smiles his understanding. I feel a mixture of exultation and relief.

'They've gone, cleared out, left an awful mess though,' Mick reports.

'I suppose that's something. Get some contract cleaners in and tell them to blitz the place. Mrs Mather doesn't need to see what they did to her home. Have everything cleaned, washed, disinfected; carpets, furniture, everything.' I shudder as I think about what was going on in that place. 'Any idea where they went?'

'No idea, but the neighbours were glad to see the back of them. I did find some bits and pieces that might help identify them.' He shovels a pile of grubby correspondence onto my desk. 'Most of the letters are addressed to a D Wasiewicz and are about Job Seeker's Allowance payments and Child Benefit.'

'Cheeky bastards,' I mutter.

'At least Mrs Mather can have her flat back,' Mick grins.

He is starting to annoy me. I don't feel he shares my deep unease at the situation, maybe it's because he's male and he sees what was going on there as a bit of harmless fun. I look at his big amiable smile, it gives me a cold feeling to think that he might easily form part of the clientele. He's a man after all and that's what they do all the time, isn't it? If there were no customers, those little girls wouldn't be abused. There'd be no business to conduct and all the customers are men like Mick.

'You don't get it, do you, Mick?' I hear myself snarling. 'It's not the flat that's the issue now, it's what was going on there and is certainly still going on somewhere else. Those girls and hundreds of others like them are being sold to men on an hourly basis. That's the issue. We need to find whoever these people are and put a stop to it.'

'It's prostitution, the oldest game in the world. It's going on everywhere, all the time. You'll never put a stop to it.'

'That doesn't mean I won't try. You men treat it as some sort of recreational fun don't you?'

'No.' Mick's eyes flicker. 'Not at all.'

'Yes you do, you're all the same.'

'No we're not. I'm not anyway.' His expression betrays his hurt feelings and I feel immediate remorse. Mick is a decent man.

'Sorry, Mick,' I say, 'I know you're not. I just got a bit angry, you know what I'm like.'

I think of Martin, my dead lover, and the last time I felt sensitivity and respect from a man's intimate touch. It's been a long time and I can't believe I'll ever feel safe in a man's arms again.

18

O'Brian is laughing now, a contrast to how he reacted when I showed him the documents I'd bought from his accountant, Simon Constable. Then, he had lapsed into frozen gloom, punctuated occasionally by the odd swear word and a kick out at one of his own polished chairs. Now he's laughing, despite the betrayal, despite the loss of six thousand pounds in hard cash. He's highly amused by my account of how I persuaded Simon to give me the information.

'He really said that?' he asks.

'Yes, really. I told him I wanted a client list so that I could use it to get more business for GOD Security. I said we'd knock on their doors and offer to look after their homes and property.'

'That's so funny.' He begins to chuckle again. 'Simon may be a smart accountant, but he's no idea about business.'

I'm beginning resent O'Brian's overblown merriment, I was much more comfortable with his initial indignation. Maybe I'm missing something here but I thought it was a plausible story. Simon Constable certainly found it entirely convincing and, to be quite honest, I have half a mind to use my copy of this list to do exactly as I promised.

'They're rich, have nice homes like yours, Peter, why wouldn't they need GOD Security? You do after all.'

'I'm sorry, Jenny, it's only that I know these people and you don't. The idea is just so amusing and the fact that Simon bought it hook, line and sinker, very funny.'

My irritation levels have risen to annoyance. O'Brian is laughing at me, belittling me as if I'm a small child. He seems less concerned about his dodgy accountant than he does about having a laugh at my expense.

'Maybe I'll try them anyway,' I say. 'Unless you have any objection?'

'Be my guest.' O'Brian stops laughing. 'Let me know how you get on though, watch out you don't get trapped in the rain by a big dog.' He starts laughing again.

All I want to do is hit someone, preferably him, and prove the old bugger wrong.

'What are you going to do about Simon Constable, are you going to be looking for new auditors?'

His face clouds, every trace of amusement has disappeared in an instant. 'Leave Simon to me, don't tell anyone about this, no one at all. And don't talk to Simon again, as I said, leave him to me.'

O'Brian is clearly less comfortable with this line of conversation than when he was laughing at my expense.

'So you will confront him, let him know you're not happy with him?'

It's O'Brian's turn to get irritated, I can see by the reddish suffusion colouring his neck.

'I'll deal with it,' he says.

I still don't see what he finds so funny.

19

Tonight I'm so tired, I can't think straight. Even with Jim Almond taking the brunt of the hard work, the Stretford job is proving more time- and energy-consuming than even Jim's direst warnings foretold. I spend most of my days in meetings with people who believe that words speak louder than actions. Most evenings, all I can manage is to flop down on my sofa and watch TV. I know it softens my mind, robs me of conscious thoughts, steals my spirit and leaves me hollow. Sometimes, though, I want to be mindless and empty. Tonight I'll switch the damned thing on and prostrate myself before it, praying for it to suck away the chaos of the day.

The door of my flat swings open as I offer it my key. The door surround is ragged and splintery, someone has smashed their way in. I rush inside, heart choking, to a scene of devastation. The TV is lying face down on the rug, surrounded by glittering shards of glass. Every cushion on my settee has been slashed and ripped apart. Drawers lie upturned, contents littering every corner of the room. Each room is similarly destroyed, even my bedroom has been systematically defiled, my clothes lie shredded, furniture bashed to pieces. The stench rolls my stomach. There are thick brown turds coiled on my once white bed sheets. I don't know what to do or where to start doing it. My mind won't think. My body wants to sink down and lie in the mess.

My tiredness begins to give way to a surge of anger and hatred. All I want now is to find the perpetrators and make them suffer. Nothing else matters. Almost mechanically I begin to clear up. By the time I dispose of the excrement and make my bed fit to sleep in, it's 2 a.m. Even so, my phone whirrs with a message from Mick. I look at it, longing to summon him, to tell someone about my pain, but resist.

The moment anyone comes here I'll lose control and break down completely. As it is, on my own, I can work through the tears, spurred on by thoughts of cruelty and torture, of severed appendages and battered faces, of burglars drowned in my bath and thrown into the Ship Canal attached to concrete blocks. Throughout all of this, there is a jangling worry trying to make itself heard through the trauma. As I lie amongst the devastation of mindless savages, I remember the phone calls, the threats, and feel the horror of it all somehow being connected.

The police want a list of what's been stolen. They did turn up eventually, took a cursory look and said there had been a lot of it about lately, especially around here. Probably kids, they offered, without elaborating on what sort of evil children might have destroyed my home. I'm not mentioning the threatening phone calls, not inviting their enquiries down the list of my potential enemies. The way I feel at the moment it would be easier to give them the names of the half dozen people I trust and let them choose from the remaining seven billion or so on the planet.

I think of ringing Doreen O'Donnell. I know how she will react, full of concern. 'Come over here, stay with us,' she'll insist. My heart dissolves at the prospect of that warm comfort and her loving support. It's what I need most right now. It's what is missing in my life, that opportunity to soften in a safe pair of arms. I resist, though every bit of me screams the opposite. The last time I sank into the warm O'Donnell household I was being pursued by murderous thugs. She lost her husband because of me, she gave me shelter and drew my troubles onto her own family. I can't let that happen again. Even though circumstances seem different now, I have a horrible feeling they may not be much different after all.

20

'I thought it was you, at first,' Jim Almond's eyebrows leap upwards, creasing his wide forehead. 'No, really.' I continue my description of the threatening phone calls. 'I thought SG might have got someone to warn me off nicking your jobs.'

'Well it wasn't.' He looks even less happy than usual after my comment. I'm used to him sitting at the desk opposite to mine, deep in anxious gloom. It's the way he is, I suppose, someone must have instilled in the young Jim's mind that cheerfulness is a crime.

'I know that, I'm only saying that I've no idea at all who might be responsible.'

'I used to get mightily pissed off with you, I admit that, but I didn't ring you with threats.'

'No, I know you didn't. I only wish it were that simple.'

'You took me on, gave me a job when all the time you thought I was making threatening phone calls?'

'No. You're getting the wrong impression. What I'm trying to say is that it would be a comfort to believe they were only someone letting off steam, a fit of pique.'

'I don't do hissy fits,' Jim looks hurt.

'No, I can see that,' I reply quickly before he proves himself a liar. 'What bothers me now is the thought that the same people trashed my home.'

'I thought the police said it was kids?'

'What do they know? Anyway, I never told them about the threats. I'm certain they're connected. What I don't understand is why someone would do it?'

'To warn you off, maybe?'

'That'd make sense if I knew what I was being warned off from.'

'You might not know, but they must think you do. So. What have you been sticking your nose into recently that involves violent criminals?'

'Nothing,' I answer automatically, but something stirs uneasily in me as I do.

21

As I enter the cavernous monstrosity and squint against the harsh lights, the hollow feeling in my stomach returns. I almost abandon my trolley and run, but I have to steel myself against my discomfort if I'm to gather some food. The atmosphere in here is antiseptic; somehow the aromas that should be jostling to enter my nostrils from this enormous range and quantity of food have been eliminated. All I can smell is cleanliness until an occasional unwashed person leans over me to grab something shiny.

There are better places to shop, better supermarkets than this one even, but the differences are marginal and this one is alluringly close to home. I throw some plastic-wrapped greenery into my basket to join cling-filmed pears and then head for the checkout escape. Mercifully, for the pressure to get out of here is mounting, the lady in front of me is quick and efficient. She even fails to look surprised when asked to pay and jabs her card into the machine automatically. My few purchases clink musically across the scanner until a dull note sounds. The girl looks suspiciously for the missing bar-code sticker and tries again. Failure is repeated. She then looks puzzled as she peers into the clear plastic.

'What's this?' she asks me.

'Kale,' I reply. More puzzlement and pressing of till buttons. Then she consults a laminated set of printed documents which she browses as if it were a clothing catalogue.

'Kale?' She looks up.

'Curly kale,' I confirm.

'I can't find a code for it.'

'It's eighty-five pence a packet,' I tell her.

'I need a code though.' She presses a button and a bell sounds and the light above the till begins to pulsate. We wait. The man behind me in the queue lets out a long sigh, we make eye contact, my look says it's not my fault, his replies you're holding me up because you eat something weird and unusual. A youth dressed in a logo-stamped fleece several sizes too large for him saunters up.

'I need a code for this.' The girl thrusts my kale at him. He walks slowly away. I look at the man's shopping displayed on the belt. Half a litre of milk, two pot noodles, chicken korma ready meal, small white loaf, tin of Heinz tomato soup, packet of McVitie's dark chocolate digestive biscuits, a six pack of Walker's ready salted crisps. I look at him again. This time his face is softer, his eyes smile first and then his mouth. There is a gentleness about him that seems out of place here.

'Sorry about the delay,' I say.

'Not your fault, we should all buy more kale so it's worth their while to give it a bar code,' he laughs. 'What exactly do you do with kale anyway?'

'Eat it,' I laugh back.

'I thought they fed it to cattle.'

'Well I'm lucky, they saved some for me.' The youth returns bearing a second pack of kale. The girl behind the till scans this successfully, puts the offending pack in my bag and the youth takes the new one away again.

'Seventeen pounds and forty-seven pence, do you have a Club Card?' I slide my credit card into the machine and wait.

'Can you try again?' she asks, 'it's not accepting it.'

I remove my card and replace it.

'Still not accepting it.' The girl looks blankly at me.

'I'll pay cash,' I say, fumbling in my purse. I have a ten pound note, some coppers and nothing else. The heat rises in my head, shame wells up. I want to abandon my kale and run. I feel like a criminal trying to rob the place.

'I'll try my debit card.' It too is declined. I am seven pounds short and I have no more options. 'I can't understand it,' I protest. 'Why would my cards stop working all of a sudden?'

The girl replies with a blank stare. I feel the pressure of the lengthening queue, already impatient over the kale incident.

The man behind me leans forward with a twenty pound note in his hand.

'Let me lend you the money,' he says.

Numbly I nod agreement, anything to escape this place with some dignity. Abandoning my purchases would be too demeaning, I'd never be able to set foot in here again. The man thrusts a twenty pound note at the cashier who accepts it with an air of suspicion. She waves the change in the air, uncertain who to give it to. Outside I try to give what money I have to him, but he refuses to take it.

'Twenty quid loan, call it that, you might be glad of some cash while you sort out your cards.' I nod my thanks and he extends his hand. 'Alex Hartley.'

'Jenny Parker.' I take his hand briefly, it feels warm and strong. 'I'll pay you back tomorrow, how can I get in touch with you?'

'Do you know the Sawyer's Arms on Deansgate?' he asks.

'Opposite John Dalton Street?'

'That's right. Shall we meet there about seven? You can give me my money and buy me a drink.'

22

It's now nearly 11 a.m. and amid the chaos and distractions of my office I finally manage to get through to someone I can talk to at my bank.

'The man at your call centre refused to talk to me and I can't log on to internet banking, what's going on?'

'Let me pull up your personal account.' She has the air of someone doing me a great personal favour. She is the business advisor for the company account. I get the feeling that my personal finances are of little or no concern. It's only my control here that holds any sway.

'Your last credit card payment was refused because of insufficient funds. You should have had a letter.'

'There's almost fifty thousand in my savings account, if I'd known I could have transferred some across. It really isn't good enough. I had to borrow twenty pounds off a stranger last night.'

'Your savings account is eight pounds twenty-three pence in credit. Your current account is one thousand seven hundred pounds overdrawn.'

A hollow feeling is developing in my stomach. Something about the situation is beginning to get through to my body, before my mind is able to grasp what's going on.

'Are you sure you have the right account?' I give her the number again.

'Yes, this is your account, I can see you withdrew all your savings over a week ago.'

'That's not right, you've made a mistake, I never did.'

'In that case you need to ring our Fraud Department.' She gives me a number.

Unlike the bank's main number, the fraud line is answered quickly and without any machine voice offering multiple choices. Even before I get an answer, I know what's happened to me. As the young-sounding man asks questions, I already know the score.

'It's because my documents were stolen, isn't it?'

'We can't be certain what's happened yet,' he replies cautiously.

'Well I can. Someone's cleared out my bank account, you must have had some reason to let them do it.'

'Let's get all the facts first.' He carries on asking questions. The usual mother's maiden name stuff and lots more about recent transactions, standing orders, electricity supplier, regular payments, salary details, other accounts. It is taking ages. All the time I'm giving him answers, I can only think about the money I've lost and feel the deep hollow it leaves inside my guts.

'Leave it with us.' He promises to get back to me tomorrow, meanwhile my accounts have been frozen. I walk into Emma's office and her warm presence prevents me collapsing into the sobbing wreck I feel.

'How much do we have in the petty cash?'

She takes the tin from her drawer and unlocks it. There's a thick wad of twenties nestling above the white receipts.

'Three thousand, seven hundred and twenty-seven pounds, thirty-two pence,' she reads off a sheet.

'All right, give me five hundred. My bank have lost all my money and frozen my accounts. I might need quite a bit more, so keep it topped up.'

She hands over the notes and I count out what I need. As she does, I feel a trickle of power flowing back into my body that triggers a warm feeling of anger. I resolve that this is a minor inconvenience in comparison with the grief I have in store for the ones who caused all this, the threats, the break-in at my flat and now my bank account. Someone has it in for me again. It's a familiar feeling, but this time I'm better able to cope. What didn't kill me last time has made me stronger now. They have the advantage of knowing who I am and where I live. I need to get on even terms and make them sorry they started this.

23

Alex Hartley is sitting on a tall stool by the entrance as I walk into the Sawyer's Arms. I am only a little late and if I allow myself to be truthful, I'm in a very nervous state. All of a flutter – my mother would have observed.

It's been a long time since the prospect of meeting a man has had this effect on me. My experiences have removed any desire for intimate relationships, my opinion of men in general is pretty well rock bottom. I know what they're like and even the seemingly nice ones aren't much different. So why am I going weak at the knees as I approach him? More disturbingly, why have I spent three hours at the hairdresser's that were badly needed at work? None of it makes sense. All I got was a brief impression of the man and a glimpse of his shopping. Re-visited he looks pretty ordinary. There have been dozens better-looking than him that I've automatically cold-shouldered. Now I'm like a schoolgirl on a first date.

The walk up from the Spinningfields car park was cold and blustery, all I can think about is the effect that wind may have had on my hair.

'What can I get you to drink?' He half rises as he asks. I'm not sure what to do so I awkwardly offer my hand which he shakes gently.

'I'm supposed to be buying you a drink, aren't I?'

'Okay, but me first. What are you having?'

'Lime and soda please, I'm driving.' The moment I make the apology for my non-alcoholic choice I regret it. I also regret driving here. I really could do with a stiff drink. The shiny plastic notice detailing special menu items isn't quite reflective enough to reassure me about my hair. I seem to have developed a halo of frizz but my image is too indistinct for me to be certain. It's not my hair that is disturbed though, it's me. Since Martin's tragic death, I haven't trusted anyone enough to allow myself to be intimate.

My life is full of energy and excitement, but seeing Alex here I realise how empty it really is.

Instead of using the moment to steady myself, by the time Alex returns with my drink, I'm even less composed than when I arrived. I'm fighting desperation now, trying to hide my neediness.

I begin with a well-rehearsed sentence. 'Thanks for rescuing me from my supermarket nightmare.'

'No problem, my pleasure.'

'Do you make a habit of rescuing damsels in distress?' As I speak I wince inwardly at how the words betray my state.

'I'd hardly call you a damsel in distress,' Alex smiles at me in a way that leaves me confused.

'So how would you describe me then?' Another sentence, another banal betrayal.

'Confident, capable, not someone to worry about being embarrassed in a supermarket queue.'

That's all very well, but I prefer words like pretty, attractive, sexy, fun, desirable, lovely. Ah, well, I suppose *capable* will have to do for now, it's better than a lot of other things he might have said. After today's revelations, though, I'm feeling a lot less confident and capable.

'My bank account has been hijacked, all my money stolen.'

His look of concern prompts me to reach into my purse and pull out his twenty pound note. 'But don't worry, I can pay you back. Here.'

'Are you sure you can afford this?' He looks suitably guilty as he accepts money from a destitute woman.

'That's the least of my worries. It's what's happened to my savings account that really concerns me.'

'How did they get access to your account?'

'I had a break-in at my flat, they stole my passport and other documents, used them to change my passwords and transfer my money. The bank is looking into it.'

'You should get your money back,' Alex says, 'it's the bank's fault.

'That's not what they're saying at the moment.'

'They want to make sure they can't wriggle out of it, to see if you're determined enough to take them to task. Keep on at them, don't let them fob you off.'

'So how come you know banks so well?'

'I don't, I've only read about similar cases. It's happening all the time. There are lots of cases like yours every day.'

He seems content to allow silence, not trying to fill it up with aimless chatter, yet he is there with me, giving me his full attention, un-preoccupied, not allowing every passing distraction to claim him.

'Has your account ever been stolen?'

'Oh no. I've had a credit card hack though. The card company cancelled it as soon as it happened. They're getting pretty vigilant these days, they have to be, it's a big problem. Bigger than anyone cares to admit.'

'What do you do for a living that makes you so knowledgeable?' I ask.

'I have a job that allows me plenty of time to read the paper and watch the news,' he grins.

'I want one of those as well, where do I get one?'

'You could try the DCLG like I did.'

'The what?'

'DCLG – Department of Communities and Local Government – I'm a civil servant.'

'Oh. I'm none the wiser, I'm afraid, it's not something I've come across before. What do you do for this DLGC?'

'DCLG. I deal with local government finance. It's all a bit boring to most people, but it's quite an important thing that we do, ensure the standards and continuity of local services.'

'Oh. So you make sure my dustbin gets emptied?'

74

'Not personally, but you're getting the idea. What about you, what do you do that makes you so attractive to fraudsters?'

As he says the word *attractive* my heart leaps and my brain stops working. I can feel the heat in my cheeks as I search for words. Before I speak though, my brain catches up and prompts me with the end of the sentence. Attractive, not to him, but to fraudsters. Disappointment and relief meet in the centre of my chest and battle it out. Neither wins decisively.

'I work for a security firm in Trafford Park, GOD Security.'

'Oh, GOD is watching you. I've seen your signs. Love it. Was that your idea?'

'No, the owner was Gary O'Donnell. It's his initials. I think it's brilliant. Most people smile about it.'

'You work for this Gary O'Donnell then?'

'No, I used to, he's dead. I work for his widow now.'

'Sounds a bit sad. What did he die of?'

'He was shot by criminals, trying to protect his family.' He was trying to protect me but the reasons for that aren't something I'm willing to reveal just yet. Maybe if I marry Alex and have half a dozen of his children, I'll take him into my confidence. Best leave those details untouched and unremembered for the time being.

'It's a rough world out there,' Alex says.

'Where do you live?' I ask.

'Salford Quays, I have a flat in the NV Building.'

'Wow, that's an impressive building, what's it like to live there?'

'It's okay, just a bit weird living on my own,' Alex says. 'Only been there for a month.'

As Alex speaks I try to place the feelings that are coursing through my body. I'm fifteen again, going through the same abandonment of sense and reason that I did then. Against all the parental counselling, all my own knowledge, I was overwhelmed by uncontrollable need. His name was Jake, I shuffled him off into a bedroom at a party and yielded him my virginity on a pile of discarded coats. I remember his face contorted in a mixture of ecstasy and embarrassment as he ejaculated as soon as I had fumbled him inside me. It was the warmth, the closeness, the deep intimacy of the act that I needed so desperately. I held on to him until he softened so much he was automatically ejected and fled in disarray.

Now I have that same irrational desire, not for sexual pleasure, but for surrender and comfort. It's as if I'd do anything at all to be close to this man, even if it means losing myself completely, giving myself up, abandoning everything.

My focus returns to the here and now but my aching persists. A nagging uncertainty intrudes. My mind races ahead of me, trying to interpret this latest remark of his. Sadness and disappointment replace reckless excitement.

'I've always lived in East Sussex and worked in the London area. A month ago I was moved up here,' Alex continues. 'It's a pain in the arse for me, but in my job you go where you're sent.'

A picture is beginning to emerge and I don't like it. I feel really stupid and let down. That pseudo-detective evaluation of his shopping and my leaped-at conclusion regarding his availability are looking very naïve.

'Worst thing is,' he says, 'I miss my kids.'

I gulp my drink, swallow my hope and abandon my expectations.

24

A black steel gate slides obligingly and allows access to a wide gravelled area, where two identical silver Mercedes are already parked. There's still plenty of room for my Range Rover and several more besides. The long, low garage building suggests more exotic automobiles may be secreted there.

The house looks modern, stonework bright and clean, every line of mortar straight and white, dark hardwood double-glazed units, shining red roof tiles perfectly aligned. According to O'Brian's list, everything I'm looking at is cosmetic surgery performed on a crumbling old edifice at the cost of over three hundred thousand pounds, half of it paid in cash.

I want to show the patronising old bugger that he is wrong and I am right. These people have possessions to protect and GOD Security are willing to protect them for a very reasonable fee. The fact that this is the only prospect willing to grant me an audience is additional incentive to push this one hard. First impressions are good, there are no dogs are barking, there doesn't seem to be any CCTV installed, the walls and gate could do with an upgrade to increase security. All positive signs, there are plenty of reasons to hire a good security firm, lots of things we can help with.

This is the only place on O'Brian's list of twenty-eight properties that would agree to see me. A pleasant-sounding man called Williams had answered my voice mail message explaining who I was and what GOD Security had to offer. Now I'm going to sort out nice Mr Williams, protect his obvious wealth and show O'Brian that his sarcastic laughter is misplaced.

The man who answers the door is not what I am expecting. He is the exact opposite of the kindly sexagenarian Englishman I visualised.

'Is Mr Williams at home?' I ask.

'Yes, it is I,' he answers in a thick accent. This man looks unpleasant and sounds nothing like the man I spoke with on the phone.

'I'm Jenny Parker.' I reach out a tentative hand which he ignores and waves me inside. The hallway is lavishly paved in white marble, I can almost hear O'Brian chuckling as he worked out the bill for all this opulence. There is an impressive staircase with stainless steel balustrades and wire posts in front of me. Ordinarily I would be captivated by the way it appears to hang in mid-air, float its way upwards, but I'm too busy grappling with the terrible feeling of anxiety in my stomach. I'm beginning to think all this is a mistake, that I should never have come. There's something here that makes me feel afraid and vulnerable.

The tall swarthy man with the prominent thin nose and slicked black hair leads me into a large room with dark wooden floors and three white leather settees. It's not only his appearance that disturbs me, it's the whole atmosphere in this house. There are no pictures on the walls, no ornaments on the shelves. No bookcases, no vases of flowers. No signs of normal life in a normal house. A bad smell pervades the whole room, a combination of stale tobacco, septic drains and diesel oil. The unpleasantness of the situation is easily matched by the unwelcoming aroma.

My mind is busily castigating me for being such a fool. The goad of pride, of getting one over O'Brian, of showing him who's the smart one, that's what got me in here. I have a sad desperate feeling that I may never get out and that it's a lesson I will never be able to apply.

'Look, I've made a mistake,' I speak to the man's back. 'I really should leave now, I have to go.'

'Wait here,' the man says as he leaves the room, closing the door after him. I sit, perched on the edge of the middle settee facing the ornate fireplace and clutching my sheaf of brochures. Trying not to panic, I breathe in and out slowly. Apart from the unexpected appearance of the man who admitted me, there's nothing to be afraid of. I'm in a perfectly respectable neighbourhood and dealing with one of O'Brian's customers. My mind turns reluctantly to the sale pitch I'm going to give. Upgrade the gate, put some razor wire on top of the walls, install CCTV linked to our central surveillance unit. We can offer a 24 hour service, Mr Williams can rest easy that his property will be monitored constantly even while he's away. Think of the peace of mind that gives, and all for an easily affordable monthly fee. The way I feel at the moment, the fee is getting smaller and smaller, I don't want to upset the rather fearsome-looking Mr Williams.

I take my phone out of my handbag to check in with the office but it's showing no signal. Williams is taking his time, I wonder if he's making some tea. If so, he needn't bother, I want to get out of here as quickly as possible. Anyway, he's not asked me whether I want a drink, or even how I take my tea. For all he knows I could be a Mormon or something and unable to drink any form of stimulant.

It's a long ten minutes, sitting alone, fiddling with my phone. I stand up and wave it in the air, hoping for some connection, but it remains awkwardly off line. Collecting my things, I move over to the door and listen. I can hear nothing through the door, no footsteps, no voices.

I visualise the front door, the drive, my car and the open road. If I can slip out now, perhaps I should. The only problem might be an embarrassing confrontation if Williams turns up in the hall. I can always say I'm looking for the toilet, I suppose.

It's taken me half an hour to drive here, that's after two hours spent on fruitless phone calls. Maybe I should hang on a bit longer. Perhaps Williams has himself been caught short and is occupying his toilet worried and embarrassed at what I might be thinking. If that's the case, he'd be really upset if I just disappear.

The room itself begins to bother me even more. It looks like a badly laid out IKEA display, not somewhere lived in. I'm in a show house, or at least a show room, somewhere designed to help sell the property by diminishing the feeling of vacant emptiness. That has to be it, and the consequences of this conclusion start to stiffen my limbs with fright. If nobody lives here then why do they want to discuss security with me?

That thought does it for me; I decide to leave before Williams returns. The door to the hallway opens easily enough. I let out a deep sigh of relief at finding it unlocked.

As I creep into the hall the silent appearance of another man bars my escape. This man I recognise. He is wearing a smart grey suit, white shirt and yellow tie speckled with blue. His shoes are polished and his hair neatly parted to one side. At first, I note only the way he looks familiar then realise that the last time I saw him he was in a grubby vest and I head-butted my way past him and out of Mrs Mather's flat. Now he's well prepared for any repeat of our last encounter and the element of surprise I had then has long since disappeared. Williams appears, grips my shoulders and pushes me back into the room. I allow myself to be manoeuvred into a sitting position back on the settee opposite the large ornamental fireplace. Both men stand over me confrontationally.

'What do you want, Jenny Parker?' Williams asks.

'Er nothing, it's all a mistake. I thought you needed security.'

'Security?' The men exchange glances.

'You mean protection?' The second man chips in.

'No, well, not exactly. Like I explained, I represent a security firm, we protect premises, you know, offices and factories and some big houses. I thought...' My voice trails away as I lose the will to say anything further.

'What do you want?' Williams repeats. 'Why are you interfering in our business, who sent you?'

'Nobody sent me, it's all a misunderstanding.'

'You have been at one of our places, you attacked Demitri. You cause big trouble, problems with police.'

'I'm sorry,' I say, the sweat dampening my hair at the back of my neck. 'Like I said, it's all a big misunderstanding.'

'Then you steal our lorry. Is that more mistake? What do you want with it? Tell me or it will be bad for you,' Williams demands.

'Let me explain,' I say. 'When I met your friend Demitri all I wanted was to find out who had taken Mrs Mather's council flat. It was she who asked me to go there. As for your lorry, I have no idea what you're talking about.' Neither man looks at all interested. 'I'm sorry for hitting Demitri.' I look at the big man's face and detect nothing to indicate he is accepting my apology. I pick up the GOD Security brochures and offer them to Williams. 'Here, take a look. This is my business, all I wanted to do was to sell you some security services. I had no idea you were the people at Mrs Mather's apartment.'

'Who are you working for?' Williams fishes a pack of cigarettes from his pocket. My fear is beginning to be replaced by excitement as the adrenalin rushes through my veins. My mind is clear now, any befuddlement blown away by the heavy waves of stimulus.

'Nobody, myself, how many times do have to tell you?' I stand up but Demitri pushes me back onto the sofa. 'Let me go,' I say, 'or you'll regret it. You can't keep me here, my people know where I am.' I jump up this time, try to twist away as William's heavy hand comes to restrain me. Demitri moves to block my exit, pulling an automatic pistol from his pocket and aiming it at my chest. I freeze, my legs weak with shock.

The gun is a very bad thing. Not only does it ruin any prospects of escape, it also provides an unwelcome complication. If they are to let me go, I have to convince them not only that I'm not a threat but that I won't report the gun to the police. Hand guns in English suburbia are taken very seriously by the authorities. I wonder if these men realise what trouble they're potentially bringing down on themselves by threatening me with a pistol. A darker thought pushes itself forward and asks me if they even care and suggests that they've no intention of allowing me any opportunity to report them; that I am going to die here and very soon.

'I'm not here to interfere. I thought you might need help, that's all. Look, I'm not going to make any trouble for you, I promise. There may be things I can help you with, money for instance. Cleaning money, making black money legitimate, it's what I do.'

Williams looks as if he might be interested. He leans forward, cigarette between his lips. The smoke from it burns my eyes and they start to water. I feel myself recoil automatically at his approach, trying to avoid the glowing tip as it threatens my face. Sucking deeply on it, he takes it from his mouth and away to the side. I feel myself breathe again and watch as his left hand reaches out. Suddenly he grabs my hair and pushes the cigarette into my face. I feel a terrible burning pain just below my eye as he grinds the cigarette into the top of my cheek. I raise my arms to try to protect myself and he hits me open-handed across my wounded cheek and throws me to the floor. As he kneels on my chest, face pressed close to mine, he repeats, 'Who sent you?'

I try to reply but can't make words out of my screams of agony. He produces a knife which he waves close to my eyes. For a moment I think he's going to stab my eyes and twist my head, desperately trying to keep away from the blade.

I hear him say, 'You have to understand we are serious,' and feel the knife slicing through my ear. It seems to take an age, sawing its way through gristle and spearing deep pain into my head. A warm gush runs down my neck, soaking my hair. The pain is all-consuming. I can't believe my ear has been hacked off, but I can believe the pain.

I feel myself half carried, half dragged into another room. I'm roughly discarded, thrown onto a settee where I bounce off onto the floor. The men slam the door as they leave. No matter how hard I press my hand to my ear, the blood flows like a river, pouring down my arm, dribbling off my elbow, making a slippery puddle. I clamber onto the sofa, grab a loose cushion and try to staunch the wound with it. The sharp pain persists and is joined by a deep throbbing hurt. All my attention is on my face and ear. I have no hope left other than that the pain will subside, that I might die in peace.

The knife returns every time my heart beats. I pray it will stop. A thick, bloody crust has glued my head to the cushion, its course fibres mingling with my ragged flesh. The pain is a constant. I try holding myself tightly and forcing it away, but it persists. Relaxing, allowing feeling into it, makes it slightly softer but I can't keep up this posture and revert to clenched wincing again and again. When they come for me they will kill me. I wish they'd hurry, get it over with, make it quick.

Toby will be all right, he has his life with her now, she is his focus. If she died it would be harder for him. Perversely it's Alex that forms the centre of my regrets. A fleeting relationship with a self-confessed family man, one tiny encounter in a shop and then an hour in a crowded pub, forms my biggest regret as I anticipate the end of my life. Out of the throbbing torment rises the wish that I hadn't flounced off, that I'd accepted what was, embraced the situation and him. How can I be so much in love with a man in an instant? Now I will never feel his embrace, never explain to him the passion in my soul, my fears and my joys, my triumphs and my disappointments. Soon I'll feel nothing but cold death and I have no fight left in me to resist it.

As soon as I saw the gun, I ought to have realised my fate. I should have taken my chances on a bullet, at least that would have been decisive. Now I wait for the inevitable. These men have no choice but to kill me. I've seen them, I've seen the gun, I've visited their house. It's a simple decision for them and one they made long before I arrived.

Once before, I fought and bit as Gary and Mick bulldozed in and laid waste to my captors. They were wielding a knife at me then, but I wasn't cut, I was naked and bound but I was still whole. Now I have a burned face and no right ear. Gary is dead and Mick has his own problems. He's no longer on babysitting duties, there's no chance of any repeat. I've had my one miracle, my entitlement is spent.

25

The stab of the needle releases a new cascade of agony. It returns a second time to the base of my ear and is pushed into the base of my eye socket. Each time it releases stinging juices which quickly cool and numb. As the pain subsides into an uncomfortable background throbbing, my mind begins to function for the first time since my ear was cut off.

There's still a large residue of resignation and acceptance. I still expect to be killed at any moment. All through the banging on the door, the crashing entry, the black-clad men carrying me out, I knew they were going to kill me. Even though I recognised their police uniforms, I had no hope left, no capacity for any more suffering and no prospect of salvation.

Now, after they wheeled me past the waiting wounded, fast tracked me into a doctor's care, I'm beginning to hope again. With the realisation that my death is no longer imminent comes grieving for my disfigurement. There is an endless loop of memory that plays constantly in my head. Hot stabbing cigarette at the top of my cheek, knife hacking through my ear, warm blood soaking my neck.

How will Toby greet a mother with one ear? Could any man desire a woman with a burnt face and a severed ear? Whatever my chances with Alex were before, they haven't been improved by my disfiguration.

All this obsession with Alex is making me ignore the important questions. How safe am I? Will those men be back to finish what they started? When I think of what happened and what might have been, I grow cold and feel completely vulnerable. Even here, in this hospital bed, there's no security. They could walk in here any time of the day or night and finish me off.

There's another thing. The origins of O'Brian's cash have always been a bit mysterious. Building work, he says, for people with cash to spend. I've always presumed this is money being hidden from the taxman but earned from legitimate, lawful work. As I lie here thinking about Williams and what he's done to me, I realise what a fool I've been. Whatever O'Brian might say or think, all his money comes from criminals, and criminals of the worst kind. My clever little schemes are helping drug dealers, child molesters, brothel keepers, pimps, thieves, murderers and ear-slicing thugs. Without people like me, they wouldn't be able to spend their ill-gotten funds. Without people like me, there would be little point to their crimes. The money would be next to useless, they'd only be able to spend small amounts and between themselves.

Emma arrives, bunch of carnations clutched proudly, big reassuring smile, bright energy dispelling my gloomy clouds.

'Oh there you are, you poor thing.' She thrusts the flowers at me.

I hate carnations, they remind me of death. They were festooned all over my mother's coffin, pink and white and red. I shudder at the recollection and push the bouquet onto the bedside cabinet.

'What happened to your ear?' The full horror is mercifully concealed by a thick bandage that winds around my whole head, giving me the look of a half-dressed mummy.

'Some thugs at the house, they cut it.'

'Did you get the bit?' I fail to understand her question.

'Get what bit?'

'The bit they cut off.' She looks at me as if I should be more aware of the procedure for aural amputation. 'If you kept the bit, they could sew it back on; you'll hardly notice the difference.'

'I don't know where it is.' I can feel the tears of self-pity welling up again. I thought I had cried enough of these and more besides. Apparently there are plenty more left.

'They shut me in a room, left me to bleed to death. I thought they were going to come back and kill me.'

Uncontrollable sobs are heaving out of me. Emma hugs me gently, avoiding any contact with my voluminous bandages. The spasms subside, I wipe away the tears running over the dressing stuck to my cheek.

'Well thank God you're safe now,' Emma smiles again. 'I'm sure they'll be able to sort out your ear. Don't worry, it'll be fine. You could always grow your hair. No one will notice.'

A young policeman in uniform hovers at the end of the bed.

'Hello,' Emma greets him. 'Are you the one who saved our Jenny from those awful men?'

'I'm only here to take a statement,' he answers, softening his defensive posture in the warmth of Emma's greeting.

'Have you seen it yet?' She turns back to me.

'Seen what?'

'Your poorly ear, do you know what it looks like?'

'Oh,' my stomach churns, 'no not really, I think it's bad though judging by all the blood and the pain.'

'It'll be okay, don't worry. They'll probably take a bit of you that you don't need, something nobody ever looks at and stick it on to mend your ear. It's amazing what they can do. You'll probably never notice, you'll have to point it out at parties when you're telling the story.'

Emma's comforting words are ludicrous and unbelievable yet they carry with them the energy of hope and life. I'm not dead, not even badly injured. Okay, I have some cosmetic injury that might be termed disfiguring, but I'm alive when I expected to be dead.

'Anyway, what's happening at the office? Did the Stretford invoice get out on time?'

Emma wrinkles her nose as if sniffing something she expects to smell badly. 'Oh invoices, they are the most boring thing ever, the big fat smelly one got done, don't worry. You had a visitor though, a man came looking for you.'

'Who?'

'A really nice man, we chatted for ages, he only popped in on the off chance, said he was passing and wanted to see you.'

'Who?'

'Apparently, at least according to him, you and him have been going out for drinks and you never even told me. What were you thinking? How long have you been seeing him? Why didn't you tell me?'

'I'm not going out with anyone.'

'Oh yes you are, you big fibber, and he looks really yummy. Good on you. But why keep it a secret?'

So Alex was looking for me. Now my mutilated ear really matters but I can't help the feeling of exultation that's breaking through my pain and anguish. It's partly Emma, but mostly Alex.

26

I can't sleep. My ear isn't hurting much at all, a dull throbbing at worst. Most of the time I can cope with the pain but I can't get my mind to stop thinking about what happened to me. The savagery, the inhuman brutality of those men sends shivers down my body. As soon as I relax and start to drift away they come back, hold me down and slice away at me.

It's all very well having someone here in the flat but they can only try to make me a bit safer physically – a security guard sitting in my lounge, watching my TV on low volume might deter them if they decide to attack me here, but I have my doubts. There's nothing anyone else can do about my mental security. Since it happened I can feel myself going crazy with fear and lack of sleep.

The only upside of my security guard is that he's an employee and therefore I have to maintain my composure while he's around. It wouldn't do to have the staff realising they were being managed by a mad woman. Even here in my bed I have to keep the sobbing and groaning to a bare minimum. I need to sleep. I have to get some rest, my energy is depleting rapidly. The more tired I get, the less able I am to cope.

Even the smallest task seems impossible to manage. Every decision I'm faced with needs effort I can no longer give. I'm scared to be here in my own home, even with a bodyguard. I'm scared to go out, even during the day, in case they're waiting for me. It's no use pretending, they'll find me and kill me whenever they decide they want to. I have the horrible feeling they've already decided.

As I turn onto my side, trying to get comfortable in this oven of a bed, I lean on my bad ear and any vestige of slumber is expelled by the sharp pain. Tomorrow I have an appointment for the stitches to be removed, then they'll take away the bandages and let me look at it for the first time.

The new me, the new lop-sided me, the new disfigured, disgusting me. My mind's eye looks at me with my missing ear. It cruelly puts sunglasses on which tilt comically to one side. It sees the grisly vestiges of flesh that were once a reasonably normal ear. It winces with embarrassment on my behalf. Maybe I should keep the bandage on permanently. Emma says I look like Mr Bump, better him than Quasimodo or Frankenstein's monster.

As for Alex, I can hardly visualise myself as the siren who distracts him from his wife and children. Even so, he shows definite interest according to Emma who can be relied on to notice; an interest, sadly, in a woman he assumes has two ears. The thought of what I could have spent my time doing with Alex instead of stupidly, pig-headedly chasing O'Brian's thuggish customers makes me want to scream out my pain.

My good ear is picking up the tinny distortions of whatever false exuberance the TV has to offer in the early hours. I think of joining my bodyguard, losing myself in the televised drivel. It's out of the question, I can't trust myself enough to show my face in this state at this time of night.

Very quietly I reach out for the bedside light and read my book while trying not to rustle the pages. *White Tiger* is an apt choice, I'm one third of the way through and being constantly reminded on every page how there are billions of people much worse off than me. Even in my present, deplorable state, the writing is still convincing.

27

'Oh,' Emma wrinkles her nose, her eyes fixed on my ear. 'Oh dear,' she says.

'I didn't think it was that bad,' I reply. It's true. When they took off my bandage I was amazed at how little of my ear was missing. It felt like he sliced most of it away, leaving me with little but a vestigial hole. In reality, all that is missing is a bit at the top.

'Oh dear, poor you,' Emma continues. 'When are they going to fix it?'

'What do you mean, fix it?'

'You know, put a bit back, make your ear normal again. You won't want to be going around like that for very long. It looks, well, weird. Not very nice at all.'

'They can't fix it, where are they going to get another bit of ear that fits?'

'Oh surely they can. They can do all sorts of things. I saw a woman on the television having her vagina neatened up.'

'Are you suggesting they use a bit of my vagina to fix my ear?'

Emma laughs and I join in.

'There,' she says when she finishes adjusting my hair. 'Can't even tell you have a manky ear. Just try not to make any sudden movements or go out when it's windy.'

Suddenly the office and the world seem welcoming and comforting. I don't feel entirely safe, perhaps I never will, but the hurt is beginning to recede, by head is back up and I'm beginning to look forward again.

'He's rung again asking when you'll be back.'

'Who?' As if I don't know.

'Alex.'

As Emma speaks his name a flush of excitement surprises me with its intensity.

'What did you tell him?'

'I told him you were having your stitches out this morning and would be back this afternoon.'

'Oh, fine, what did he say?'

'He said he'd pop round and see how you were.' A man's voice, Alex's. I turn so quickly we almost collide, he reaches out to steady me.

'I'll make a brew.' Emma leaves us in her office.

'I was attacked.' My hand touches my ear as if I need to show him I'm speaking the truth.

'So Emma said. What happened?'

'I was on a sales visit in Radcliffe and two thugs attacked me. They burnt me with a cigarette then cut off a piece of my ear.'

'My God, that's awful. Shouldn't you still be in hospital?'

'I'm okay, it's not so bad.' I slump back in Emma's chair, my feelings are in direct contradiction to my words.

'How did you get away from them?' Alex asks.

'They locked me in a room, the police let me out. They just left me there. I was so certain they were going to kill me.' I can feel the tears, this isn't how I want to appear in front of Alex. I bury my face in a clump of tissues until the sobbing subsides. When I emerge, Alex is quietly standing next to me, his strong presence bringing me comfort and strength. 'When I didn't ring in to the office, Emma called the police and told them the address, bless her.'

'Did the police get the men?'

'No, they must have been long gone by the time the police arrived. I can identify them though, if they ever catch them.'

'I'm amazed you came back to work so quickly. Shouldn't you be taking some time off to recover, to heal?'

I can't tell him this is the one place I feel at all comfortable. Everywhere else, especially my flat, is threatening.

'Oh, I have to keep them all beavering away, you know how it is.' The lameness of my reply is left hanging in the air.

'Well, when you feel up to it, maybe I could take you out for a meal. When you're better of course, no rush.'

Take me now, I want to say. And not only for a meal. Take me home with you, take me away from danger, take me in your arms. Take me.

'I'd like that,' I reply, trying not to let the thought of his wife and children intrude too far into my thoughts. At least they're down south, somewhere far away. At least Alex is interested. At least I have a chance with him.

Emma comes back with three cups of tea, sits with us like some auntie chaperone making sure we connect properly and firm arrangements are made.

'Tomorrow night,' she decides, as if she is included. 'At the Lowry. It's nice there, I'll book it for you if you like, best to make sure you get a table. There might be something good on and it could be busy.'

28

The Lowry restaurant is small, open, exposed, crowded – none of the things I want for my first meal with Alex. Somewhere dark, intimate, quiet and discreet is what I need; the Lowry is none of these. At first I thought we had booked a table in a plastic-tabled café but Alex's enquiries discovered a more exclusive area for diners and I breathed a sigh of relief. It's much better here, even if it's not ideal. The menu is simple, no precious time lost leafing through pages and pages of stuff. Beef for Alex, salmon for me, done. Now for the part I've been nervously dreading and longing for all at the same time.

What if he doesn't like me, finds me boring? All I do is work after all, work, eat, sleep, oh and get myself attacked and hacked to pieces.

'How was work today?' His face opens as he speaks, his eyes invite me to reply, offering their total attention when I do.

Work? It was shit, as usual. Worse than usual in fact, Jim asked me to do without my babysitter tonight. He's desperately needed to cover Trafford Trailers. I really do need to get lucky with Alex tonight otherwise I'll be on my own in an empty flat. The thought makes me very afraid. Now I've worked myself into a state of incoherent desperation. All Alex did was ask a simple question.

'Fine,' I reply. 'Same old problems – not enough men, too much work.'

'Better that than the other way round.'

'I suppose you're right but I'd like to try it just to see. How about you, how was your day?'

'Very good, very exciting, lots of fun and laughter.' He smiles. 'Every day is like that if you're involved in local government.'

'Very funny.'

'Why do we do it then? Money? Fame and fortune? Habit? Or because everyone else does and we don't want to be left out?'

'Don't mention money,' I grimace, 'the bank is still being awkward, I don't know if I'll ever see my savings again.'

'Give them grief at least once a day. Get Emma to pester them on your behalf, that should do the trick.'

I become aware that the couple to our right are not only sitting uncomfortably close to us but also that their attention has shifted this way. He is mid-twenties, head shaved, apart from a wide strip of stubble on his crown. Ear-rings, nose piercing, black t-shirt with a grinning green skull. His companion is dainty, petite, short black hair, cotton flower-print dress, fingers and wrists festooned with jewellery, eyes fixed on Alex.

'Should we have booked the play?' Alex asks.

I stare distractedly at him. 'Book what?' I ask. I half expect the girl to my right to provide an explanation, so enwrapped is she in Alex.

'The play here, Ibsen, *A Doll's House*. Is it something you'd like to see?'

'Sorry, the play, I've never seen an Ibsen play. I don't go to the theatre much. Though when I do I generally enjoy it.'

'What was the last play you saw?' Alex asks.

I wonder if he's testing me, then realise we're both trying to find some topic to connect about, something that transcends banal small talk.

'*The Crucible*.' I have seen it, I also read it at school so I'm pretty safe with this one. The last one I actually saw was Shakespeare, *Hamlet*. I don't want to show my ignorance and admit I understood very little of it.

'Where was that?'

'The Octagon at Bolton, do you know it?'

'No.'

'Oh of course you don't,' I laugh, 'you've only been up north for a week or two. How could you possibly have been to Bolton?'

'Is it a good theatre, we could go there if you prefer?'

My heart floods with warmth, my body with energy, he's committing himself, seeking to commit me to much more than a casual dinner.

'Very good, small, intimate, in the round, a bit like the Royal Exchange in Manchester.' I try to appear like a proper theatregoer. It's something that might keep Alex's interest.

'Next time there's a good play on, we'll go,' he says. 'We'll both keep a look out, shall we?'

'Love to.' I really mean it.

'I've not seen *The Crucible*. I thought it was where they played the snooker,' Alex smiles.

'You men,' I laugh back. 'You care nowt for anything but sport.'

'I think you'll find we do.' Alex's eyes twinkle. 'At least this one does.'

'You'll be telling me you can read next.'

'Love it, do it all the time.'

'Who's your favourite author then?' I ask, hoping it's someone I've read or at least heard of.

'Vonnegut.'

'Who?' My heart sinks but only a little, after all he can't expect me to have heard of every writer going.

'Kurt Vonnegut, he's American or he was. He's dead now.'

'Ah, that explains it,' I say.

'Explains what?'

'Why he's not phoned me for advice lately.'

Alex laughs. I don't even have to add the only-kidding bit that my ex-husband always needed to avoid lapsing into total confusion.

We chatter excitedly about books, the couple on the right lose interest in anything apart from their rapid intake of alcohol. Neither Alex nor I are drinking. I want to leave my options open. If I do end up having to go home alone I might just go out to see Doreen O'Donnell after all.

He promises to lend me *Cat's Cradle*. I offer *White Tiger* as soon as I'm finished with it. Now we are a supper club, a theatregoer's club and a book circle. More connections all the time.

Outside, I get nervous again. All those nice connections, but are we going to be a couple? Does he want to hold me, to make passionate love to me, as well as improve my reading?

29

Chris greets me at his front door, his uncharacteristic nervousness betrayed by clasping hands and unsteady stance.

'There's somebody I want you to meet,' he says.

'Who?'

'My wife.' He smiles thinly, as if expecting some negative comment.

'I didn't know you were married, this is a surprise, Chris. I'd love to meet her.'

I've known Chris for a year or so, he once helped me get some important information which saved my life. He's always portrayed himself as a loner, a geekish technophile with little time for social niceties.

He leads me through the long hall and into his dining room where a young girl sits at the table. She has a wide smile, perfect teeth, round eyes, a cascade of blonde curls. She is dressed simply, but her clothes accentuate her slim figure.

'This is my wife, Lottie,' Chris says.

As we exchange greetings I am staggered by her perfection. I look at Chris, untidy Beatle-mop hair, prominent nose, bad skin, old jumper which is liberally decorated with food stains, sad old, baggy, corduroy trousers. Then I look at her pristine perfection. She must be half his age, if that.

'How long have you two…?' I ask.

'Two months,' Chris answers quickly, 'we've been married two months. Lottie is from the Ukraine, she's finding it a bit difficult here in Salford.'

'Maybe she needs some female company,' I say, 'someone to show her around, take her shopping. How about it, Lottie?'

She looks at Chris for approval, he nods and she answers. 'That would be good. I miss my girlfriends in Ukraine, especially my sister.'

'You should get her over here to keep you company,' I say.

Her face clouds over. 'We try, but she can't get visa, it's not possible for her to come.'

'Then I'll have to do instead,' I say. It's the least I can do for Chris, he helped me out so much in the past, anyway I need him to do an urgent job for me. Taking Lottie's distracting charms out of his way for a few hours might help speed things up.

'Tomorrow,' I say. 'I'll pick you up at ten, we'll go into Manchester. Spend the day.' I can see by her expression that she's very pleased at the prospect.

'Thank you, that will be very fine. Can I get you some tea perhaps?'

'I'll have a brew, as well,' Chris says.

'I need you to build me a tracking device,' I say.

'Okay,' he says, 'come in to the workshop, I'll see what I can sort out.'

I'm not even sure this is something Chris can do for me. The front room of his terraced house is piled with carcasses of dead electronic equipment, stacked shelves and dusty components, tangles of wire lying underfoot. I need him to make me a tracker, like we use on our vans, but this one is a bit special.

'How long do you want it to work for?'

'I don't know.'

'Well, are we talking years, days? It's important to know how big the power supply needs to be. That determines the size of the whole thing, pretty much.'

'It needs to be small, nobody must find it, that's important. Nobody could ever know it was there. If they did I'm likely to get killed or worse.'

He returns my earnest look with concern. 'Don't do it then, someone like me could detect it easily, even if it can't be spotted by eye.'

'That's a risk I have to take.'

'Where do you want to hide it? In a car? If it's a car I can tap into its power supply and it will last forever, just about.'

'No. I thought a video tape.'

'Oh.'

'Isn't that possible?'

'It's possible, but why a video tape?'

'It fits in with how I intend to deliver it.'

'Bad choice,' Chris shrugs. 'Think again.'

'Why, is it too big to fit?' I have to get this tracker device, I've been racking my brains how I can get out of this mess and this is what I've come up with. A tracker on a video tape.

'It's not that, there's nowhere to put it. I'd have to try to open up the tape and glue it back together. Does the tape have to work with the tracker inside?'

'Yes of course.'

'Sorry, there's no room then. The tape will snag on the tracker.'

'I need it to be a video for a security camera, that's the thing.'

'Simple then, we'll not use a video tape, I have something much better. I can easily fit a tracker and it will be almost undetectable, even to someone who might be suspicious.'

'How long will it take you to make it?'

30

'Well?'

'Well what?'

'You know what.' Emma's eyes are ablaze with excitement.

'Oh, my dinner with Alex.' I stop teasing her. 'It was fine, actually it was better than that, it was really good.'

'So you two got on then?'

'Yes, you could say that. We got on really well.'

'How well?'

'I already told you, really well.'

'Tell me what he said to you.'

Emma settles on the edge of my desk, she won't go until she has extracted every morsel. The thought strikes me that I should have taken her along, save all this badgering and I laugh.

'He said lots, we talked about films and books and all sorts. He's really interesting.'

'And?' Emma prompts.

'And the meal was good, at least the food was nice. . . My ear was hurting a bit, especially when I chewed my food. Anyway I didn't let it spoil the meal.'

'What did you do after the meal?'

'Nothing.'

'Nothing, nothing at all?'

'Alex walked me home, that's all.'

'Didn't you invite him in for a…ahem…coffee?' She grins.

'It didn't seem the right thing to do.'

'Oh.' She looks glum. 'Did he kiss you?'

'No.' I'm a little put out by her questioning and find myself reacting automatically in defensive mode. 'He gave me a nice hug though.' I soften at the memory.

'Ah.' Emma seems satisfied. 'So no rumpy-pumpy, no argy-bargy until next time. Is that tonight?'

'Actually it's tomorrow night if you must know. We're going to the Bridgewater Hall to see Dylan Moran.'

'Oh I like him, he's funny. Prefer Bill Bailey though, I've see him three times, he's hilarious.'

'I don't really know Dylan Moran, it's Alex's idea.'

'He seems keen then, your Alex. Did he mention your ear?'

'No, I showed it to him though, told him I was going to have some more surgery.'

'Good idea. If he suddenly saw it for the first time while you were having a bit of nookie it might have put him off. Now he knows to put a paper bag over your head first.'

She scampers off as I pretend to attack her. Her laughter lingers in the air for an instant, then the awful feelings of vulnerability and helplessness begin to close in on me again.

31

I park at Blackfriars Bridge, it's the only place I feel okay with the big Range Rover. All the multi-storey car parks are much too tight for me to manoeuvre comfortably. Here, there's open air and lots of space. Not only that, but it's just as handy for the shops.

Lottie pours herself out of the car, her long legs slightly unsteady on the combination of heels and cobbles beneath. Her legs seem to go on for ever, her microscopic skirt accentuating the illusion. She's dressed for a night on the town, silky eye-catching multi-coloured top, sumptuous man-catching body.

I'm wearing my usual flat shoes, simple black skirt down almost to my knees. The familiar black and white ensemble that was my daily work-wear as an accountant and which I've never bothered to change. We both need to do something about the way we dress, now we have the perfect opportunity.

'Typical Manchester weather.' I point up at the almost cloudless sky. Lottie laughs, she already knows better. Even in Odessa, Manchester's chronic tendency for continuous precipitation must be legendary. Today, though, there's a beautiful breathless brightness. In this light, even the nasty Urbis building behind the Cathedral looks stunning.

'We'll buy you some new outfits, I'll bet you've not had a chance for a proper shop, Lottie.'

'Chris takes me, he's okay, he lets me buy anything I want.'

'Like I said, you've not had a proper shop, then. It's not the same having a man hopping impatiently from one foot to the other, telling you everything looks great just to get you out of the shop as quickly as possible. Am I right?'

She laughs, nods her head. Her bright eyes show her appreciation of what I'm telling her.

We dive into Top Shop. She grabs a collection of tiny skirts and slinky tops, parades herself in front of me, seeking approval. I find myself shaking my head on a regular basis, watching her bottom lip pout with increasing disappointment.

'Lottie, you're picking clothes for a summer holiday. It'll be winter all too soon, you need to be planning ahead a bit more.'

'Don't you think Chris will like me in this?' She stands there in tight shorts up to her bum, purple top with a deep vee that leaves very little of her chest to the imagination.

'Chris loves you even if you wear a sack. What we need to think about is how you look to everyone else.'

'But it's only Chris I dress for, as long as he's happy that's all that matters.'

'Men aren't always happy when their wives go out looking so sexy,' I say. Her face drops, she looks at herself in the long mirror.

'You think I look like a whore in this?' she asks.

'No, you look very beautiful. But you can look even better in something a bit more subtle.'

She allows me to extricate her from the booming cacophony in Top Shop and lead her into the more refined ambience in Jackpot. As she pulls dresses from the hangers, she looks at the tags and frowns. 'I can't afford any of this,' she says.

'Oh yes you can,' I say. 'This is how it works, Lottie. Chris is making something for me. He thinks he's doing it as a favour, he's not going to ask me for any payment. In return, you get to buy some really nice clothes and I'll pay for them. So, you get some clothes, I get my device and Chris does me a favour. Everyone wins, everyone is happy.'

Her crinkled forehead indicates puzzlement at the complicated arrangement, so I explain again. 'Chris is happy to make the thing for nothing, but I want to pay for it. This way, we both get what we want and you get some nice things. Don't worry, Lottie, I'm an accountant, I know how these arrangements work. Get whatever you want, if there's a problem with money, I'll tell you.'

Festooned with paper bags advertising the success of our shopping mission, I steer Lottie into Katsouri's Deli on the corner of Deansgate and John Dalton Street. The place is full of people milling about in apparent chaos. We collapse gratefully into chairs that suddenly become vacant as if by magical arrangement. There's barely enough room to stuff our bags out of the way of careless feet.

We share a large platter of meze served with delicious warm flatbread.

'I've never been to Ukraine, what's it like?' I ask.

'Some of it is very beautiful. Where I come from, Odessa, it's especially good. Very nice, people having holidays there.'

'So now you're living in Salford, it's not so beautiful eh?' I ask, knowing the answer but intrigued about how this gorgeous woman has arrived in this less than gorgeous neighbourhood.

'Salford okay,' she smiles, 'lots to do, lots of nice shops here in Manchester. I like.'

'How did you meet Chris?' I can't resist being nosey.

'We meet on internet, he's so nice, so kind.'

'Yes he is, though he's a bit older than you, isn't he?'

'No matter, how old doesn't matter. He looks after me well. I've no complaints.' She looks uncomfortable and I am feeling sorry for being so rude.

'Excuse me for asking, I don't mean to upset you. It's just that I'm a bit surprised he's not mentioned you before.'

'We fell in love.' Her face is reddening. She is speaking in gasps. 'It's true, we fall in love, I with him also. He choose me, I am happy.' She is almost belligerent now.

'Well, I'm very happy for you both,' I say, holding her gaze and making her listen. 'Chris is a good guy, you've done well. I'm sorry, I don't mean to upset you with my questions.'

Her forehead crinkles but the rest of her face is more relaxed now. 'Thank you, you are kind.'

'Have you any family or friends here in England?' I ask.

'No, not here. Only in Odessa back home. My sister, Kat. We are very close, we always do everything together. She's so funny, she always makes me laugh. I really miss her.'

'How old is she?' I ask. 'Are you the big sensible sister or the little one of the family?'

'Neither, we're the same age. Look.' Lottie takes a photograph out of her purse, it shows two identical laughing faces. 'We used to cut our hair, wear the same clothes, everything the same. It was so much fun. Now we're older we have different styles. Kat likes to have crazy hair, I like mine natural.'

'You said she'd had problems getting a visa, is there any chance she can sort that out?'

'I don't know, it's hard for us to come here. Maybe she can get a student visa, I don't know if that's possible. She desperately wants to join me here.'

'There's one more shop we need to take you to,' I say. 'Finish your coffee and we'll go to Marks and Spencer and get you a bra or two.'

Why?' Lottie looks puzzled. 'I already have a bra at home, you know, for sports and jogging.'

'You really need to wear one under your clothes here in England. It's a sort of tradition. Believe me, Chris will be more comfortable if you do. Over here, girls without bras are considered a bit, well, naughty.'

Her face colours itself bright red in an instant. 'Do I look naughty? Like a whore? Is that what you're saying?'

'You look lovely, really pretty. It's only that customs differ from place to place. Where you come from it's normal to dress like you do, here there's a more conservative attitude.'

'Oh my God!' She puts her face in her hands. 'You think my Chris married a whore. Everyone must think it.'

'Don't be daft, I don't think that for one minute. All I'm saying is that you might want to blend in a little more. Wearing a bra is part of it. Believe me, that's all I'm saying.'

By the time we arrive at M&S Lottie has recovered her exuberance and lets a lady measure her and tell her she's a 34B. We find some nice bras and join the long queue for the changing rooms.

Before I can say anything, Lottie pulls her top over her head and hands it to me, then puts on a dark blue T-shirt bra.

'Does this look nice? It feels a bit strange.' She holds a breast in each hand and adjusts the bra. 'That's better.'

I recover the power of speech and as she removes it and reaches out to try the next one, I push her top back at her. 'Put this back on,' I say. 'We should wait for a cubicle, you can't try your bras on out here.'

She looks all around slowly. 'Why not?' she says. 'There's only women here, there's nobody to look.' She drops her top back into my arms and fits the new bra. 'Perfect,' she announces, 'I'll take them both, come on.'

I look at her face and see the mischievous grin and flashing eyes. One Lottie is enough of a challenge. If her twin makes it to England, I wonder if Chris, or anyone for that matter, could possibly cope with two of them.

32

'Hello George.' I place the thick jiffy bag on his desk. It makes a solid sound as I let it drop.

'What's that?' he asks.

'That's the hard disc from our server, it's where all our video files are stored, including the ones from Trafford Trailers.'

A look of alarm is beginning to form on his round face.

'The recording from the night of your break-in is on here.'

The alarm is turning to panic.

'I've not looked at it, neither has anyone else, nobody even knows it exists.'

He is calmer now, but only fractionally.

'This is the only copy and I'm giving it to you.'

'Why?' He manages a word at last. His hands dance on his desk top, drumming away his discomfiture.

'Because you are the client, George, you had the break-in. It was your trailer that was stolen.'

'But it was your man who got himself killed.' George looks down at the package as if trying to resist an urge to grab it before I change my mind.

'That was unfortunate, tragic, nothing you or I could do to change it, is there, George?'

'No, I suppose not.' He finally picks up the jiffy bag and weighs it in his hands. 'I suppose you expect me to hand this over to the police, then?' He looks into my eyes for the first time since I walked in.

'No.' He looks puzzled. 'No, George, I don't expect you to give it to the police.'

I reach out and hold his wrist. 'I need you to listen to me carefully. I don't want you to say anything, don't even shake your head, don't try to confirm or deny anything I say.' I look hard into his eyes and see that I have his attention. 'George, I need to get these people off my back. I need to convince them that I don't pose a threat to them. I need them to leave me alone.'

His eyes widen but he says nothing.

'I don't care about anything else. I don't care about you, or the people who are doing this. They stole your trailer, they killed my employee, they cut my ear, they're still threatening me. Enough. I want it to stop, at least as far as I'm concerned. Call it a peace offering. Give it to them. Tell them what I say, there's no copy, no threats, no 'you back off or I'll tell the police', nothing like that. A peace offering, security, one less problem for them to deal with. Right, now I'm finished.' I take my hand away. 'You can deny all knowledge now, George.'

'I don't know what you're talking about,' George gasps. 'What makes you think I know the people who attacked you or the ones who stole our trailer? That would make me an accessory. Is that what you're implying?'

'No, George, I'm making no implications. I'm accusing you of nothing. All I'm doing now is giving you this disc and saying my piece. Now I'm going to leave. As far as I'm concerned we never had this conversation. Next time I see you it'll be to discuss our service and agree some better rates.'

He sits transfixed in his chair, not even bothering to see me out or say goodbye. I feel exhausted now that the excitement is fading. I know I have to get this exactly right. Talking to George is the easy bit. Things are going to get harder from now on.

33

'Better now.' Toby kisses the ragged edge of what he calls my poorly ear. I clasp him hard to me, his body reacts by going entirely limp in protest.

Outside the house the August sunshine should feel much warmer than it does. A surprisingly chilly breeze sweeps my hair away, exposing my ear. I wish I'd brought a hat.

The children's play area is sparsely populated, a couple of tentative princesses are swept aside by Toby's brash entrance. He invades the elaborate climbing frame, dashing across the wobbly bridge, clambering through the tube, sliding down the pole then back again for more. It's a route he's taken many times, one that I watch with trepidation. The contraption appears to consist of snares and pitfalls, an accident zone waiting to claim Toby as its next statistic. Sure enough he trips, falls headlong, lies trapped in rope netting, red-faced, teary-eyed and a few inches from falling from a great height onto his head.

I rush over to extricate him, carefully lifting him out and saving him from more serious injury. There are a few spots of blood appearing on his right knee which I wipe away quickly, then dab the tears with the same tissue. A few gulps of breath is all Toby needs and then he's off and running, climbing, slipping, falling, crashing to the ground, picking himself up, smearing mud on the polished steel as he struggles to ascend the slide.

By the time his energy is spent and I can persuade him that sitting in the café eating chips is an essential part of the park experience, I am old with worry, exhausted with fear, weary of holding onto my concern. It's only been a couple of hours. I wonder with a heavy heart if full-time motherhood would be survivable.

34

It's my phone choosing the most inconvenient moment. I am stark naked, dripping wet, in a hurry trying to get myself ready for Alex. The show starts at seven-thirty, it'll be a miracle if we get there on time as it is.

It's Chris, my heart beats faster. 'Your package is on the move, again.'

Yesterday it moved from George's office to George's house. It's been there all day. I was wondering if George had decided to stick it in his attic and forget about it. Now he's taking it somewhere.

'I'll be right there.' It'll take me five minutes to dress and ten minutes for the drive, I have to go but my heart lurches at the prospect of missing out on an evening with Alex. He'll be on his way here already, it's too late to ring and tell him I can't make it tonight.

My doorbell rings. It's either the ear-cutting thugs or Alex, neither of whom are welcome in my current state of undress and confusion. I throw on my dressing gown and answer the door.

'Sorry, Alex, something's come up. I can't make the theatre tonight.' He looks suitably disconsolate and hands me a bunch of tulips. 'Come in for a minute,' I say, 'I'll get dressed and explain.'

The excitement of the package and its importance overwhelms even Alex's presence. I bustle around, throwing on clothes, unsnagging my hair, snapping on shoes. All the time I talk, tell him I'm sorry, that I've been looking forward to the theatre, that it's lousy timing.

'What is it?' he asks.

'What's what?' I stop chattering, stop moving about and stand by the door, ready to leave.

'The work thing you have to do, will it take all night? Can't we salvage some of our evening?'

I look at him, smart blue sweater, navy blue chinos, dark brown hair neatly trimmed. His broad shoulders are tensed, he looks taller than I remember him now that he's framed in my doorway. He's bought the tickets, made the effort, turned up and I'm brushing him off. The reality of how it must look sinks in and I know I can't risk him thinking I'm fobbing him off and that I have something in my life more attractive than him.

'It would take too long to explain, Alex, I'm sorry. It's something I really have to do, not something I want to do.'

'Then tell me about it, Jenny.'

'I can't.'

'Why not? You said it's work, what is there about your work that I can't be trusted with? Do you think I'll start robbing the places you're guarding?' He's starting to look like Toby when I refuse him a visit to McDonald's.

'No, of course not, but it's not entirely work, it's also personal.'

'So, you don't want me interfering in your personal life. Okay, I get the picture. Maybe I can sell the tickets outside the theatre, I might as well go and try.' He shrugs his shoulders and turns away.

'Wait.' I can't help myself. I can't let him walk away like this. 'I am sorry, it's not fair on you, I'm being awful. I don't mean to. I'll come to the theatre, I don't want to spoil our evening. I really do want to go out with you.'

He turns slowly, his shoulders are relaxing, arms out by his side, hands open and pointing at me.

'It's me that should be sorry,' he says. 'I'm acting like a spoilt kid. It's what I do – go off in a huff when I don't get what I want.' He smiles.

I go to him, stand close, let those arms wrap around me, it's warm and safe in here, this is where I want to be. I look up at his face. He tilts his head and kisses me on the lips. His soft strength spreads a warmth throughout my body, awakening every cell. The heat is starting to intensify in my belly. His hands move slowly, one holding the small of my back, the other slides gently up to the back of my neck, caresses me, pulls me in even deeper. Then he releases me gradually, places me back into my own separate world. Now I'm standing close to him and we are apart.

'It's those men.' I look into his eyes. 'The ones who killed my security guard.' He looks puzzled then concerned.

'What about them?'

'I'm trying to find out where they are.'

'How?'

'I sent them a parcel, it has a tracking device in it.'

'If you know where to send the parcel, you must know where they are already,' he says.

'No, it's not that simple. I've planted the device with a man who I know is mixed up in the break-in where he was killed.'

His face tells me he needs a much better explanation. My excitement shows me I have to join Chris, to watch the position of the device, to see the action unfold.

'Come with me,' I suggest. 'Let's go together, I'll explain on the way.' His face brightens up. 'Are you okay with missing the theatre, though?' I ask.

'Sure, when you said you had better things to do I was a bit miffed. Now I understand completely. This is much more important, let's go.'

By the time we pull up outside Chris's house I've told Alex everything, about the child brothel, the trailer theft, Alan's murder, my suspicions about George Bottomley.
Something inside me starts to release. I feel lighter, as if part of my heavy load has been passed on.

'I don't understand,' Alex says. 'Do you think the brothel keepers who cut off your ear are the men who robbed the trailer park?'

'I'm sure they are. The threatening phone calls started after I told George I had a surveillance tape showing what went on at the trailer park. When they cut my ear they went on about

113

me stealing their lorry. At the time I didn't understand what that meant but it must be the trailer they were referring to. From the questions they asked, they assume that I'm working for someone, a rival gang perhaps. That's why they're so concerned about the security camera record. I think they may have trashed my flat looking for it, I'm sure they killed Alan to cover their activities. If there's a film showing what went on they know it means big trouble for them. That's why I gave the tracker to George. He's got to be in on it.'

Chris drags an extra chair for me in front of the monitor, leaving Alex to hover uncomfortably in the rear.

'This is the trace so far.' Chris brings up a map with a red line on it. 'He's driven from Eccles to Pendleton, down Frederick Road and stopped on Seaford Road. That's it, the package is in there now. Hasn't moved for half an hour.'

Lottie comes in bearing a tray laden with tea and biscuits. I sense Alex's reaction to this vision of young loveliness and am comforted that it feels like genuine surprise and pleasure without any hint of lustful longing. I need him to be lustfully longing for me, not my radiant Ukrainian friend.

'This is Alex,' I say, 'the man I told you about.'

Lottie smiles. 'Hello, Alex, Jenny has told me lots about you. It's nice to meet you.' There's something about Lottie's manner that's worrying me, she appears subdued, maybe a little sad.

We drink tea, make small talk. Alex is interested in the tracker, asking Chris for technical details which he is all too happy to provide. Lottie disappears after bringing the drinks. I find myself wondering what has upset her. It's not something I can ask Chris, I doubt he's even noticed.

'I need the loo,' I announce.

'Upstairs, first door on the right,' Chris tells me. I leave the morass of technical debris and walk out into the tidy hall.

35

Lottie is sitting at the kitchen table reading a book which has an indecipherable title and a lurid picture on the cover. She looks nervous as she sees me, puts down the book and stands up. The kitchen is pristine, worktops clear and sparkling, the tidiness is so intense it leaves me with a hollow feeling.

'Hi Lottie,' I say. 'Didn't mean to disturb you, I got fed up sitting in there with Chris. '

'Can I get you something? Are you hungry?' she asks.

I sit down uninvited and wave her back to her chair. 'Relax,' I say. 'I just got bored. What are you reading?'

'Oh.' She looks at the discarded book. 'It's about a Polish girl called Vavara in eighteenth century Russia.'

'No, I meant what language?'

'Ah, Russian, it's a Russian book.'

'I thought you were Ukrainian, aren't you?'

'Yes.' She wrinkles her nose. 'Ukrainian, not Russian. They teach us Russian at school. It's still a big influence, how you say, control from Moscow.'

'Are you okay? You look a little sad today. You're not depressed because I made you wear a bra, are you?'

Lottie smiles, 'No, I like my bra. You are right, I think Chris is a little less crazy when we go out these days. He says he really likes my new look.'

'Great, so why so sad?'

'It's Kat,' she says. 'I've not heard anything from her for three days now.'

'That's not so long, maybe she's busy.'

'You don't understand.' Lottie leans forward over the table, fists clenched. 'Kat emails me every day, five or ten times. Always she keeps in touch. Suddenly now, nothing.'

'Could there be a problem with her computer or her email account? There's all sorts of things that could explain it.'

'No, then she would text me or phone or something. Also my mother doesn't know where she is, she's worried as well.'

'You must miss your family, it's hard for you when they're so far away.'

I think of my own situation, that I don't even have somewhere to return to, a family to visit, anyone to worry about me. I think of Alex and suddenly I want to be back in there with him.

'My sister tries to come here,' Lottie is saying. 'She told me she met this man who said he would get her a job in Manchester.' Her face is sad and worried.

'I'm sure she'll be okay,' I say automatically. 'Give her time.'

'You don't understand.' Lottie is crying softly now.

36

'It's stopped transmitting,' Chris says.

'What? It's stopped working?' My disappointment makes me irritable, despite the presence of Alex. We've been sat here half the night and now the dammed thing's gone faulty, just when we might be getting somewhere.

'I don't think it's a fault in the tracker. Something or someone has interfered with it, or it could be somewhere where the signal is shielded, like in a metal cabinet.'

Chris is fiddling with his computer, scrolling through pages of numbers. I feel upset at this outcome. The excitement of the chase has vanished and I'm left only with dread. If someone has found it, I'm in desperate trouble. They will know that I'm still interfering in their business, despite the warning of the severed ear, and that they have to finish the job they started and kill me properly.

As uncomfortable as this tangled electronic graveyard is, I don't want to go home and wait for death. I look longingly at Alex, peering over Chris's shoulder, as if this were a computer game. The implications seem lost on both of them.

'I need to know what's happened to it,' I say. The two men look at me.

'Hang on. I've a good idea where it is and why it's not transmitting,' Chris says, pointing to a map on the screen. 'It moved down Seaford Road, turned right down Gerald Road and stopped at the end. It was moving slowly, someone was carrying it on foot. The last transmission was from here.' His finger stabs the monitor. 'I reckon they've thrown it in the river.'

A long breath finally escapes from where I've been holding it in. Some of my tension releases with it. 'That'd make sense, wouldn't it? If you had a computer disc that you wanted to get rid of, what would you do?'

'I'd wipe it,' Chris says. 'Format it, then check it's clean.'

'But you'd have to put it into the computer and get it working,' I say.

'That's not difficult.'

'Not to you.' I wave my hands at the computer carcasses all around us. 'But anyone without all this paraphernalia might think differently.'

'You're right,' Alex says. 'Without installing it on a computer they couldn't know what was on it. Chucking it in the river is probably the best option to get rid, it's what I'd have done. Better than throwing it in the bin where it might be salvaged.'

'But I need to know for sure. If they've found the tracker and destroyed it, they'll be after me again.'

'That's not likely,' Chris says. 'It was still working when it left the house on Seaford Road, that's where they would have found it. You're safe, don't worry. It's in the river, you're in the clear and we have their address. That's what you wanted, wasn't it?'

'Well yes,' I answer. 'But not really.'

Chris looks puzzled.

'Look, the whole point is to get them off my back, give them something that tells them I'm no threat, that I'll leave them alone.'

'But why the tracker then, you could have just given them the disc?' Alex asks.

'I have to know my message has got through. How else can I be sure it worked? I wasn't even certain that George could deliver it, that he knew where to take it.'

'Maybe George has thrown it in the river,' Alex suggests unhelpfully.

'If he has then we're back to square one. We need to check that address, see who lives in the house on Seaford Road,' I say.

'I'll do it,' Alex says.

118

'No don't be silly, you're not going down there.'

'I don't intend to.' He smiles. 'Do you imagine I would knock on the door and see who answered?'

'Yes,' I say. 'It's what I would do if I wasn't so scared of being recognised.'

'I'll get all the details from work,' Alex says. 'The electoral role and council tax records, that sort of thing.'

'When?'

'It won't be until Monday.' He smiles and I resign myself to a weekend of uncertainty.

37

The weather has deteriorated by the time I reach the Tesco car park. I find three empty spaces together that allow easy access to my Range Rover's bulk. I hate all that squeezing slowly between cars, waiting for the horrible scraping noise that tells me I've misjudged things again. My car is lovely to drive, I like sitting up high but I have to confess I don't have an accurate idea of where its corners are or exactly how long it is. Most of the time, I'm pleasantly surprised at how I manage to manoeuvre myself into an inadequate space. If I can avoid all that effort though, I do.

The three consecutive spaces are towards the end of the car park furthest from the entrance but I welcome the marginal benefits of an extra fifty metre walk, I've been sitting on my bum all day. The little plastic hut for returned trolleys has but a single occupant, attesting to the relative remoteness of its location. As I walk towards the store, I snuggle into my lovely raincoat, pulling up the hood against the drizzle. Ahead, I see another lone woman climb out of a white Mini and walk ahead of me. There's something familiar about her, at first I wonder if I might know her then realise it's the coat she's wearing. It's very similar to mine, black with narrow horizontal quilting, fur-trimmed hood, cute belt that accentuates her nice figure. I hope I look as good in mine as she does in hers.

It's the fact that I was able to treat myself for the first time in ages that makes my coat so special. I bought it at a tiny shop in Kirkby Lonsdale when I'd taken Toby out for the day and couldn't think of anything to do other than go for a drive in the Lune Valley. It was so expensive, nearly three hundred pounds, that I'd become breathless and sweaty at the thought of spending all that money on a coat when I had several perfectly serviceable ones already. I've never regretted it, though. My coat is wonderful and I deserve it.

The other coat is only a few paces ahead of me, I hang back, make some distance. I'm in no mood to connect with someone who might want to compare clothing, she'll only tell me how she bought her coat in a sale for fifty quid and then I'll never feel good about mine again. Now I'm a bit closer, I realise her coat isn't exactly the same as mine, it lacks the detailing around the pockets, the hood is a bit shapeless and floppy, the fabric isn't the same quality as I know mine to be. I guess it's a cheap mass market equivalent, she probably did pay fifty quid for it, and I'm still happy with my choice.

I hear a squeal of tyres, a big car comes hurtling around the corner, heading down the line of parked cars towards me. It's going much too fast, hardly manages to make the turn, seems out of control, sliding on the wet road surface. Instinctively, I duck into the gap between two cars. I hear a piercing scream, a soft thud. A loose trolley comes clattering past followed by the car which is now going even faster. The headlight nearest to me is smashed. I glimpse two men in the car as it hurtles past, slides around the bottom of the row and speeds towards the exit. In what seems a brief moment, it's gone.

When I emerge from my sanctuary, a small group of people is gathered around the fallen figure. The adjacent car has its front smashed in. The woman lies awkwardly, head at an unnatural angle, still, lifeless. She's wearing my coat.

Shocked, I turn away, walk slowly back to my car. As I tread nervously, looking over my shoulder at frequent intervals, cowering at the sound of any car, I replay the incident in my head. I hear the tyres squeal, feel the terribly soft thud as her body was broken, watch the grim-faced men as they make their escape.

My coat. She's wearing my coat. That's what killed her, it was my coat. It should have been me, they were after me. I know it. My thoughts make me hurry, my legs feel weak, hardly able to propel me back to my car.

As I pull the solid door shut and sit in the protective steel, I begin to cry. Desperate sobs convulse me, I can't control myself. My whole system is shut down, all I can do is heave and shudder, feel the anguish. I sit transfixed until I'm roused from my catatonic state by flashing blue lights.

When I get home, I take off my lovely coat, fold it neatly, place it in a black plastic bin liner, take it downstairs and throw it in the dustbin.

Whenever I close my eyes, I see the woman's sightless eyes staring accusingly at me from inside her fur-trimmed hood.

38

'You're very clever.' Alex hovers over the bed, holding a mug of tea. He obviously thinks I've decided to wake up. He's wrong. I try a tired sigh and turn over, burying my head in his pillow.

'I've been thinking about what you did, very smart and brave.'

I let him talk. I don't feel clever and I'm certainly not brave enough to tell him about the woman in the Tesco car park. He started off with clever and brave, maybe he'll get round to some attributes I want to hear like passionate, sexy, beautiful, desirable. There are plenty for him to choose from.

He clunks the mug on the bedside table, sits softly on the bed and places his hands on the only bit of me left exposed, my neck and head. I feel his warmth and my whole body stirs with longing.

'Sending them that computer disc with the tracker, that's a brilliant piece of work, I don't know how you thought of it.'

I love his gentle touch, but I wish he would stop talking and come back to bed.

'On the one hand they get a peace offering from you, something that ought to get them off your back. On the other, you find where they are, you get the upper hand. Brilliant.'

I don't feel like I have the upper hand, they're still out to get me and can kill me any time they like. The tracker idea is looking more foolhardy by the minute. Something is badly wrong, either they know I'm trying to find them or they're not the ones who stole the lorry. Could they be the ones who owned it, and they've got the idea from somewhere that I'm implicated in its theft? The more I think about it the more I realise I must be missing something. They asked me why I stole their lorry. Why would they do that? Were they the ones George took the disc to, or not? Maybe they did check the disc and see that it was blank? Now I wonder how that must seem to them. Was the message they got the one I intended?

I've been having my first proper sleep since the accident at Tesco and I'm not finished. I don't care if they're wondering where I am at the office. It's Saturday, surely I'm allowed a day off once in a while. A pang of guilt stabs me, then I struggle back to life and sit up.

'What time is it?' I ask.

'Eleven-thirty.' Alex smiles as if proud of the good job his bed has been doing.

'Shit.' I can't help it, but regret the unladylike expletive as soon as I utter it. 'I have to go.' He hands me the tea, my awkward position makes me dribble down my naked chest and I flinch, spilling even more hot liquid down my front.

'It's the first home match of the season,' I explain.

'You never said you were a football fan.'

'I'm not. My lads do the parking, I have to supervise.' I'm really there to collect the money, dole out the wages, make sure there's no temptation for the guys to pocket a bit extra. Also, with my bank problems, I need all the cash I can get just to pay the bills.

'Can't I come with you?' he asks.

My heart sinks. I can't take him to see my bunch of yellow-jacketed chancers taking cash off motorists to allow them to park in areas where they could park anyway, if we weren't there. Some of the parking is subject to informal arrangements with the site owners, some of it isn't. Sometimes we have to cut through a fence or knock down a gate to get access. Occasionally the police query our rights to be doing what we do but they're usually satisfied by the spurious documents I have created. An official-looking letter on a fake letterhead generally does the trick.

Gary was doing this for a long time before I arrived on the scene. It was he who established territorial rights.

Alex, a government official, can't risk being involved, even if he approves of what I'm doing, which I doubt.

'No,' I speak softly. 'Not your scene. I'll only be gone a couple of hours, I can come back here if you want.'

'What I want is for you to stay here, let someone else look after work.' He clambers onto the bed, puts his warm hand on my naked stomach. I feel a deep urge to melt back into his arms, to allow his touch deep inside me, to surrender to this moment and let the world out there take whatever course it will. Instead I slide deftly to one side, slip out of the bed and start dressing.

'Later,' I say. 'Keep that thought, I'll be back for it soon enough.'

Alex wrinkles his face in disappointment, but makes no further move to stop me leaving. I realise how close I am to staying when I feel a twinge of doubt rapidly dispelled by my practical mind. Two thousand pounds in cash. I need this money. Alex will be here when I get back.

39

I don't recognise the black youth who is taking the money. I park the Range Rover across the car park entrance and wind down my window.

'Five pounds,' he says.

'Who are you?' I ask.

'You want to park or what? Five pounds.'

There are no familiar faces amongst the yellow jacketed lads who are waving cars in. None of my men are here. It's still early, two hours to kick off, so they should be arriving any minute now.

'Who told you to man this car park?' I ask.

'Five pounds, missy, or fuck off.'

I open the door and step out of the car, leaving it blocking the way in. 'This is our car park, you have no right to be here,' I tell him. 'I suggest you clear off now before there's any trouble.' He towers over me but his arms are slack, his face confused rather than angry.

It's the first match of the season, an opportune time for someone to muscle in on our business, and that's what they're trying to do. I should wait for Mick and the lads to arrive; they'll see this bunch off in no time.

The youth looks nervously over his shoulder, shouts to one of his mates, 'Get Leroy.' None of the interlopers are out of their teens by the look of them. The boy in front of me could still be at school.

In response, a man gets out of a black Audi parked untidily in the far corner of the yard. He walks slowly towards me with a rolling, swaggering gait. A small man in comparison to the ones who accompany him. As he gets nearer, I realise that he is even younger than the rest. Leroy looks like a school kid dressed in ridiculously baggy trousers, worn so low they threaten to drop to his ankles with every step.

Behind me van doors slam and my men arrive. 'Perfect timing,' I say as Mick looms over my shoulder. The youth who told me to fuck off steps back, looking as if he's now having different ideas.

'What's going on?' Mick asks unnecessarily, maybe as a way of announcing his arrival. As if anyone could fail to notice a man of his bulk dressed in a fluorescent jacket so big it seems to illuminate the whole street.

Leroy finishes his unhurried saunter across the car park and stands flanked by his helpers. By now I have four of my own at my shoulders. Leroy is a child and has kids to back him up. I almost feel sorry for the inequality of the situation. He is hopelessly out of his depth. I only hope he realises it and leaves gracefully.

'There seems to have been a mistake,' I say. 'This is our car park. Whoever has sent you here must have been mistaken.'

'No mistake.' Leroy's voice has a high-pitched, pseudo American whine to it. 'This was your park, it ain't no more.'

He stands with his head tilted to one side, arms held stiffly, fingers pointing towards me. It's a pose I've seen rappers take on TV. The thick gold chain around Leroy's neck is another testament to their influence.

It's almost laughable, this childish bluster and foolish bravado. When I look into Leroy's eyes I don't see any fear. He is obviously outmatched here, will have to back down to avoid a beating. He's going to lose face in front of his teenage gang, yet he holds my gaze unwaveringly, head cocked to one side as if trying to peer around the corner.

I get a sudden rush of terror as I realise what must happen next. I take half a step back, ready to turn away, disperse my men, leave quietly. Before I can, the inevitable gun is poked at my face.

Leroy's face contorts as he spits out words. 'Fuck off, you whore. If I see you on my land again I'll blow your face away.'

Gary's kindly face flashes through my mind. No guns, walk away; his words, his mantra. Don't get involved with fire arms, he was adamant about it. He once explained that a gun couldn't protect anyone, only put them at risk. A gun wouldn't have saved him the night he was killed. I might have, if I'd followed my instinct and kept away from his home.

Whether it's the thought of Gary or my more recent encounter with threatening behaviour, I don't know. Something moves deep inside me. I feel a great anger born out of mistreatment and savage abuse. My hands rise reflexively, as if they carry a will of their own. My right sweeps the pistol aside, my left grasps the gun arm at the elbow, folding it back towards Leroy and bearing down hard. The explosion jolts me but I still cling on, locking the arm in place.

Leroy's face shows he is as surprised as I am that the gun has discharged. The surprised look is quickly followed by concern and then pain, confirming that Leroy has shot himself. I twist away the weapon, stand back and allow Leroy to sink to his knees clutching his stomach. A dark wet patch is spreading quickly from his groin. He begins to whimper and shake. All his bravado is lost, there is now only a frightened boy crying with pain.

Mick and two lads push past me and pick up Leroy, then half carry, half drag him to his car. A thin dribble of blood stains the dusty concrete as they go.

'Get him out of here,' Mick orders the black youths. They need no persuading but leap into the big Audi and drive steadily towards me. I throw the gun onto the passenger seat and back the Range Rover into the road to allow them passage. Cars begin to enter the car park and Mick calmly relieves them of their money. The rest of the lads fan out, direct the traffic, waving in new customers. Business as usual.

I look up and down the road expecting flashing blue lights, police rushing to the incident, SWAT teams being deployed from black vans. Nothing. The pedestrians walk by unconcernedly, the punters roll up in ever increasing numbers.

40

I'm still trembling when I reach the sanctuary of my flat. My hands shake as I fill the kettle, my nerves are jumping all over my body. I feel wretched. As I stand waiting for the kettle to boil I remember the gun. A fit of panic pictures it where it lies on the front seat of my car. I imagine curious faces pressed to the window, gazing at the deadly instrument.

After clattering down the stairs, I arrive breathless back at the Range Rover and yank open the passenger door. The gun rests quietly on the brown leather, as if it belonged there.

I snatch it up, looking wildly around me for witnesses, and thrust it under my blouse where it nestles cold and uncomfortable against my belly. Slamming the door I take a few steps homeward, then freeze with indecision. Am I going to take this weapon and hide it in my home? The last time I hid contraband the police raided me, seized the guilty money and imprisoned me. It's bound to happen again if I have a gun.

I consider taking it to one of the big steel bins and lobbing it in, then I remember all the security cameras around the place, one of which must be watching me right now. It might even have seen the pistol when I retrieved it. I go back to the car and climb in. I slip the gun out of my clothes and push it into the glove compartment. I resolve to dispose of it properly, I need time to think what that might look like. Melt it down for scrap metal perhaps, but I have to find the means.

Back upstairs, the tea steadies me, the exertion from the stairs has cleared my head, pumped blood through my system. I ring Mick.

'What's happening?' I ask.

'Nothing, business as usual,' he answers. 'Are you at home? Do you want me to dish out the wages then bring the takings back for you?'

'Yes please, that would be good. I'm still in shock, Mick, I can't believe what just happened.'

'The little toe-rag had it coming, you were lucky he didn't shoot you. He would have if you'd let him.'

'What about the police, have they been round?'

'No, it's all cool, no sign of any interest.'

'But the gunshot, surely it would have been reported?'

'Not necessarily, lots of bangs around here. Cars backfiring, fireworks, all sorts of noises. It's no surprise if one muffled shot goes unnoticed. Apart from our young friend, of course, he noticed it all right.'

'Okay, let me know if there's any sign of trouble. I'll wait here for you.'

41

I'm still wondering what to say to Alex when he rings.

'Are you on your way back here yet?' His voice is light and cheerful.

'No.' I hesitate, story not formed; no tale devised suitable for Alex's consumption. 'Not yet, I'm at home sorting something out.'

'Are you okay?' he asks. His note of concern makes me think he can tell the voice of a woman who has recently been in a gun fight.

'Yes, fine,' I lie.

'You don't sound fine,' Alex says. 'Shall I come over now and cheer you up?'

'No, don't.' I recognise my abruptness, try to soften it. 'Yes, sorry, but later.' I look at the kitchen clock. 'This evening, can you come about six maybe?' By that time I hope I will have gained some composure and concocted something to explain my mood.

The whole Alex thing is unravelling. He thinks I'm an accountant who's fallen foul of unspeakable evil through no fault of her own, that I lead an unblemished life and earn an honest living. I haven't bothered him with any details that demonstrate the exact opposite. I left out my prison sentence for money-laundering and neglected to mention any continuing activity in that business. Hard working and honest, that's what Alex thinks. And unlucky. Our brief joy can't possibly stand up to the truth of who I really am. Now I have to add assault with a deadly weapon to the list. I only hope that Leroy received timely medical intervention and that it isn't murder. My worst nightmare has him bleeding slowly to death in his bedroom, scared to tell his parents what happened to him.

Alex is touching me, caressing me gently. I lie naked, splayed, trying to be receptive and failing. Last night when he did the exact same movements I opened and blossomed every time. I felt every thrill of energy, I abandoned myself to his loving care. I rocked and whimpered and shouted with joy.

'It's not working, is it?' Alex says. His own enthusiasm for love-making is evidenced by his unwavering erection that points accusingly in my direction.

'Sorry,' I mutter. I take hold of his cock, begin to rub it, intent on providing him some relief, some recompense for his journey over here.

'That's okay.' He takes my hand, disengages it. 'We'll wait for a better moment, shall we?'

'I'm sorry.' I feel the dread of inconsolable loss, I'm excluding him, rejecting him, lying here clenched and unavailable. I know what I'm doing, but it can't be helped, there's too much to hide, too many lies inside me. The foul river between us seems unbridgeable.

42

Jim Almond looks as if he hasn't been enjoying himself either. Normally morose, Jim brings a new level of dissatisfaction with him this afternoon. Wherever he's been all morning, it doesn't appear to have agreed with him. He slumps down in his seat opposite mine and stares glumly at me.

'Well,' I ask, 'what's your problem?' I'm in no mood to put up with someone else's tantrums, not after the way Alex left me last night. There is a gaping hole in my being that can't be filled by anything but Alex.

'How long have you got?' Jim grimaces. There's an air of resignation about him today that I like even less than his usual pessimism.

'As long as it takes. Tell me about it, Jim.'

'I've been to Trafford Trailers, they asked me in for a meeting.'

'Oh really, I normally deal with George.'

'George isn't there any more, his director knows me from when I worked at SG, wanted to tell me personally.'

'Tell you what?'

'That we are no longer required, that GOD Security is out and SG are in.'

'Oh shit!' I feel uneasy on two counts. Firstly we need the work and secondly I now have no direct access to George, when I know he's implicated in the trailer theft and Alan's death and who knows what else.

'It's a big loss, three jobs gone, three men we don't need any more. I've already told the men involved, dished out the bad news. It's a tough situation, but it has to be managed properly, swift action taken, you understand?'

I'm only glad I don't have to do all the dirty work myself for a change. I forgive Jim his miserable face, any man who looks happy after he's made people redundant can't be trusted.

'Who did you lay off?' I asked.

'Johnny Harris, Danny Williams and Mick.'

'Mick?' My heart stops.

'Yes, Mick. He's overweight, his knees are so bad he can hardly walk. He's been a passenger since I got here.'

'Now hang on,' I say, feeling very aggrieved. 'Mick is practically management these days, you can't just fire him.'

'Yes I can and I did. You hired me as manager, not Mick; if you would rather he did this job you only have to say.'

'That's not an issue, it's just that Mick and I worked closely together, have done for a while. I owe him a lot. What did he say when you told him?'

'He seemed happy enough, said he'd been wanting to spend more time at home. His wife isn't well and there's his motorbikes to keep him busy.'

'I don't care, I need him here. I'll tell him if you don't want to.'

'That would undermine my credibility.' Jim's eyes narrow. 'You put me in charge of the personnel, I've hired and fired dozens of men for you. You can't expect me to run everything by you first, you might as well not employ me. I am sorry, Jenny, but it's a point of principle for me. Either you let me do the job you pay me for or I might as well go now. If you want Mick back, you'll have to do without me.'

'It's my business, I decide who stays and who goes.' I'm getting riled at his pompous attitude.

'I never said it wasn't your choice.' Jim remains stony-faced. I have to leave my own office before I burst with frustration.

43

Mick is sitting in John's Diner with several more GOD Security men clustered around him. When he sees me he brings his mug of tea over and ushers me to an empty table.

'I'm so sorry, Mick, Jim's way out of order on this one. He never consulted me.'

'That's not what I wanted to talk to you about. Jim's done me a favour, I should have left ages ago, it's just that...' He looks down awkwardly and stops in mid-sentence.

'What?' I ask, suspecting that I'm not going to be happy with his explanation.

'Well you know, after what happened to you and Gary being gone and all.'

'You think I need looking after, is that it?'

'Not exactly.' He looks up, round head nestling in concentric rings of flab.

'Then what exactly?'

'Well, sort of that I suppose. I thought you needed back-up, it's a tough world.'

'I did.' I smile at his concerned look. 'I still do, but you really need to take care of yourself, Mick, and your Joan.' A flicker of concern across that big open face tells me that he's not convinced I can look after myself. He's absolutely right but I can't have his life compromised by the danger I've put myself in. These are dangerous criminals with guns, I can't have Mick taking them on and getting himself killed.

'You've done well for me, Mick,' I continue. 'I don't know what I would have done without your support. But you've no need to worry about me any more, though you can have your old job back any time you like.' And to hell with Jim Almond.

'Thanks, Jenny, but no thanks. I'm already too old for the business. My hip is giving me bother, never mind my blasted knees. Okay, I guess it's the easy life for me from now on.'

'How will you manage for money?'

'I'm fine.' He nods. 'We aren't short, don't worry, we'll manage.'

'Listen, Mick, I'll split the football with you. You organise it, sort it out as usual, and I'll give you a cut of the proceeds. It's the least I can do. That will give you enough to get by on.'

'Thanks.' Mick looks unimpressed by my generous offer. 'But I can't see there being any parking for much longer, it's getting too dangerous even for me.' He grins.

'What do you mean?'

'Do you remember Deelon Carruthers?' he asks.

'Can't say I do.'

'He did a few shifts for us last year, helped out on the riots.'

'Was he a big black lad?' I ask.

'That's a fair description. Long dreadlocks, in a big pony tail.'

'Yes, I remember him, didn't I sack him for stealing?'

'Yes, you did. It was only a minor incident, a bit of petty theft.' Mick smiles.

'If I remember rightly, he stole Alan's leather jacket then turned up to work in it, swore it was his own.'

'Ah poor Alan, I miss him.' Mick sighs. 'Deelon was twice his size, didn't stop Alan having a real go when he saw him wearing that jacket. There was a right old barney. We all laughed about it afterwards.'

'What's Deelon got to do with the match day parking?' I remembered Deelon as a troubled young man with no obvious redeeming features. 'Is he threatening us?'

'No,' Mick laughs. A large waitress in a large pinafore with large blue checks hovers, dripping dishcloth in hand. She smiles coquettishly at Mick, leans over the table and flicks soggy crumbs on my lap.

'Hello, Mick,' she says. 'Who's your girlfriend?'

137

I presume she means me. I am toying with appropriate uses for that dishcloth involving her fat mouth when Mick answers.

'You are, Sadie, you are the woman of my dreams.' She waddles over to the next table and repeats her performance. Mick's eyes follow her as she goes by.

'Deelon,' I bring him back to the matter in hand. 'You were telling me about him.'

'Oh yes, he's a good lad really, never means any harm,' Mick answers. 'Anyway he tells me there's a bit of trouble brewing. Apparently Leroy is a bit of a player...'

'Then he should limp back to Moss Side and stay there,' I say. 'Do we know how he is, whether he's recovered from his self-inflicted injury?'

'It seems you got him in the crown jewels.' Mick's eyes twinkle. 'Shot off his bollocks. He's not best pleased by all accounts. Facing a long stay in hospital while they try to patch him up.'

'So he's not dead then? That's a relief.'

'Not necessarily, Jenny. He'll no doubt have another go at the football parking when he's recovered. And he's going to be looking for you. Might be best if you lay low for a while, maybe go up to Fleetwood again.'

'No, not there, the last time I tried to hide there it didn't work out at all well, did it?'

'True.' Mick grimaces at the memory. 'If not Fleetwood, somewhere then. It'll not take long for him to find out where you are. He probably saw the GOD Security van anyway. That would tell him all he needs to know.'

'I still don't see why we have to give up our car parks just because some teenage hoodlum decides he wants to take over. This must have happened before, what did Gary do?'

'Gary brought in Popov to deal with it last time. Those East Europeans don't like blacks and the feeling is mutual.

Popov's men are very scary, even to the Moss Side gangs. Just having them on site was enough of a deterrent.'

'So we do the same. Get Popov.'

'No can do. He only dealt with Gary as some sort of favour, something he owed him personally. Popov won't deal with you or me.'

'Then we turf them off ourselves, like we did with Leroy.' I can't help my feelings of resentment at the prospect of having to relinquish Gary's long established business.

'That's not what we do, Jenny, you know that well enough. They're not going to hesitate to use their firearms, we can't compete with that. We'll be getting our lads killed.'

'I suppose you're right. But there must be something we can do.'

'If there is I can't think of it,' Mick says.

His friendly waitress brings him a plate piled with three donuts. 'Made fresh,' she simpers. Mick pops one into his mouth as if it might aid his thought process.

'This Leroy, how serious a threat do you think he is?' I ask.

'Bad, I reckon. If he's permanently damaged his love life and holds you responsible, he'll not rest until he gets revenge and according to Deelon he's a total nutter. They say he's shot a few people.'

'Thanks, Mick, let me know if you hear anything else.'

'Well, there's old George. Funny business, that.'

'He's left Trafford Trailers, that's all I heard.'

'Died last Wednesday. Car accident, hit and run. He wasn't far from his home, just popped round to fetch a paper. That's why SG are in and we're out. He was always good to us was George.'

My heart freezes as I recall the squealing of tyres and the sightless eyes beneath the fur-trimmed hood. George as well. He must have upset them too. Maybe carrying the tracker to them was enough to get him killed. In that case, I'm to blame.

139

Mick is looking at me with concern on his face and a frosting of sugar around his mouth.

'What are you going to do, Jenny?' Mick sounds even more worried than when I arrived.

'I'll think of something,' I say. 'I'll not let go of the football income if I can help it. As for you, there's a job at GOD Security for you as long as you want it, just say the word and you're back on the payroll.'

'Thanks, Jenny, I'll keep in touch.'

44

Alex is on his way. I'm tidying up frantically. The flat looks like it hasn't been cleaned for months. Come to think of it, I've not felt inclined to hoover or polish since the break-in. My ear is an excuse I have relied on, but one that's now well past its sell-by date. I ought to concentrate on getting the living room shipshape, leave the bedroom and kitchen, but I'm tidying my clothes, changing the sheets, plumping the pillows. My priorities are obvious, even though I won't admit them, even to myself. It's been a very long time since I felt this way.

The thought that this might change tonight leaves me frozen with terror. Unless I can be open and honest with Alex, my body is back to its closed, clenched, defensive norm. Nothing is allowed through, not even the man I most desperately need. My automatic systems kick in, I can't help it if I'm withholding my true self. If I tell him who I really am he's going to run a mile. At the moment he is a little bit in love with a bright, business-like, interesting career woman, divorced with one estranged child. What he is really cosying up to is a habitual criminal, a jail bird, engaged in serious money-laundering and outrageous fraud, a woman who is being hunted by gangs of organised criminals and who shot and seriously wounded a child only two days ago.

If I don't tell him I seize up and any meaningful relationship is over. If I do tell him he'll be party to information that would lock me up and throw away the key. It feels like every word I say to Alex has to be carefully weighed and selected in case I give myself away.

I desperately need Alex, I want to be close to him. I have to be honest and open to achieve these things. There's only one choice – tell him everything and be prepared to take the consequences. If he runs away, even if he puts me back in prison, it's a chance I'm willing to take. My life without Alex is not good enough to warrant preservation at all costs. I will tell him all, every bit, nothing left out – but only if he asks. I'll truthfully answer any of his questions, but my life story can wait for the right moment.

I feel a sense of release, a lightness as if I've shed a heavy load from my shoulders. My breathing is deeper, my anticipation of his imminent arrival turns from trepidation and uncertainty to excitement and joy.

'Wow!' Alex returns my hug with interest. 'You seem glad to see me.' He looks me in the eyes, holds me by the shoulders. 'Amazing, you've lost that faraway look.' He smiles. 'Nice to see you again, Jenny Parker.'

His words have an instant effect, I melt into him. Only he exists and only now. As we make love there is only Alex's touch left in my world. Every doubt, care and worry has evaporated.

45

Alex puts a sheet of paper on the table.

'What's that?' I ask.

'The information I promised you,' he grins smugly.

'Oh. The house where George took the disc, what did you find?' Using the poor man's name makes shudder. It's quite possible that I'm at least partially responsible for his death and that thought really saddens me. Maybe if I'd left things as they were, neither of us would have become a target.

'I checked out the electoral roll.' He picks up the top sheet and hands it to me. 'Looks like a normal family; father, mother and two daughters. The name is Wasiewicz.'

The last name gives me a jolt big enough for Alex to notice.

'What's up,' he asks, 'do you recognise them?'

'Yes, I think so. I've seen that name somewhere before, I'm sure I have.'

'Where?' Alex asks.

It comes to me in a flood of certainty and a gush of relief. I no longer need to speculate, now I can be sure that the brothel keepers are involved with Trafford Trailers. Wasiewicz is the name on the letters that Mick found in Mrs Mather's flat.

I want to talk to Alex about everything, to involve him fully in my world, but I can't be entirely sure about George's death and I'm not certain how he's going to react when he finds out his girlfriend has recently shot a teenager in the genitals. My thoughts turn to Leroy and what I need to do about him.

46

Hospitals are very much like hotels. They were conceived, designed and built in an age when fairness and honesty were the norm. In other words, their security is almost non-existent. Okay, there are a few bits of sticking plaster over some of the biggest holes, but the overall situation remains the same. Anyone can wander freely, take what they like and leave. This includes furniture, valuables and even the occasional patient. The security guards they employ are few and far between. I have even known them help carry stolen items for a thief who appears to be struggling a bit.

The pity is that act of kindness nearly lost GOD Security the contract at Salford Royal. I managed to persuade them to give us another chance, to be a little more heartless and a tiny bit thorough. The fact that their previous security firm was caught actually doing the stealing might have swung it my way. I'm in the fortunate position today where if I get into a situation where the staff decide they need to call for security, I do at least have that aspect covered.

They used to call this place Hope Hospital, aptly named on two counts. First this area of Salford between Weaste and Eccles is actually called Hope. Secondly there is something uplifting about hope that fits in nicely with a medical establishment. Without hope we are all lost. I sometimes wonder where mine went.

Unfortunately, they renamed it Salford Royal Hospital when they converted what was Salford's main hospital into apartments which would fit nicely into a Stephen King novel. I walk into the main entrance and follow signs for the Hope Building where I believe the answer to my most pressing question may lie.

The Hope Building is ultra modern, everything a new hospital is designed to be. Soulless, antiseptic, unwelcoming and irresponsibly bright. If the shock of admission here isn't enough to kill you, then your soul is of a less sensitive nature than mine. The person I am looking for is insensitive enough to be immune, if my assessment based on a very brief acquaintance is correct.

It's very quiet in here. A few inhabitants sit quietly as if in a library or hide in alcoves behind computer screens. Nobody is interested in a woman with a security pass around her neck carrying a black leather briefcase and looking like she is none too happy about life in general and being here in particular. If they knew I had a loaded firearm in the bag they might take a different view.

There is a nurse sitting at a desk in the entrance to Ward H3. I smile at her and breeze past. She makes an inquisitive face but no other movement. There are two private rooms at the entrance to the general ward, both empty. I walk slowly along the line of beds examining each occupant in turn. The last bed on the left has curtains drawn around it, hiding the incumbent from view.

I march over and pull them open. The black youth is lying in a half-slumber, his eyes flick towards me as I appear, his face screws up as if in pain or it might be recognition. I take the gun, wrapped in a piece of cloth, and slide it gently into his bedside cabinet.

'Hello Leroy,' I speak softly, then leave before I get an answer.

47

Hector Brighouse is a big man, corporately important and corpulently large. If I put Mick on the scales opposite Mr Brighouse it would be a close run thing, and Mick is enormous. The effect of Hector's size is modified by the immaculate suit he is wearing, designed to make the best of his large frame and doing an excellent job. He looks imposing, rather than flabby, a man of stature. Atop that thick neck is the bespectacled face of a choirboy, if a rather well-fed one. His eyes hold me in a supplicant gaze as if he is begging for morsels at my table. As the table is in the French Restaurant at the Midland Hotel and I am his guest, the impression is a bit misleading.

'So glad you could make it.' The chairman of SG half rises to greet me and grasps my hand firmly. 'This is Arthur Wilkinson, Group Finance Director, and Jim you know of course.'

I ought to know Jim Almond, he's been working for me long enough. The way Hector phrases his introduction niggles at me, makes me wonder if anyone told him Jim has left Security Group. The wine waiter is already hovering at Hector's side.

'Do you like red wine?' Hector addresses me.

'Yes,' I answer, wondering if I should tell him the name of my favourite Rioja.

'What have you got for me?' Hector turns to the waiter who waves his hand to beckon two others, one carrying a decanter containing wine, the other an empty bottle and a cork.

'Gevrey Chambertin, Almond Leusiex 2005. I took the liberty of decanting a bottle this morning, I'm sure you will like it.'

Hector sniffs the proffered cork then sips at a sample dribbled into his glass.

'Very nice,' he pronounces, 'you may pour. We will certainly be requiring another bottle. If you haven't done so already, please decant it immediately.'

The wine is nice, not up to Rioja Grand Reserva standard, but drinkable. I don't intend to drink very much of it, coping with these men won't be made easier by my guzzling wine, however much I feel tempted. It's been a hard day, a difficult week, a horrendous month, but alcohol won't improve my life, only make it even more challenging.

Tonight I need to pluck up the courage to confront Alex. It's long overdue. I keep skating around the subject of his wife and children. I have the feeling I won't like the answers to the questions I need to ask. There is also the delicate subject of me. How much of me I reveal, what Alex can be trusted with. I feel nervous. Does he already know all about me? Is he waiting for me to tell him?

The three men are looking over their menus at me. A waiter is poised to take my order.

'You all go first,' I say, 'I haven't decided.' As they order, I try to find something I like that won't take too much concentration. I don't want to be spitting out fish bones or dissecting some small bird. 'Scallops,' I say, 'then the beef.'

Hector begins to ask impersonal questions in a gentle, avuncular way.

'Where did you go to school, Jenny?' he asks.

'Parklands,' I say. He wrinkles his brow. 'In Chorley,' I add.

'Ah,' he says, obviously none the wiser. 'And your father, what does he do?'

'I have no idea,' I admit. 'He left when I was six years old. Where he is now and what he might be doing I don't know and I really don't care.'

Hector takes my brusque rebuff on his plushy chin and perseveres. 'I am told you started your career as an accountant, is that right?'

'Yes.'

'What attracted you to the security industry, why did you make the switch?'

'It was a challenge,' I say, leaving out the fact that I was destitute, recently out of prison and Gary saved my life when he gave me a job.

'A challenge you have responded to magnificently,' Hector smiles. 'You've transformed GOD Security into a very good business.'

'You own all the shares, don't you Jenny?' Arthur asks. He is mid-fifties, probably ten years Hector's junior. He has a deep Scottish voice and a friendly smile.

'That's the way Gary set the business up,' I explain, 'but it's really still his business, or rather his widow's.

'Yes but you run it, you call the shots as it were.'

'Doreen O'Donnell relies on me for her livelihood if that's what you mean.'

'But if the business were to be sold, it would be you who made the decision?'

A wave of excitement makes me pause mid-scallop, almost making me choke and justifying my choice of easy eating. Something more substantial might have stuck in my gullet and asphyxiated me. It never occurred that they might want to buy the business. I expected something along the lines of them offering some loose agreement not to compete amid a wealth of thinly veiled threats.

GOD has been treading hard on SG's toes lately. I have aggressively priced them out of several big jobs in an attempt to cover the loss of Trafford Trailers. As it happens, I had a call from them this only morning and we're back in there from next week. There's a new man in charge of our contract and I get the feeling that he doesn't like the way that SG are working and needs things to go back to how they were before Alan's death.

'All the business decisions are mine, Jim will have told you that.'

Jim nods and makes a thin smile, as if uncertain of his role in all this. He needn't be. If SG want to buy GOD, Jim has to be helping them put a deal together. He's only looking after his own interests. If the sale goes through he'll be back with his old employers.

'That's what we thought,' Hector says. 'Have you ever considered selling GOD Security, Jenny?'

No, but I should have. Ever since I discovered the tainted origins of O'Brian's money the other week, I've wrestled with my desire to get as far away from the business as possible. All that stops me is Doreen and the debt I owe to Gary and his family. Now I'm being offered a way out that would leave her financially secure and let me get on with my life with Toby, away from the constant threat of prosecution and imprisonment. My heart is beating loudly, the prospect of escape is so enticing I can hardly restrain myself.

'No,' I reply. 'The situation has never arisen. GOD Security isn't for sale. It provides livelihoods for its employees and financial stability for Gary's family.'

'What if those things could be maintained, where would you stand, Jenny?' Hector asks.

'As far away as I can,' I laugh. 'I'm sure I could find something to keep me busy.'

'Good,' Hector smiles. 'So you won't be insulted if we make you an offer?'

'It depends on the offer.' I smile, hoping my desperation can't be detected.

Arthur leans forward. 'I think you'll agree that as the largest security provider in the UK we should know the value of a similar business. We have to be realistic, you understand, we have a policy of rapid expansion but not at the cost of profitability.'

'Look, Arthur,' I give him the hardest, least-bothered stare I can manage. 'You are buying, I'm not even on the market. Be careful how much you're offering. I'm hungry and don't want to have to leave the table before I've eaten my main course.'

Hector laughs too loudly then continues to guffaw at Arthur's discomfort. Jim sits meekly in the middle of them, po-faced.

'Jenny, you have done a great job putting GOD where it is today. Let us take it from here. As part of SG your employees will have better conditions and more job security. Doreen O'Donnell will have her income guaranteed and you will be able to seek new pastures with a tidy sum in your pocket to finance whatever opportunities might attract you,' Hector says. 'Now eat your lunch and let us get back to you with some suggestions. No need to rush into things on an empty stomach.'

As if on cue the main courses arrive. Mine turns out to be a fillet steak with a lobster crammed onto the same plate. I should have read the menu more thoroughly. Hector tucks into his chateaubriand, he seems to have had the same problem. When the waiter asks who is sharing it with him, all he gets is a stony silence.

48

'Are you okay?' Alex looks as though he has run up the staircase to my flat. 'I got your message and came as soon as I could.'

'I'm fine,' I purr, and throw my arms around him. We stagger crab-wise to the settee and flop down.

'You've been drinking.' Alex isn't asking a question.

'I certainly have,' I answer. 'I've drunk about oh, two hundred pounds' worth of wine, that's what I've done.'

'That's a lot of wine.' Alex grins.

'No so much as you might think. If you must know, it's less than a bottle full, so there.'

'I've never seen you like this before,' Alex says.

'What, drunk or happy?'

'Both. Either, if the truth were known, what's the occasion?'

'I've been to lunch with a very nice man who wants to buy GOD Security. That's where I've been.'

'And do you want to sell?' Alex asks.

'Dammed right I do. The further I get from this smelly place the better. Present company excluded, of course.' I lean over to kiss him.

'I really didn't know you wanted to leave. I thought you were pretty well committed to GOD Security.'

'Committed? Yes. Want to leave? Also yes. I only stay for Gary and Doreen. I owe them. Without me Doreen would have nothing to live off. Her children and horses would starve.' I can see Alex needs more explanation so I carry on. 'Gary saved my life. They were trying to kill me. So that's why I owe Gary and why I have to look after his family.'

'Who?' Alex asks.

'Gary's family,' I repeat.

'No, who was it trying to kill you?'

'It's a long story,' I say, vaguely realising that I may have said too much, too quickly. I can't even remember how we got on to the subject.

'But one I would really like to hear.' Alex shuffles closer and holds me around my shoulders.

I tell him the tale, sparing only a few gory details.

'I need a drink,' I say, feeling desperately thirsty all of a sudden. 'Water,' I add to avoid confusion.

The long cold glass of water gives me time to gather my wits, I can't believe I've told him everything in a few quick sentences. He's still here, that's the main thing. It may be curiosity that holds him, but at least that's something.

'So you've been in prison, that must have been hard. Especially with Toby being so young,' he says.

'I told you, it wasn't my fault, none of it was. I made one mistake, that's all. Trying to make a better life for myself.'

'You're amazing,' Alex smiles. 'To come through all that and be as positive as you are. That's real bravery.'

Problem is I seem to be in as much trouble as ever, attracting the wrong sort of attention from the wrong sort of people. That's a good reason to sell up, get out and take Toby somewhere. The sooner I can get away, the better.

'You've come through it all astonishingly well,' Alex says, then hesitates. 'Apart from your ear of course, what happened about that?'

'It's healed up into a weird shape, I look like an orc out of *Lord of the Rings*.'

'No, that's not what I meant. Anyway it's cute, makes you look special.'

'Special? Like a pirate with one eye and one leg looks special? All I need is a parrot pecking at my ear.'

'I was only wondering if anything's happened about the tracker, the address on Seaford Road?'

I'm feeling very tired, Alex's aliveness is no longer enough to sustain me. I need to close my eyes and rest them for a while. 'Tell you later,' I mutter and relax into his arms.

49

It's a beautiful day with not a cloud in the sky, warm and inviting. Today I miss having a garden, somewhere I can sit amongst greenery and absorb the delights of the season. Alex and I are sitting on a blanket, sharing a flask of tea in the middle of Buile Hill Park. Most of the population of Salford, those, like me, who live in gardenless flats, have the same idea. The women are stretched out on the grass, as naked as they dare to be. The men sit attentively watching over their property and keeping an eye on the competition. The children run and dance and squeal.

'Why don't you ever have an orgasm?' I ask.

Alex looks surprised at my sudden question. I am a tiny bit disappointed he doesn't look more shocked. Judging by one or two heads twitching locally, my words have reached a wider audience. I don't care. The warm sun and Alex's presence make me feel good enough to enjoy a little mischief-making.

'What?'

'You heard, you never have an orgasm when we make love. It's a bit off-putting if I'm honest. It's like you don't want to join in with me.'

'But I do,' Alex grins. 'And I am joined in with you, completely, don't you feel it?'

'I suppose I do. It's like you're there with me, part of me, having my experience, my pleasure. I love it, Alex, don't get me wrong, you make me feel so amazingly good. It's only that I'm worried about you. Whether you need something from me that you're not getting.'

'All I need is your attention, your presence,' Alex smiles. 'And I really do get that most of the time, when your head's not still at work. Don't make the mistake of confusing orgasm with ejaculation. It's not the same thing.'

'But isn't that the whole point of it for a man? Don't men need to ejaculate? I thought that's what it's all about for them, that's why they do it. So why don't you come like everyone else?'

A stray plastic football bounces past, pursued by a horde of small boys. Alex fields it expertly and returns it into play.

I think of Toby, what he might be up to on this glorious day, whether he wishes his mother were with him. Does he even think about me when I'm not there?

'Don't confuse orgasm with the release of semen,' Alex is speaking in a very low tone, trying to keep this very intimate conversation between the two of us.

I give him great credit that he is persevering, that he meets my impertinence with direct answers, that he is prepared to be honest, even out in the open.

'Ejaculation isn't necessary for an orgasm, though I'll admit most men think it is.'

'So why not you? Why don't you squirt like every other man I've been with?'

'Well, there's lots of reasons. First I believe that it's important for a woman to be able to trust her lover. If all he wants to do is ejaculate, then she can't rely on him. His attention should be on her, not getting to his own climax. Second it's a question of energy. When I release semen, I lose a lot of energy. This takes a long time to build up again. Losing energy like that not only affects my sexual desire, but everything I do. The way I feel about life. The effort I can put into things. How good I feel generally. It's something I've learnt from experience. I have a choice and I know the consequences that choice brings.'

'What about your wife, is she happy with a man who doesn't ejaculate?' I am beginning to like the word *ejaculate*. It brings up an image for me of exactly what it describes. I also like the effect it has on the casual listeners around us. Every time I say *ejaculate* or *ejaculation* they react enough to let me know they're trying to listen to every word of our very private conversation.

'My wife,' Alex says, 'makes other arrangements that I'm not party to. I have no idea what her current preference might be. We've been separated for over three years now. It's amicable, based on the fact that she's very happy with her new man and I'm anxious not to lose my access to the girls.'

'Oh,' is all I can say without giving away my feelings of exhilaration. He's free. No, he's mine. He's free to be mine. We can be together without complication and guilt. Why didn't I ask him sooner? I could have avoided all those nights of worry and uncertainty about him, about his intentions. I know why I never asked until now. I thought I wouldn't be able to cope with the answer, whichever way it went.

'You think I've been cheating on my wife, don't you?' Alex smiles. 'What sort of man does that make me?'

'If I did, what sort of woman am I?' I smile back. The moment is gentle, humorous and utterly connected. A bright light is shining into my darkest recesses, the air I breathe is lighter, more life-giving. I put my head in his lap, look up to watch his lips approach, draw him to me. To hell with the audience.

50

It's cool in the stables, a welcome respite from the heat of the day. Doreen O'Donnell is rubbing down Donovan, a large bay gelding who stands nonchalantly as she works. It's as if he accepts all this attention as his right, but isn't afraid to enjoy every minute of it. I love the smell in here, earthy, cheesy, horsey. We can talk here, away from the house and the mild bickering, raucous laughter and constant drone of the television.

'They're making us an offer for the business, Doreen.'

'It's yours to sell, Jenny. God love you for all you've done for us.'

I wince inwardly as the sharp dagger of guilt pierces my guts. 'If it weren't for you and Gary I'd not be here to do anything. As far as I'm concerned it's your call, Doreen, I'll go along with whatever you decide. Whatever's best for you and the kids.'

'Don't be so soft, Jenny. Look at all this. Gary left us well set, debt-free, you've no need to concern yourself about us. You've done your bit and more.'

'My instinct is to sell if the offer's at all reasonable,' I say.

'Then do it, I'll not be complaining.'

'If we do sell, you should have enough to be able to live comfortably.'

'What about you?'

'I'll move on, get another job.'

'And you'll not be worrying about me, Jenny Parker. I'll not accept a single penny, it's your business, you made it what it is. The kids are older now, we're capable of making our own way in life. That's for the best, you know it is. If you let them, they'll sit on their backsides and get up to God knows what mischief. Look at all those lottery winners, are they happy? No, they are not. Every single one of them dies from drugs and drink and suicide and who can blame them? All the point's taken out of their lives. I'll not have that happen to my children, Jenny Parker, not even if you have the very best of intentions.'

'You'll need money just for basic living, Doreen. You've lost your family bread-winner and that's my fault.'

'No it's not. You can't be blamed. Gary was just being Gary. There's a dozen times he could have got himself in real bother. It's the way he was. You were unlucky it happened to involve yourself.'

'Look, Doreen, if I'm right SG will be offering us about two million pounds for GOD Security. It might even be more.'

'Then you have it, dear, you deserve it. Haven't you been the one with all the good ideas and all the hard work?'

'Two million, Doreen. It would make me feel better knowing you and your family were taken care of. We'll split it. Down the middle. I'll not say another word on the subject.'

Doreen looks like she might wear right through the horse's thick hide the way she is brushing now. I feel content with the situation. I can't be any more persuasive and half the proceeds is more money than I ever imagined I'd have. She's right. I do work hard and I do have all the good ideas. Without me GOD Security would have gone under long ago.

'Okay,' Doreen says, 'if it'll make you feel better and it's what you want than that's fine by me as long as you're sure.' Her mock-evil stare confirms her certainty and her beaming smile attests her satisfaction with the outcome of our conversation.

'Won't they want to keep you on?' Doreen asks.

'That's not the deal,' I explain. 'They already have Jim Almond to run the business, and Jim worked for them for twelve years.'

'And probably does to this day, even though you pay him,' Doreen observes.

'I couldn't manage without Jim though, that's another reason for doing the deal.'

'But not the main one?' she asks me.

'No, to be honest, I'll be glad to get away. Things haven't gone well lately, I need to get out.'

'I'm sorry, dear, is there anything I can do?'

'No, thanks. It all started when I reported that brothel. There's been threats, my flat turned over and now this.' I pull back my hair to show my bad ear. 'It's not over by any means, someone's out to get me. I think they'll kill me now if they get a chance.'

'Can't you go to the police, tell them what's going on?'

'No, that's the problem. Our business doesn't bear close scrutiny. There's money passing through it that isn't legitimate. If I get the police involved we might all end up in prison.'

'Ah yes, O'Brian and his cash.' She smiles. 'What does the great man himself have to say to all this?'

'Nothing, I've not told him.'

'Don't you think you should?'

'Only when I'm ready.'

'And what about selling the business, won't the purchaser want to look at what we do very closely? How can we sell it without revealing the little bit of irregularity we indulge ourselves in?'

'I've thought about that, Doreen, I think I have a way of dealing with it, at least I hope I have.'

51

Gaggles of excited Chinese are gathered on the narrow footpath outside the Yang Sing. These appear to be Chinese people from China, rather than Chinese people from Manchester, judging by the cameras and backpacks. Every time one of them moves too close, the glass doors of the restaurant slide invitingly open, then shut with a reluctant swish when the invitation is declined.

I pick my way through the throng into the building and walk down the wide staircase into the restaurant. The place is heaving with diners and an even greater number of aspirants facing almost certain disappointment. All Chinese, whether customers or staff, all bright and animated. The noise and intensity reminds me of a school visit to the swimming baths, apart from the deep-fried food aromas that replace the chlorine.

I am received amongst all the chaos by an exquisite lady in a tunic dress who offers to take my non-existent coat after I tell her I'm having lunch with Peter O'Brian.

'He's not here yet,' she explains apologetically, as if somehow I'm holding her personally responsible. 'I'll take you to his table if you like.' We weave our way through the seated masses and she directs me to the only empty table in the whole place, next to a deep alcove where a convoluted dragon is staring out at me. My insistence at meeting somewhere other than his house is beginning to look like a mistake. I want O'Brian's attention and I need somewhere to explain my unwelcome news. This seething hubbub is singularly unsuited to serious discussion.

Twelve-thirty we agreed. Twelve-twenty I arrived. O'Brian lurches into view at one-fifteen, I've been kicking my heels in here for almost an hour. By the time he arrives at the table I've drunk so much water I have to excuse myself and head for the Ladies. When I get back I've acquired a large glass of red wine and the table is festooned with bamboo baskets containing morsels of hot food. O'Brian is already tucking in.

'What's this?' I point to what looks like a lump of gristle, clad in a cabbage leaf.

'Pork,' O'Brian says, 'I think so anyway. Maybe it's something else.'

I eat it tentatively. It's absolutely delicious but I've little idea what I'm chewing and am none the wiser when I swallow it. O'Brian waves his arms; six more dishes arrive, each with two bite-size morsels. He's getting way ahead of me.

'I need to talk to you, Peter.'

'Eat up, there's plenty more coming. The chef knows what I like. Good isn't it?'

'Yes, delicious.' I would happily settle for a nice green salad but at least I'm spared the need to extract something appropriate from a menu which, judging by the number of dishes we have been served already, must rival *War and Peace* for size.

'I'm considering selling GOD Security.'

'Why?' Peter pauses. A prawn dumpling, clenched between chop sticks, hovers in front of his face. 'Why would you do that?'

'I need to get away. I have to get out now while I'm still alive.'

'Surely it's not that bad, the job I mean.'

'It's not the work, it's everything else. Somebody has it in for me. They've already chopped off my ear. I'm convinced they won't stop at that.'

'Look. The business with the ear, that's not something I can take responsibility for, Jenny. It was you who decided to put yourself at risk. I did warn you.'

No he didn't warn me. He did nothing of the sort. All he did was laugh at me when I told him I was going to try to get business from his clients. He must have had a good idea of how dodgy his customers were. I should hold him partially responsible, I realise that now. Before he spoke I was content to blame only myself.

'It's not that. I think they saw their opportunity and took it, but whether I walked into their den or they grabbed me off the street, it makes little difference. They know where to find me, they know where I live, where I work, who I associate with. They must know about you, Peter. I have a feeling they also know about our arrangement, about the money you pass through my company.'

O'Brian is no longer interested in the food. Even the appearance of a gigantic whole fish festooned with chopped leeks and swimming in soy sauce fails to divert his attention.

'What makes you think that?' His face has lost all its customary good humour.

'They could have killed me at that house you renovated, or at my flat or anywhere for that matter. Instead they broke in and trashed the place. They stole my documents and used them to transfer all the money out of my bank accounts. They know what they're doing. None of this is random. Maybe they're wondering how you managed to salt away so much of their cash, when they find it almost impossible to spend these days. I don't know, Peter, I just don't know.'

'I don't think that's a reason to drop everything and run, Jenny.' Peter resumes eating. I gave up almost before I began. Meanwhile, un-summoned waiters bring more unwanted food. 'Think of the consequences. The caravan parks, they produce a tidy income for us both and you need GOD Security to siphon off the profits. Hang on.' His face is getting redder. 'If you try to sell they'll find out what we're doing when they do the due diligence. Their accountants will flag up all the payments and we'll be in real trouble. It's not on, Jenny, you can't sell GOD Security.'

'I have to do something, Peter, otherwise I'll get sucked deeper into whatever's going on, and so will you. Better a clean break now before the authorities get word of what we've been doing. We've had a good run and we'll still have the caravan sites, don't forget.'

'The caravan sites aren't much use on their own, the money will slow down to a trickle.'

'Better that than we get collared or worse.'

'Even if you wanted to you couldn't sell GOD Security, not to a legitimate buyer anyway.' Peter insists.

'I have to make it work, there's no other way.'

Peter stops eating altogether, surveys the myriad dishes littering the table and rises from his seat.

'Don't,' he says. 'Leave it as it is, you're rushing to conclusions that can't be substantiated. Do nothing until I get back to you.'

He walks over to the reception desk and hands over his credit card. I ask the waiter to box up all the spare food.

52

Alex is impressed with me. I've been out to lunch and arrived home not just completely sober but also bearing food.

'Is all this for just the two of us?' he asks, eyes wide with gluttony.

'It's all for you,' I answer. 'I've had far too much already.'

'How did your lunch go, was it the people who want to buy your business again?'

'No, it was a client, O'Brian. He has a construction business, we provide all the security for his sites.'

'So you had to pay for all this?' Alex smiles. 'I'd better not waste it.'

'No, actually O'Brian paid. It was his choice of restaurant.'

'Ah yes, one of the old school, I'll bet. There's advantages to being female.'

Alex's words provoke a reaction in my body, an upsurge of fury. I try to suppress the bitterness but it's too strong.

'So that's what you really think of me, some kind of weak girl who has to be taken care of? Well, I don't need anybody. I can take care of myself. Here,' I start throwing food back into containers. 'Take the food and go home and stuff yourself.' Something compels me to run into my bedroom, slam the door by savagely kicking backwards and then dive headlong onto the mattress, trying to muffle my sobs of anguish.

I stop crying when I hear the bedroom door open surreptitiously. Alex enters, heralded by an aroma of Chinese food. I feel him sit softly at the foot of the bed. His hands gently take one of my feet and hold it. I like the feel of his soft touch but I keep still and rigid. He begins to stroke my instep, massage my toes, press the sole of my foot with his thumbs. I move my head slightly to get it out of the soggy mess my tears and snot have made on the bedclothes. I'm beginning to enjoy what he's doing and appreciate even more the silent way he's doing it.

Gradually his hands reach my ankle, manipulating it, enlivening it. He runs his thumbs up the back of my calf, smoothing out the muscle, then they slowly return down to my foot. As his hands work, I start to long for his touch on my thighs, my buttocks. Every time he slides his hands underneath my skirt up to my knee, I anticipate the thrill of them continuing upwards, inside my thigh, touching me where I'm already beginning to feel aroused.

Instead, I catch my breath as he descends again back to my foot. I lie still, breathing shallowly to avoid giving him any encouragement. My initial impulse to lash out with my foot and try to catch him in the groin, send him on his way, recedes as quickly as it came.

Now I am loving his touch, appreciating his gentle stillness. There's no wheedling, no cajoling, no 'what's the matter with you' from Alex. Only being here, standing up to my tantrums, giving me space, offering support. Now I want more than a massage. I shift my legs to what I hope is a provocative position, leaving room between them for his hands to pleasure me. Instead he moves nearer, places one warm hand at the base of my spine, the other just below my neck. My body begins to feel lighter, my neediness is lifting. I'm conscious that my breathing is becoming longer and deeper.

The hands remain motionless, but I'm becoming increasingly aware of them and of my connection to Alex. I let myself relax. As I do, I realise how tightly my body is clenched. Now the constriction I hold in my chest begins to give way to a spaciousness and breathing becomes a real pleasure.

Still Alex says nothing. His presence is all the more powerful for his silence. There is nothing he can say to me that can possibly be as nourishing to my soul as this. The clouds of distress waft away, lulled by his gentle breath.

'It's Toby,' I say when I'm ready. 'It's the way I abandoned my little boy. How I'm never there when he needs me. I've lost him, Alex, she's got him now, Tim's new wife. She's the one he can rely on. She's there every day to look after him. I'm nothing to him any more, some old woman who insists in intruding into his life, unasked and unwanted.'

Alex stays still, allows his hands to remain resting on my back, touching me in a way that no words might.

'It wasn't my fault, you know,' I continue. 'I was set up.

'So you didn't abandon Toby, he was taken from you, or you from him,' Alex says. His hands move to my shoulders and he turns me around to face him, still lying on the crumpled bed. I look up at him sitting calmly next to me.

'It was my fault, I took the money thinking I could use it to get me and Toby away from Tim. That's why they put me in prison. I only have myself to blame.'

'And you took ten grand in cash, what for?'

'Nothing really. I was supposed to be conducting a due diligence exercise. I took the money, but I didn't actually do anything for it.'

'Except keep quiet.' Something in Alex's voice shocks me out of my train of reminiscence.

'I suppose you're right,' I say, but suddenly I become aware of all the stuff I'm telling Alex and how much interest he is showing.

'But there wasn't anything to keep quiet about really. Everything was okay on the face of it. All I had then were vague suspicions, some uneasiness about the people involved. Nothing to go to the police with, if that's what you mean.'

Alex slips his arms underneath my shoulders, draws me close to him. My head is resting on his chest, I can feel the warmth and protection I desperately need. Now I have Alex I don't have to face these nightmares on my own.

53

'They want to meet to put their offer to you,' Jim Almond greets me as I slump into my chair.

'They've got my number, why don't they ring me?' I ask.

Jim looks uncomfortable. 'It's easier for them to get me to make the arrangements, I suppose.'

'They're doing it through you because they know I'll ask them how much. There wouldn't be any point in asking you that question, would there?'

'No, you're right. I suppose they want to make it a bit of a presentation, give you the whole picture, make sure you're comfortable.'

'Okay, when and where?'

'They said to ask you that.'

'In that case today at their office. I don't need a fancy lunch, just a cup of tea and the price they're willing to pay.'

'I have to meet Stretford today,' Jim says. 'Do you want me to put that off?'

'No, certainly not. I don't need you for my meeting with Hector.' As I speak I realise that I don't want Jim involved at all. My negotiations with SG have to be done without Jim's presence. The more I think about his position in all this the less I like it. I dial SG's office myself and get put through to Hector's PA.

'Jenny Parker here, Hector wants to meet me. Tell him I'll come round to his office today at three o'clock.'

'I'm sorry, Ms Parker, Mr Brighouse is unavailable this afternoon. I can offer you next Thursday, 9 a.m., that's the earliest he can do. He's very busy, you do understand.'

'Thanks but three this afternoon is better for me. Tell him I'll be there unless I hear to the contrary.'

'But, as I already said, he's unavailable.'

'Then tell him to ring me himself and explain why he can't meet me. Thank you. Goodbye.'

I ring off, look at Jim's pallid complexion. 'You go off to see Trafford,' I say. 'Leave Hector to me from now on.' He looks like a whipped dog, it makes me wonder which of us he thinks is his master.

Hector's PA has the air of an upmarket doctor's receptionist. I've dealt with her kind before, ladies of indiscriminate age with little interest in anything outside their protection duties. Letting someone near their important charge makes them feel violated and ineffective. I'm getting a tight-lipped 'told you not to come' look from her, which dissolves into a rictus of disappointment when Hector bulldozes his way into the office at three minutes past three.

'Sorry I'm late,' he gasps, 'police liaison meeting, terrible bunch of self-important incompetents. This country is going to the dogs. Nobody has any idea how to run things properly any more. Everything is about cutting corners, chopping staff, saving money. They remove one security guard, save forty grand a year and get three million pounds of theft and arson. As long as the three million comes off someone else's budget they're happy.'

He sits at his enormous antique desk, top inlaid with green leather. There is nothing on it except a telephone and a single sheet of paper, carefully aligned to be exactly equidistant between us. He pushes this slightly towards me. It is now in my territory and I reach out to take it. As I read, Hector's PA brings him a tray containing a floral teapot, two large white bone china cups with matching saucers, milk jug and sugar bowl, complete with cubes and tongs.

The document's title is Heads of Terms of Agreement. It goes on to list the parties to the transaction, what is being purchased and eventually the financial consideration involved. Two million, one hundred and twenty thousand pounds. My heart thumps faster, my excitement must be obvious to even the most casual observer and Hector is watching me closely for my reaction. Breathing carefully and fully I calm down, read the whole page, start again and make sure I understand it. There is one problem I can see immediately. A big one. I try not to be too deflated by it, reasoning that this document is only Hector's starting position. I must adopt a contrary position so that we can negotiate our way to a situation which feels hard-won but fair. My biggest mistake here would be to concede too much too quickly. If I'm being honest, though, I feel desperate enough to take what's on the table and run. It means a new life, a chance to get out while I'm still able, a chance to shake off the people who want to cause me harm. A new home for me and Toby.

I push the paper back to Hector's side of the desk. 'GOD Security made a quarter of a million profit this year, we'll clear at least half a million this current year. Two million isn't enough and you know it, Hector. That's only four years' earnings.' What I'm saying is true if I include O'Brian's money. The profit I make relies on the cash O'Brian gives me. It also works its way back to him. If only Doreen and I could keep it, we would be wealthy women already.

'We have to continue to make that profit,' Hector speaks softly, as if there's a small delicate man inside his massive body. 'We might make nothing, there's always a risk when you project forward. Two point one two five million is a fair price in an uncertain market. The way GOD Security is expanding your earnings will be insufficient to provide cash-flow for the business, you're in danger of running out of money.'

He would be absolutely right under normal business conditions. I can't tell him we are awash with cash, that the volume of money provided by O'Brian is almost embarrassing.

'We get by,' I say, hoping I maintain my deadpan face but fearing I'm an open book, desperately eager to conclude the deal. Hector pours two cups of pale yellowish tea and passes me one. It has the colour of urine rather than the dark brown I'm

169

used to. He sips his appreciatively without adding any milk or sugar.

'Darjeeling,' he says, 'light and refreshing. My one weakness, I'm afraid. I am addicted to good tea.'

I put a drop of milk into my cup and the entire contents turn off-white.

'Our valuation is a generous one,' Hector says. 'It reflects our real interest in acquiring GOD Security.'

'Not generous enough, Hector. Our order book is full and our cash reserves are more than adequate. I have ambitions for the business. If you come back in two years' time, you'll have to pay double your offer.'

'Then stay on and help us expand the business, Jenny.'

'No. The only reason we're still talking is that my ambitions lie outside the security industry.'

'You can't expect to be paid for value that we might add, my offer already includes an element of hope value.'

My mind is filled with the prospect of two million pounds, one for Doreen and one for me. A fortune. Even after I pay half of it in tax, it's more than enough to get me away from all this anguish. I have to take this offer. I want to grab it, to dance around this plush office waving it in the air.

'The proceeds of any sale have to be distributed amongst Gary's family. By the time I've done that, there's not enough for me to do what I want. I'm inclined to keep going, grow the business and look for an exit in a few years' time, when it might be more worthwhile.' I can hardly believe my own words, I hope that Hector has more success.

'As I've already told you, this is a fair offer in today's market and I can't improve it. What I am willing to do is offer you a consultancy contract. Something that allows me access to your talents on an agreed basis. It needn't interfere with anything else you might want to do, unless it involved a rival business. It would mean that I have you at the end of a phone and you're unable to engage in anything that might be detrimental to SG. Would that be of interest?'

'It might be. I won't be setting up my own security business, or doing anything to compete with GOD Security.'

'Good, I'll have something drawn up. I suggest we make it five thousand pounds per month for a minimum two year period, would that be okay?'

'As long as it doesn't tie me down to set hours.'

'Then we have a deal,' Hector smiles.

'No, not yet. The consideration has to be paid on completion, no stage payments.'

'But it's normal practice, we pay half up front and the remainder over two years.'

'That's not acceptable. I have to have all the money up front, otherwise I can't do the deal.'

Hector frowns. It's not a very convincing frown and I know I am home and dry.

54

The door to my solicitor's office is firmly locked, stranding me in the wind and rain that inevitably follow any period of sunshine in these parts. I push hard, barge it with my shoulder, but it remains immovable. There's a new box fastened to the wall with a button to press for entry. I rest my thumb on it and keep it there, a slightly satisfying continuous whine is created which eventually receives a response. A voice crackles from the box, there's a metallic click from the door.

Stephen Bailey greets my bedraggled appearance with joviality.

'What happened to your door?' I ask.

'Oh, you mean the new entry system. That's to stop people coming in off the street, security.'

'It works. I'm wet through.'

'This is Suriya Melling.' Stephen ignores my moans and introduces me to a tiny Asian girl already seated in the meeting room. She half rises and we touch hands briefly. 'Suriya will be handling the sale of GOD Security. She's our corporate law specialist.'

She looks far too young to be entrusted with such an important role. I feel like asking for someone else but recoil from all the awkwardness that that would entail.

'Oh,' I hear myself say and leave my reaction to hang in the air.

If he's noticed my discomfort Stephen chooses to ignore it. 'Before I leave you two to discuss the deal, I have some good news for you, Jenny. Arrangements have been agreed for access to your son at long last. I think you'll be pleased with what we've managed to negotiate.'

Stephen gives me a single typed sheet which details arrangements. Every other weekend, one week during summer holidays; it's not much better than I used to have. I was unhappy then and I'm more upset now. Yet a gnawing feeling tells me I

172

can't have Toby at the flat, not after the way that poor woman was killed. Imagine what would happen if they burst in while he was with me. I'm spending most of my nights at Alex's these days and I certainly can't take him there.

'It's the best we could do,' he says.

'I know, but it all seems a bit inflexible.'

'Look, Jenny, these terms were hard-fought and hard-won, you can't just take them or leave them. The commitment is binding on both sides.'

'What if I want to alter them?'

'Then you'll need to talk to your ex-husband and his wife.'

This prospect is a difficult one but I'll have to manage if things are to run smoothly now for Toby. I have to face it, they've got the upper hand and I'm going to have to bide my time and bite my tongue. At least there's a starting point at last, a firm foundation to work from.

I turn to the diminutive Asian lady. 'Suriya, I need this deal done quickly and smoothly. I can't afford any delay. Push them hard to make them sign, the sooner I get the money the sooner I can get on with my life and be a proper mother to Toby.'

'You won't get any delays from our side,' Suriya promises. 'I'll make sure everything gets turned around as quickly as possible. You do realise that they will require you to answer an awful lot of detailed questions? It'll be a lot of work for you and take up a lot of your time.'

'No problem, I'll work all day and all night if I have to. How long do you think it will take?'

'From when we get their initial heads of terms of agreement I'd say six or seven months realistically.'

'Six months! This is a tiny deal, two million, that's all. I have a small, very simple company to sell. Six months is what it takes for a large corporate merger, I can't wait six months.'

'I've been involved in transactions that have proceeded more quickly but not very many. I'm only giving you a realistic timescale, that's what you asked for.'

Six months. There's a lot that can go wrong in six months.

55

Alex is away all week, working in London and spending some time with his daughters. It's good for him, I know. He sees so little of them, he's missing all the best parts of them growing up. At least I'm never far from Toby, it must be horrible for him to have all that distance between them. But now I miss him, I know I should be more understanding but I don't like that he has to be down there when I so badly need him here with me. Now I have to try to sleep alone in my gloomy flat, waiting for someone scary to kick my door down and murder me. Every little click, every distant voice, each passing car, holds menace. I try to comfort myself that nothing else is going to happen and that the hit and run on George might not be connected after all.

At least Leroy is still in no fit state to run up three flights of stairs looking for revenge. And even when he is, I don't think he'll be going anywhere apart from prison. The call I made after I left the hospital has made sure of that. Leroy's arrest even made the front page of the Manchester Evening News.

It's no wonder that I'm feeling less than on top of the world, even Emma is getting it in the neck and that's neither fair nor reasonable. I am tired, lack of sleep-weary, but most of all I'm realising that I'm in a constant state of fear. It's the fear that takes most out of me. Ever since the police raided my house, disturbed Toby, found the cash, I've been constantly afraid. Being scared is my default mode and it's a debilitating one. That's why I have to make this drastic change, get out while I can, leave all this terror behind me. At least Hector has given me a way out, and at exactly the right time. Maybe things aren't completely against me after all. I remind myself that I've been in a lot worse situations than this one. All I have to do is find a way to influence things in my favour and I know I'm damn good at that kind of thing, there's nobody better.

Stuart Donaldson, the head of SG's accountants, sits in his glass-fronted corner office overlooking Manchester city centre, a position very similar to the one I commanded long ago at Landers Hoffman. I can see the front of my old building from here. They have installed a swish Italian restaurant in the cavernous entrance space on the ground floor. Spinningfields is looking very chic, shiny and new, amongst the black-stained, crumbling mess all around it. I do get a pang of regret when I see what should have provided the backdrop for my non-contentious career in accountancy. A place where I should have enjoyed a normal life, doing a routine job. If life were in any way fair I would be sitting in comfort, distracted only by staff squabbles, work capacity and other trivial details. Instead, the Stuart Donaldsons of this world sit in these glass and steel towers, with no idea how scared the rest of us can get in the real world.

That's my default setting now, fear. It bubbles like a sulphurous pool inside me, belching poison. Even those fleeting moments of joy when I'm with Alex or Toby are soon corroded by the terror of their impermanence. When I'm unhappy I think I'm unhappy for ever. When I feel good I know it's only a transitional state. It's only a habit, though, and one I can get rid of. It's a matter of taking things one at a time, living in the present moment, not projecting my worries into the future. Alex will help me do this, I know he will.

Stuart knows about the proposed acquisition of GOD Security by SG. It's his firm that will be conducting the due diligence exercise and it's his report that will form the basis for the transaction. I find myself in very familiar territory.

The soft, inconsequential pleasantries are slipping by, his family are well, my Toby is likewise. His eldest placed at Oxford, the younger brother's aspirations are the same. Business is difficult, the traffic a nightmare, property prices unpredictable, insolvencies abound.

As we talk my resentment of all he has that might be mine dissolves into gratitude. He has everything to lose, exactly as I did.

'I have something for you,' I say, pushing the thick envelope across his desk. His eyes betray his panic as his hands reach out for it and feel the wads of currency inside.

'What's this?' he asks.

'A token of my appreciation, Stuart. I don't believe this takeover would be on the cards if it weren't for the help you gave me. That information on the Stretford contract not only won me the job, but it brought SG to the table. They would never have bothered to approach GOD Security otherwise.'

'No, Jenny, I can't take this.'

'Of course you can, Stuart, it's only the same as the cash I gave you before.'

His eyes widen. His hand hovers over the money. I press home my point.

'Take it. It will help with the university costs, think of it as a second instalment, a bonus if you like.'

He reluctantly scrapes the offending item off his desk and into the obscurity of a drawer. I stand up, reach out my hand. He half rises to clasp it briefly.

'I need to be going now, Stuart, I've a lot to do. I'll not be popping in again, at least not until the deal is completed, we wouldn't want Hector thinking we were in cahoots, would we?'

56

It shows what little I know about the intricacies of business. After all my worrying and heart-searching, our insurance company paid up a sizeable sum to Alan's widow. Enough so I certainly don't mind sitting at her kitchen table with a mug of tea in my hand.

'Thanks for all you've done, Jenny,' she says, as if I had carefully made financial provision for her misfortune. 'How's GOD Security getting on? I heard they were prosecuting you over Alan's death. Ridiculous if you ask me, there's nothing anyone could have done, least of all you.'

'It's the way of the world these days, Alice. The authorities always have to have a scapegoat and we're it. They say we were negligent and there's nothing we can do to prove otherwise. We had to plead guilty and they fined us twenty thousand pounds, would you believe it?'

'You should have got them to listen to me. I'd have stood up in court for you, Jenny. I'd have told them it wasn't anything that GOD Security did. I told him to be careful, but he said it was perfectly safe, that nobody was going to get hurt.'

This unexpected turn of the conversation jolts me out of my placid conciliatory posing.

'What are you saying, Alice?'

'He died because of their special trailers.'

'What's so special about their trailers?'

'Alan told me that they fabricate them in the big shed on site, that they're used to hide people. Someone else must have found out about them and decided they wanted one.'

'How do you know all this?'

'Alan told me what he was doing for George Bottomley.'

'Which was what?'

'He helped out with special consignments, the lorries with people in. About once a week, he told me. One of the special lorries would be there and men would come with vans to take the people out. Alan had to let them in and help them.'

'Did he say what sort of people?'

'The ones he saw were young people, mainly girls. Alan said they were here to get jobs. He made a joke every time we saw a Starbucks that he should get a commission for providing staff.'

My heart is thumping. Aware or not, it sickens me that Alan was assisting the importation of these poor women and that GOD Security is implicated in the whole business. It shocks me to think that someone at Trafford Trailers has almost certainly made the same arrangement with Alan's replacement by now. After all, if a customer instructs us to allow access to certain people, we're not going to deny him. It's their business. We're under their instructions. It can be argued that Alan was doing nothing wrong, but I don't accept that. He should have informed me or Mick about what was going on. Alan must have known full well that he was involved in people-trafficking, even if he didn't fully realise the fate of the girls being brought in.

My breath is shallow, restricted, too fast. I look at Alice, her face drooping with sadness, her eyes wide with anxiety. I decide that whatever the cost might be, I can't walk away from what's been happening.

57

Lottie looks puzzled when she opens her front door. 'Chris is away, working, he never said you were coming here.'

'He doesn't know, Lottie, it's you I want to talk to. Can I come in?'

'Sure.' She waves me into the kitchen and boils a kettle. I wait until she brings the mug of tea before I get down to the reason for my visit.

'Your sister, have you heard from her?'

A dark cloud crosses her pretty face, the sadness in her eyes tells me the answer to my question before she speaks. 'No, nothing.'

'I want you to tell me what you know, how she was supposed to travel to England, who arranged it, what she was expecting when she got here.'

Lottie's eyes fill with tears. 'I can't tell you, I'm so ashamed.'

'Please, Lottie, you don't have to worry about anything you tell me. I'm your friend. You can trust me.'

'It's too horrible, I can't tell anyone.'

'What about Chris, surely you can tell him, then?'

Panic shows on her face, her hand grips the table tightly. 'No,' she gasps, 'not Chris, especially not Chris. If he knew then he would send me home. He'd never look at me ever again. It would be over between us.'

I watch her as she rocks backwards and forwards in her chair, head down, groaning and wailing as if in pain. After a few minutes of this she looks up at me, her face streaked by tears.

'I told you lies.' Her sobbing begins again. 'I told Chris lies, it's all so very bad. I'm a horrible person, I've been doing such horrible things.'

'I don't believe you,' I say. 'I know you, Lottie. You wouldn't hurt Chris, I know you wouldn't.'

'No, that's true, but if Chris knew who I really was, he'd hate me.'

She looks at me and meets my eyes. 'The way I told you, how I met Chris, that wasn't true.'

'You said that you met on the internet, then he came over to meet you in person,' I say.

'We agreed to tell people that, Chris said it sounded better.'

'So what really happened?'

'Chris came to Odessa on holiday. A special sort of holiday where foreign men meet Ukrainian girls. That's how we met.'

'So it was a sort of dating agency. What's wrong with that?'

'That's what Chris believes. He thinks he met a normal girl, that we fell in love. That I was so in love with him right from the start that I stayed with him and made love with him. That it was special.'

'And wasn't it?'

'No. I worked at that hotel, meeting foreign men, having sex with them. That was my job. I'd already met hundreds of men like Chris, he wasn't even the first one I'd had sex with that day.'

'But he was special, Lottie. He married you,' I say.

'You don't understand, Jenny. I'd do anything to get away from Ukraine, to get a foreign husband. If Chris knew, he'd never forgive me. He'd never trust me.'

'And can he trust you, Lottie?'

'Of course he can. I love him. I'd never hurt him, I'd never let him down.'

'Then he need never know. Although I've a feeling he must know a lot more than you think. Why are you telling me all this?'

'It's Kat. She worked at the same place as me, she tried to do the same, find a nice Englishman. Then she said she'd got a

181

job in England through an agency, she was very happy for it. A good job, secretarial work, good wages, so she could easily send good money back to our family in Odessa. But now she's disappeared. I think she's in really bad trouble.'

'How old is she?'

'Seventeen, same as me of course. Here, I have a photo, look.' She shows me a stunningly beautiful girl with short blond hair who looks much younger than Lottie because of her boyish figure and unflattering plain dress. 'What's her full name?' I ask.

'Ekaterina,' Lottie replies. 'Ekaterina Federenco.'

'Write it down for me, please, also her date of birth and her address.'

As she writes slowly and neatly, she asks 'Why are you wanting this, Jenny, what are you doing?'

'I don't know yet, Lottie, I need to start somewhere if I'm going to help you find your sister. I have a friend in the government, you met Alex didn't you? He might be able to help, you know, pass on the information to the right people maybe. We'll try to find something out. Can you let me have the name of the agency?'

'I'll ask my mother if she knows, I think they were Bulgarian, Kat went by boat to Varna when she left. What do you think has happened to her, Jenny?'

'I really don't know, Lottie. There are some bad people that I've come across who are doing this kind of thing, bringing in young girls to this country and forcing them to do very unpleasant things. I imagine that's how they do it, pretend to have good jobs for them then transport them illegally into this country. Once they are here they're at the mercy of the men who brought them. I hope Ekaterina isn't one of the girls I'm talking about.'

'But what can you do?' Lottie looks sad and worried, but not shocked by my reading of the situation.

'I don't know what I can do, all I know is that it's happening right here in Manchester and I'm going to try to stop it.'

'I'll help,' Lottie says. 'Tell me what to do.'

'The men involved are very dangerous, if you help there's a chance that you and your family in Odessa could be put in danger. You need them to be very careful if they start asking questions about the men who took Ekaterina. We need to find out how they operate over in Ukraine, though.'

'We'll do anything if it will help Kat.'

'Then get them to find details of these Bulgarians, the name of their organisation, telephone numbers, addresses, the people who work there. As much information as they can, but please tell them to be discreet. They might be putting themselves at risk.'

'Anything else?' Lottie asks.

'Yes, I need your Chris to build another one of his special trackers.'

58

Alex is sitting cross-legged on the carpet, supporting me with a strong hand on my lower back. I can feel the tip of his penis resting at the entrance to my vagina as I sit astride his warm nakedness. He holds me gently in position, his other hand soft between my breasts. I want to feel more of him, I need to impale myself completely. As I shift my lower body to bring him further inside me, he adjusts our position to prevent it.

'Keep still,' he instructs in a low voice 'Feel into how this is. Breathe in down your front. Follow your breath down your body, enjoy the sensations it brings then let them travel up your back and through the top of your head. Be still. Only breathe. See how that is, how it feels.'

He places my hand over his heart and looks deep into my eyes. I obey. I visualise my breath, it is flowing like water down my front, it suffuses my genitals with warm desire. I can feel myself expanding, opening. Then the tingling passes up my spine and into my head. Each breath is a nourishing pleasure.

The feelings in my groin are getting stronger. Alex remains perfectly still apart from the rise and fall of his chest under my hand. His penis is barely touching me, yet I am getting those beautifully familiar ripples of pleasure. I concentrate on them, holding on to them, urging them to intensify.

'Breathe,' Alex whispers. 'Let the energy flow into you and then away again. Let go. Relax. Don't try to control what you feel, let it be how it is.'

I'm trying to understand what he's telling me to do but I really do need him to fuck me properly now. He's got me going, now I want him to get on with the job. I'm so desperate for him, a few deep thrusts is all it's going to take and I'll be there. I manage to get more of him inside me by slowly moving my hips. I feel the beginnings of a more satisfactory fullness as I manoeuvre myself.

'Breathe,' Alex repeats. 'Breathe deeply and fully. Touch the roof of your mouth with your tongue, keep it there. Relax.'

As he speaks, he draws me towards him slightly and enters me very slowly. I gasp, give out little moans of pleasure, see Alex's calm face. I breathe in deeply, then out completely. I feel like my breath is sucking his cock inside me, I can feel it sliding deeper with every breath. I breathe in, hold the feeling, breathe out and release it.

He's moving us both, rocking slightly now. I try not to tense into orgasm, and instead continue to enjoy my blissful breathing. It's getting more difficult to breathe away the pleasure as it suffuses my whole body. I want to grab it and hold it. I want it to concentrate and intensify. My head feels as if it might explode, I'm tempted to stop breathing altogether and let it.

We gaze at each other, I hold his eyes, watch his ecstasy, feel my own.

Then they start. Unstoppable waves coming from deep inside my belly, a white heat that builds until I can no longer breathe it away. My head can't contain it any more, I convulse and scream and rejoice. Still they come, coursing through all of me until I try to catch them, hold them still, make them stay. Then the waves dissipate, lap gently until the waters still completely and I collapse, shuddering with tears, into Alex's arms, wrapping myself around him.

Alex takes me gently over to the bed, places me on the edge, penetrates me fully and begins long, slow gentle thrusting. It's what I've been longing for, he fills me with searing pleasure, brings me crashing into spasms of release. As I lie back, spent and glowing, he withdraws and stands over me, both his hands resting on my thighs and his penis above my belly.

I see him draw in a deep breath then the tip of his cock begins to twitch. A long stream of ejaculate squirts past my head, then several more in quick succession. The whole length of my body is striped by warm pearlescent liquid by the time his unaided cock quietens.

Alex slides onto the bed and we lie together, entwined in the sticky mess.

59

The entrance to Trafford Trailers is almost opposite the huge Unilever complex on Ashburton Road that most of the lads refer to as the Typhoo. The gatehouse is a modest affair, sitting in the middle of two red and white striped barriers. For good measure at night, the black steel gates are drawn across and padlocked. Ian Telfer, GOD Security's replacement for the sadly departed Alan, clumsily unfastens the chains and allows me entry.

It's not often I experience the quiet tedium of being a security guard. Three-thirty in the morning is a challenge to anybody's senses. To be expected to stay alert and capable in the early hours is probably too much to ask, even of men who are alert and capable normally. Most of my guys, bless them, are neither at any time of the day or night. Ian is pleasant enough, red haired, tall, rangy and able to brew a cup of tea without scalding himself too severely. He has a rather stale odour, a state common to workers who work long hours and bathe infrequently. Being cooped up in this stuffy cabin with him on a tepid summer night isn't high on my bucket list.

'They said it's tonight, boss,' he repeats as if I'm holding him to account for them keeping me waiting.

'When you say *they* who exactly are *they*?'

'Don't know. I just get the word from the manager. He says, "they're on for tonight", or "they're coming tonight, watch out for them".'

'And these aren't the same people who did for Alan?'

'No, course not. Alan was helping this gang, just like I do now.'

'So that was another lot, the ones who stole the trailer and killed Alan?'

Ian shrugs. 'Must have been.'

'You don't know anything about them?'

'Not me.'

'So who are these people then, the ones bringing in the girls?'

'No idea. All I do is let them in and keep my head down. I'm not sure telling you about tonight is a good idea. We could all get into big trouble.'

'Yes, but you let them in, don't you, you must see who they are?'

'Only the drivers and they don't say much on account of them being foreign.'

'Where are they from?'

'Europe, at least the truck is, I've seen BL and PL plates on them, that's Bulgaria and Poland. My mate once went on a holiday to Bulgaria, said it was a terrible long way away, on the plane for hours and hours and when he got there he said it wasn't a patch on Greece, sort of dull he said, nobody doing anything much, bland I think he described the place.'

'If they've driven all the way from Bulgaria, we'll have to expect them to be a little flexible on time.'

'Talk of the devil...' Ian points out headlights in the distance. 'I think that's the van now, the truck won't be far behind.'

He saunters out of the gatehouse and fiddles with the lock. Two headlights envelop him with brightness as he struggles to pull the gates apart. I sit in the shadows hidden by the high counter, hoping nobody decides they need to come in here. The twelve-seater passes noisily by. Two men sitting in the front, nobody that I recognise. I'm surprised at how disappointed I am about this. I must have expected a nice neat package, all wrapped up, more than I realised.

Almost as soon as the van disappears behind the maintenance building, the lorry turns up. The driver is perched high in his Scania unit, hauling a long curtain-side semi-trailer in his wake. If he bothers to look down he could see me sitting here. Once the truck's back end clears the gatehouse I make my move. Taking care to avoid being caught in his mirrors I follow in a crouching run. Lying flat on the greasy tarmac underneath a parked trailer, I watch as an electric forklift is used to remove one pallet of shrink-wrapped goods from the curtain-sider.

One man clambers onto the deck, a female appears tottering on the edge, uncertain how to get off. The forklift returns with an empty pallet and offers this as a platform. As she steps unsteadily out of the shadows, I can see she is young, late teens maybe, dressed in a tiny skirt and short sleeved top. She is clutching a sports bag. Voices are raised, male and female, girls are being ushered off the truck, lowered to the ground and directed into the waiting mini bus.

One girl is standing by the truck shouting, refusing to move. A man grabs her roughly and tries to push her towards the van but she resists, kicks out with her foot, screaming loudly. A second man runs over, begins punching the girl in the face. He throws her to the ground and kicks her viciously. I'm feeling the sickening blows in my own stomach and I half rise, desperate to intervene, to put a stop to the horrible cruelty. Then I remember my ear being cut, my overwhelming sense of helplessness and I duck back into the shadows. Her screams turn to moans, he keeps lashing out at her with his foot, even when she goes silent and is lying still. The two men half drag, half carry her to the mini bus and throw her inside. The other girls' voices diminish in volume, the doors are slammed shut and I am left shaking with frustration at my own powerlessness to intervene and help.

I wait while the two remaining men de-couple the trailer unit and leave it parked in a row of identical ones. I make sure the lorry and the men are long gone before I venture out of my hiding place and with unsteady hands attach the device that Chris supplied to the trailer with the secret compartment.

60

'They could be gay.'

Emma laughs at my suggestion. The office atmosphere is becoming lighter every day now as the acquisition proceeds. I've had to take Emma into my confidence, she has been heavily engaged in feeding information to Security Group's accountants, but her natural exuberance remains undiminished. She is the one element of this business that I will miss.

'Then they could try with a man, it's the same result.' Emma twists her face in distaste. 'Either way it's a sure giveaway.'

'Are you sure what the police procedures are?' I ask.

'Yes, Ben says they've been tested in the courts and everything. It was all to do with some peace protestors or green activists or something similar. The undercover policeman was having a relationship with a woman in the camp, even though he was already married and had children.'

'And you're saying that the police condone that sort of thing?'

'Encourage it,' Emma says with disgust. 'I'm not letting them send Ben on undercover work.'

'But surely it's a matter for the individual. Your Ben wouldn't get up to anything like that.'

'But it's like I already said, they test you to find out if you are a policeman, if you don't have sex then you're suspicious, I mean it stands to reason doesn't it?'

'I thought you said the police allowed sex for undercover officers?'

'Yes, that's my point, Ben said in the case he's talking about, the undercover cop spent four years getting the activists' trust. When he testified in court they were really pissed off and tried to get his evidence thrown out on the basis that he was having an affair with one of the main women. The judge said it was perfectly reasonable, he would wouldn't he, being a man. I bet he wished he could do it.'

'So, it's legally permissible for an undercover policeman to have sex with a suspect?'

'Exactly, how awful is that? It's practically encouraging them to do it.'

'Does Ben work undercover?'

'No, don't be silly. I'm just saying that if he did, then that would be it as far as I'm concerned. He could tell them to stick their lousy job up their smelly bottoms, I'm fed up with him being a policeman anyway. Because of the cuts they're getting no pay rises, less overtime and no promotions for five years. But at the same time Ben has to suffer they're spending millions and millions and millions on things like the National Crime Agency that the politicians have dreamed up.'

'What's that?'

'The NCA, I don't know. Ben says it's the only way to get promotion, but normal policemen probably won't get a look in. The adverts he's seen want specialists like forensic accountants, not policemen at all.' She looks at me, her eyes widen. 'That would be a good job for you, Jenny, you know when SG take you over, you could do that sort of thing, I bet you'd be good at it.'

'Damn right I would,' I laugh. 'As long as it involves lots of undercover sex.' We collapse into fits of giggles, but when I emerge from the laughter, something about our conversation continues to gnaw at my insides.

61

'How's your retirement going, Mick?'

The uncertainty that flickers in his eyes tells me more than his words can.

'Fine thanks, Jenny, life is good.'

'I was just checking that you were still up for the football parking. It's the City match on Sunday, we can double the prices.'

Joan waddles into the lounge bearing mugs of tea and a plate piled high with chocolate digestives.

'He's driving me mad,' she says as she delivers the refreshment. 'Can't you get him out from under my feet?'

Mick's eyes swivel to the ceiling and back to the biscuits.

'I'll try, Joan,' I say to her broad back as she leaves the room.

'Well,' I say, 'Joan seems to think it's a good idea.'

Mick frowns. 'What about all the palaver with those black lads, they'll be back. That Leroy will be gunning for us, you in particular. I'm surprised you haven't had a visit already.'

'Leroy won't be bothering us and I doubt any of his mates will.'

'How can you be so sure of that?'

'Leroy's in prison. He got five years for possession of a firearm.'

'Never. I heard he was in hospital for a while after his accident.'

'He was, they transferred him straight to custody as soon as he was well enough. I doubt he'll be interested in trying to muscle in on our car parks or in any position to do it, even if he was.'

'So it's business as usual?'

'That's right, Mick, and the offer I made still stands. After the lads are paid we'll split the proceeds. Should help keep you and Joan in biscuits, maybe even a holiday somewhere warm.'

'She wouldn't go, I've tried.' Mick grins. 'She doesn't like foreign food, can't get on with it – and that was only the Isle of Man when we went for the TT Races.'

Chris lives only a few minutes' drive from Mick. Lottie opens the door to me, her big eyes are swollen with tears, her hair tangled and uncared for.

'Come in,' she says. 'Chris is in his study.'

'What's happened?'

'I don't know, Chris will tell you. The truck is on the move, he says, he likes to be mysterious.' Her eyes try to twinkle but fail.

'No, that's not what I meant, Lottie. You look upset, I'm asking about you.'

She takes me through to the kitchen and flops down on a chair. 'It's my father,' she says, tears making soft tracks over her cheeks. 'He's very ill in hospital, my mother says he might die.'

Chris comes in and hovers by the door, obviously distressed by Lottie's state.

'Oh dear, I'm so sorry.' I reach out to comfort her but her shoulders remain stiff and unyielding. 'It's because of the questions about Kat, they attacked him.'

I swallow. 'Tell me what happened.' My heart is heavy but my anger is simmering close to the surface.

'One of Kat's friends told them about a man called Grublauskis in Odessa. She thought he might have been the one who made the arrangements for Kat.' Her eyes avoid mine as she speaks. 'My father went to confront this man at his hotel.'

'And he was attacked?' I ask.

'Not there. He came home and told my mother Grublauskis was to blame for Kat's disappearance, that he had sent her to Bulgaria.'

'Did he say where Kat was supposed to be going in England?'

'He told my father that Kat had asked to go to Manchester, he had introduced her to someone who would arrange transport and all the necessary papers. When he wouldn't say who this man was my father was angry and said that he would tell the police. The next day he was leaving home and two men started fighting with him on the street, that's how he got hurt. Now he is very bad, he may die at any moment, my mother is with him.'

'You should go, Lottie, go and see your father, make sure your mother's okay.'

'I'm scared,' she says. 'I don't know what to do.'

'You must go home to Odessa, you won't forgive yourself if you don't. If it'll help I'll come with you.'

Her eyes brighten. 'Really?'

'Yes, really,' I say, hardly believing my own ears.

My car squeals with discomfort as its wheels try to retain contact with the slippery cobbles. To my left a steep, crumbling bank cascades down to a torrent of dark water. To my right a gorse-clad hill squeezes me towards the river. O'Brian's offices are at the end of this long cobbled road which is barely fit for any sort of vehicle. His offices consist of a series of inter-connected old, green, temporary portable buildings, amidst a landscape of discarded debris. There are trees as thick as elephant's legs growing through steel roof sections, piles of stones, concrete bricks, timbers and tiles. Anything in fact that might once have been useful for the construction of a building, now awaiting its time to be resurrected and used again.

As I enter the floor sags beneath my feet. As I walk down the corridor my feet bounce so that I can't help swaying like a drunken mariner. I'm left waiting for Peter in what the receptionist refers to as the board room. This is a cabin looking out on the most overgrown areas of detritus, with a raft of tables occupying the centre of the large area. Each of the tables is unique in size and construction, each one a different shade of brown, each a slightly different height. The one I am leaning on rocks violently if I exert any pressure on it. The chairs are similarly piecemeal and in various stages of dysfunction. Mine has lost one of its wheels, which makes it lean awkwardly but has the advantage of reducing its mobility. The first one I tried insisted on taking me sideways on a journey to the centre of the room where the floor sags the most.

It's rare for Peter to meet me in his office. Normally he comes to me or I go to his house. I have a feeling he's still upset about the sale of GOD Security. He's been very quiet lately for which I'm grateful. There's been no more visits to my office, no recent sitting on my desk and mercifully no complicating bag of cash for me to deal with. As for SG, the questions being asked are detailed, pedantic, pernickety even, but not intrusive or awkward. Stuart Donaldson may be carefully controlling things behind the scenes but I doubt it. I think that SG's accountants are merely demonstrating a high incompetence level in examining small aspects minutely but failing to comprehend the big picture. It's quite possible I could have saved the money I bribed Stuart with, but the added comfort of having a fall-back position is probably worth every penny. I can't take the chance that something might be raised with SG that puts them off the deal before I get a chance to sort out Stuart.

As for O'Brian, I am done with his filthy money and glad of it. The caravan sites are not part of the SG deal, they are owned by me as a proxy for O'Brian. If he wants his money out I'll sell. If not, they'll continue to provide an income stream for his business, albeit a much smaller one with GOD Security out of the picture. He'll have to live with it, find some other patsy to do his bidding. I'm not touching any more of his prostitution earnings, even if he doesn't consider them in that way. As far as I'm concerned, by accepting the black money from those appalling men, he's condoning everything they do. I can't believe he's unaware of the source of his ill-gotten gains or hasn't at least a vague notion of the kind of activity that generates his income.

O'Brian won't like it when he has to find another way to launder his cash but that's not my problem. I'm nervous about it, but I am determined to tell him straight. The sale of GOD Security is my decision not his. There's nothing he can do about it now, the deal's nearing completion and I'll soon be on my way and out of his way in particular. Just a few more days and I'll be signing the contracts. SG will be transferring the money. I've already put my flat on the market and put in an offer on a beautiful little house close to Toby's school where we can be together more and more. My plan is to make it so convenient for Tim and his wife to use me as Toby-sitter, Toby-minder, Toby after school club, Toby sick nurse, Toby everything. It's all going to be so much better.

O'Brian is exhibiting his customary lateness. I've been sitting on this wobbly chair for nearly an hour. My irritation is rising to a point where I feel like walking out, telling O'Brian to learn some manners, explaining how disgusted I am at how he takes filthy money that has been generated by all manner of unspeakable crimes. By the time O'Brian walks into the room I'm ready for him and in no mood to pull any punches. That friendly, innocent smile of his, the twinkle in his mischievous eyes, the lazy gentle manner he has, are no longer enough to deflect me from letting him have it. What does stop me is the man accompanying him.

Peter O'Brian and Hector Brighouse enter with the comfortable air of old friends.

63

My urge to inflict physical suffering on that wispy grey head narrowly loses out to my fear. Seeing the two of them together hits me hard, reduces me to helplessness. I can't begin to guess the plans they are hatching together, but I can be sure that they're to my disadvantage. As I sit in stunned silence Hector breezes over to clasp my hand. He even leans down and places a delicate kiss on my left cheek.

'Ah, Jenny, so nice to see you. Peter has been scolding me for being responsible for keeping you waiting. I thought it only decent to come down here and apologise personally.'

Before I can make any kind of response he clasps O'Brian on the shoulder and strides away. Now I'm in turmoil, uncertain what if anything that little charade is all about. I haven't told O'Brian I'm definitely selling, and to SG, nor am I going to. I want the deal to be complete before he has a chance to do anything to stop it. Now it looks like he may know all about it, otherwise why would he display Hector in front of me?

'It's hard to stop old Hector when he gets talking,' O'Brian says. I take this to confirm that they have been discussing me, but refuse to rise to his bait.

'You two know each other then?' I ask.

'Oh yes. We were in Round Table together for years. Got up to all sorts of fun and games. I actually succeeded Hector as chairman. He's something of a legend, a hard act to follow. Oh we've had some laughs, Hector and me. He can drink anyone I've ever met well and truly under the table and be fresh as a daisy the next day. Great guy.'

So that's how these captains of industry measure each other's worth, by the quantity of alcohol they can consume. It's pretty pathetic, a competition I'm glad to stay out of.

'I suppose you're still convinced you'll be better off out of the security business with a nice lump of money behind you?' O'Brian asks, then continues without waiting for my reply. 'I've been thinking about it for quite a while, that's why you've heard nothing from me these last few months. Look, Jenny, unless I can convince you not to sell at all I'm willing to buy the business myself. That way I can protect my own interests, keep the caravan operation and make sure the arrangement remains intact.'

'You want to buy GOD Security?' Now I'm uncertain about what's going on. If Hector was here to talk to O'Brian about GOD Security, why is O'Brian acting like he knows nothing?

'Yes. It's the only thing that makes sense. We both end up with what we want. You get some money, I continue with business as usual.'

'How much are you offering?'

'Oh don't worry, Jenny, you'll get fair value. I'll pay you what you're due. It'll be market value less of course an allowance for what I've put into your business already.'

'Market value is two and a half million.' I watch as his face reddens.

'Really?' he asks. 'I didn't think the market was that buoyant.'

'Don't forget we got the Stretford contract, it's made a big difference to our turnover.'

'Yes, but we both know that it only makes money because of my contributions, don't we.'

'Actually it's better than I expected, Peter, we got a good deal there.'

'Even so it would be difficult to sell to anyone else, the nature of some of your transactions is bound to raise a few eyebrows. The due diligence would uncover a lot of things we can neither of us have out in the open.'

'So what are you proposing?'

'Like I said, a fair deal. Something to keep you going. I'll pay you half a million, Jenny. Fifty thousand a year for ten years.'

199

'What about Doreen?'

'What about her?'

'She relies on the business for her livelihood as well as me.'

'That's up to you. If you want to give her something I'll not object to that.'

'So you're offering me five hundred thousand pounds over ten years and I have to share that with Doreen?'

'Yes, I thought you'd be pleased.'

'Leave it with me, Peter, let me think about it and get back to you.' His smug grin tells me he thinks I'm out of options. My only hope is that Hector isn't party to this act of highway robbery. If he is, I'll find out soon enough when the SG offer gets rescinded.

64

'This is where my family live.' Lottie points to the enormous slab-sided apartment block. My heart sinks. As the taxi ride progressed it seemed to take us ever deeper into deprivation. These monstrous blocks are clustered together a dozen at a time, ten storeys high and in various states of disrepair. The predominant colours are bare concrete with a light blue patchwork. Washing streams from balconies, rust-stained metal boxes on some of the windows testify to the debilitating heat. Promislova Street is cracked and pitted, crisp brown vegetation protrudes from the fractured pavements. In comparison, Salford seems like a closer relative to Monaco than here. Opposite the block of flats there is a haphazard array of asbestos-roofed sheds, made from odd bits of wood and concrete. The heat is intense, oppressive. I am struggling to breathe as I lug my too-heavy suitcase up the steps.

Lottie's mother is a short, stocky lady with sad eyes. She greets her daughter with copious affection and strong hugs before taking my hand stiffly. The Ukrainian chatter is loud and excited from both women. As the conversation progresses, Lottie's mother flashes sideways glances at me with increasing regularity.

'She says my father is still very sick, he has a ruptured organ, I don't know what the English word is. They have to do an operation if he is to survive.'

'When will they operate?'

'Nobody knows. My mother goes to the hospital every day to be with him. She pays the doctors and nurses, she cleans him and takes him food. She can't do any more.'

'You have to pay for everything?'

'Officially everything is free but doctors are paid so little salary they only treat people that give them money. It's normal. The problem is the operation. Up to now nobody knows if it can bc done.

'Look Lottie, I'll help pay for the operation, don't worry about the cost.'

'It's not that. At the moment there's no surgeon to do it. They don't know when they might have one.'

'Then he needs to go to another hospital, surely.'

'That's not possible. Anyway he's in the best one already. You can't blame our doctors, there's no money here. Look around, Jenny, would you stay here unless you had to? Doctors get less than two hundred pounds a month. My Chris earns twice that every day.'

'Then we take him away from here, take him somewhere he can get the proper treatment.'

'He's too ill to be moved, they say. Anyway, where would we take him?'

A horrible trapped feeling squeezes my abdomen, her desperation communicates directly into my own nervous system. I have seen squalor before, lived in it, but never imagined it existed on such a massive scale. No wonder pretty young girls throw themselves at fat old westerners. In their circumstances I'm certain I'd take my chance to get the hell out of this place.

At my insistence, Lottie takes me to meet the men who operate the sex tourism business that she and Kat were involved in. As soon as we enter the hotel, her nervousness increases to the extent that it becomes contagious. I look at the false glitz and sad faces, taste the hopelessness all around me.

She leads me over to where two of the more unsavoury characters are sitting.

'Tell them I'm from Manchester, that I operate an escort agency, say I need some young girls to work in my business.' I can see that Lottie is nervous to the point of stupefaction. The two men opposite may not be the ones who attacked her father but they might just as well be, the way Lottie is reacting. She struggles with her words, looking everywhere apart from directly at the men. When she stops talking the younger man shrugs his shoulders and glares brazenly at me.

I look right back. The two men both stink of tobacco and sweat. The older man, probably in his late fifties, scratches his groin in an instinctive rather than provocative gesture. It's as if he has a severe irritation in that region, one he returns to often. I'm feeling very uncomfortable, it's so hot, and I'm not at all sure these unsavoury characters are going to be of any help. One of them grunts, the other grunts back.

'How many?' Lottie says. 'They want to know how many?'

'Tell them two or three immediately, more later on.'

'Five thousand,' Lottie translates. 'Pounds, they say.'

'For three?'

'They say for each, five thousand pounds for each.'

'Tell them they are crazy, I can do it cheaper myself, tell them that.'

'They say that girls in England earn you fifty thousand pounds every year. Their girls are good for two or three years at least. They are very young and fresh.' Lottie's eyes are streaming with tears now but the men's eyes are fixed on me.

'Tell them I'll pay two thousand five hundred, but only on delivery and only when I see the girls.'

The older man shrugs his shoulders. A white froth of spittle appears between his lips which he discharges in my direction.

Lottie translates his mutterings. 'He says the transport costs more than that, he asks if you have any idea how hard it is to get into your country?'

'Ask him who deals with the transport, tell him I need to speak with them.'

The old man raises his eyebrows and shakes his head as he replies.

'He says you must deal with him, that you can take it or leave it. He doesn't care either way.'

'Ask him when his next delivery will arrive in England.'

They listen to Lottie's translation then the older man shrugs his shoulders. 'Every week,' she says, 'he can send them any time you want. Just pay the money.'

'Tell them I'll let them know, that I have to talk to Grublauskis first. That I'll get a better deal from him.'

At the sound of the name, the two men exchange a glance, then the younger one answers while drawing his finger across his throat. Lottie translates but I already know what is being said.

'Grublauskis is dead,' she says.

We leave the grisly duo sitting there and return to the warm sunshine and fresh air outside. I feel drained even from such a short exposure to those men. I shudder when I think how vulnerable young girls like Lottie and Kat find themselves under the control of nasty pieces of work like them. Lottie looks at me with a puzzled frown. 'Why did you say that, about the transport I mean?'

'Because that's what I'm interested in, Lottie. These aren't the sort of men who might know where Kat is now. Once she's left Ukraine and they have their money for her, they have no interest in where she is or what's happening to her. It's the ones who took her to England that we need to find.'

'But how do we do that?'

'I don't know, we need to change our approach, that's for sure.'

65

This man speaks good English, but I'm not getting the answers I need from him. Lottie left me to visit her father in hospital. It seems he will surely die very soon without an operation and there is no prospect of surgery in the near future. There are no doctors available, it's not a question of money, only of personnel. Lottie has become increasingly distraught the last few days. The brutes in the hotel made her fear for Kat's life, as well as her dad's. One of her school friends set up this meeting with an elderly man with scholarly leather patches on the elbows of his dark green jacket.

My thin cotton t-shirt is clinging wetly to my armpits as we sit in the harbour side café, how he manages to justify that jacket I have no idea.

'I don't understand, don't you have some transport arrangement, you know, someone who puts the girls into a lorry and smuggles them into England that way?'

'Why would anybody want to do that?' he frowns. 'You say you have two girls both eighteen and you want to employ them in England. As long as they are willing, there is no need to take such trouble. Are they willing?'

'Oh yes.' I hope he can't see the lies in everything I'm saying.

'Then let me have their documents, I'll arrange student visas for them.'

'Student visas?'

'Of course, anyone under twenty-five has no problem with a visa.'

'Don't they need to be accepted at a university or something?'

'Yes, but that's no problem either. I have good contacts in England.'

'At universities?'

'Yes, and colleges, mainly colleges.'

'Don't the girls have to apply for a course, have qualifications, all that kind of thing?'

'No, as I say, I have good contacts. Your girls will be registered officially at the college. They'll get confirmation of their places, everything. And for this all I require is their papers and two thousand pounds per girl. It's a trouble-free way for you.'

'Do you arrange many of these?'

The man smiles. 'Hundreds, every year. An old academic like me has to do something in his retirement to make ends meet.'

'What about the girls who have to be smuggled into England by lorry, why don't they use you instead?'

'I can't help you. Human trafficking is a different matter. Those people deal in children and slaves, you don't want to get involved in that business, it's very dangerous. Better to get your girls my way, much better.'

66

The apartment has even fewer items in it than the one Lottie's parents occupy. A smell of over-cooked cabbage pervades the whole place, at least I hope that's the origin of the smell. I dread to imagine what else might be causing it. The threadbare sofa is occupied by Lottie and a small girl a few years younger with cropped black hair. Her name is Alisiya and she is Kat's friend, the one who put us in touch with the old guy with the student visa racket.

'Why didn't Kat get herself a student visa, surely that would have been her best way to get to England?'

'No money.' Alisiya's sad brown eyes betray a sense of hopelessness, an air of resignation that feels out of place in one so young. 'Only the very rich can afford that man's prices.'

'She could have had the money from me.' Lottie's voice is shaking with emotion.

'I know,' Alisiya says, 'I told her to ask you but she wouldn't. She said she'd do it herself, just like you did.'

'So what did she do?' I ask, watching Lottie's face twisting with distress.

'She stopped working at the big hotels and started trying to make friends with the tourists, hoping one of them would fall in love with her and take her home with him. She's very pretty, she had lots of men interested in her but not as a wife.'

'So she stopped?' I ask.

'No, she didn't stop meeting men, though she did begin to take their money. I suppose she hoped to save enough to buy a visa.'

Lottie bursts into tears and begins to shout at Alisiya in her own language. The exchanges are angry and acrimonious as if Lottie's holding Alisiya responsible for her twin sister's actions. Alisiya stands up and points to the door, screaming wildly.

When we emerge from the dank apartment block into the dazzling sunlight, Lottie is still sobbing. Parked next to our waiting taxi is a police car. Two blue-shirted men with French style flat hats and white gun holsters are talking to our driver. As we approach they look up and move to intercept us. I feel Lottie's body stiffen with shock as she sees the policemen.

'Run,' she says, grabbing my arm and bundling me back inside the apartment stairwell.

'It's only the police,' I say, 'there's no need to run.'

'Yes there is,' she pants, as she leads me down a grimy concrete-walled corridor, through a door and out into the desolation that forms the open space at the rear of the tower block. Four more policemen are waiting for us, complete with their ridiculous gendarme style hats. One of them grabs me roughly by my forearm. Another clamps his arms around me from behind. I relax instantly, buckle my legs, become a dead weight. When I feel the man behind me bending his back and bracing himself to bear my unexpected weight I stiffen, drive my legs hard into the ground, smash the top of my head into the face that overhangs me. The grip slackens. I kick hard at the knee of the man in front of me, wriggle my way free, turn to look for Lottie, take a savage blow to my jaw, see the gun being held to my head. For a brief moment I'm confused, it looks just like Leroy's gun. I wonder why the same gun is threatening me again, whether everybody has a gun like this in the dreadful world I'm living in. Another blow to the back of my head knocks me to the ground. As I lie tasting my own blood, the kicking begins.

67

The fat woman with dirty blonde hair hanging in lank strands comes over to my corner of the cell as I try to eat. My mouth and jaw are aching badly; at least one of my teeth is broken or missing. The thin brown soup and dry black bread smell unappetising, but it's all I've been given. She grabs at the enamel dish I'm holding and as I resist the soup spills over the side and the bread drops to the filthy floor. I stand up and smash the dish, soup and all, into her face, then I grab her disgusting greasy hair and use it to throw her over my right hip so that she lands heavily on the back of her head. As I stand over her, the spark of anger in her eyes diminishes. I continue to stare, daring her to rise up and fight me, but she has no stomach for it any more.

I'm back in prison. I know this game, I've played it before. Now she knows I don't represent easy pickings she'll leave me alone. It's simply a matter of risk and reward to her. Her beaten look tells me she's no longer interested. I turn and pick up her dish which she carefully placed on the small wooden table in the centre of the cell before she came over to grab my food. Slowly, so that the others can also get the full effect, I pour the lukewarm liquid over her head then crumble the bread onto the floor. Now they can see I don't care, that I have nothing to lose. That if they fight with me I'll injure them whether they win or lose. I am hungry but I'm not starving and I'm certainly not showing my cellmates any form of weakness.

Nobody seems to speak any English. My repeated questions and requests go unheeded by both inmates and prison officers. Once a day we are let out to wash in an area as filthy as the cell we live in. No showers, only cold water taps. Most of the women don't bother, they drink the water thirstily, splash a little over their faces and nowhere else. There's no soap, no incentive to keep clean, but I do my best.

My meals go unmolested, the days and nights merge into grinding tedium. At least my jaw pain eases and the stench of the place is reduced with familiarity. As my own fears subside into numbed indifference, they are replaced by the terrible realisation that Lottie may be even worse off. She hasn't had my experience, the hardening that this brings. Her food may be confiscated, she could be beaten half to death. If she were in here with me, I could help her, protect her. But Lottie is not here with me and I've no way of finding out where she is. My hope is that she's back with her mother, that the police only took me, that she did nothing to aggravate them like I did. I have a horrible feeling that I probably did enough to get both of us imprisoned indefinitely. At least the policeman I injured hasn't been around to exact vengeance. Maybe they won't let him at me in a women's prison. Maybe he's in no fit state.

This time it's only me they want. Two female officers lead me down the corridor and I get visions of the police waiting to give me another good kicking. They take me into a toilet block. This one is passably clean with flush toilets and showers. They wait patiently as I strip off the prison uniform and stand under the lukewarm water. I even find a small sliver of soap to aid the process. There's no shampoo, no conditioner, no shower gel, but after what I've been used to, this is five star quality. I dry my hair on the rough grey towel, look at myself in the mirror. There's a red and black bruise on the left of my face, extending from my neck up to my cheekbone. My own clothes are produced, I am encouraged to put them on. Then the women bring out my handbag and push cosmetics at me so that I can repair my damaged face as far as possible. It's quite clear that they're going to stand there until I finally apply some lipstick, so I oblige.

My hopes of being released are increasing with every moment. Why would they clean me up and make me dress in my street clothes if they weren't going to let me go? The man in the interview room is the answer. He is my age, maybe a little older, forty at the most, neat black hair, grey flannels, dark blue blazer with shiny brass buttons.

'Charles Smith.' He stands stiffly and shakes my not quite so grubby hand. 'I'm from the British Consulate, Mrs Parker.'

I sit down opposite him, the guards leave us alone. Charles sinks sadly into his seat.

'Bit of a problem, I'm afraid.' He indicates a manila envelope in front of him. 'The Ukrainian authorities have rather taken exception to your behaviour. I must admit I expected you to be a lot more – how should I say – beefy. Putting one of their police officers in hospital has made you somewhat unpopular, though looking at you I can see why they're so embarrassed. With the greatest respect, Mrs Parker, you don't look like a major threat to Ukrainian national security.'

'They chased me, grabbed hold of me, and then they kicked me while I was on the ground.'

'Very unsporting, I'm sure.'

'They knocked out my teeth, I desperately need a dentist.' I'm not impressed with this junior assistant consul, or whatever he is. 'I need to see someone who can help me, the ambassador, isn't it? Can you get him here, surely he can do something?'

He smiles a thin reluctant smile. 'I'm afraid the ambassador is unlikely to intervene personally every time a British tourist roughs up a Ukrainian policeman. You will have to make do with me, I'm afraid.'

'What's going to happen to me then?' I ask, knowing full well now that I'm going to be in this cess pit for a very long time.

'That depends.' Charles opens the envelope and slides out a sheath of documents and a passport. 'What exactly are you doing here in Odessa?'

'My friend Lottie is Ukrainian, her father is ill. I came over to help and support her. She lives near me in Salford, she's married to a friend of mine, Christopher Worthington. Do you know what's happened to her? She was with me when the police arrested me.'

'I'll see if I can find out,' Charles says flatly. I detect more than a note of insincerity in his answer.

'Why aren't you writing any of this down?' I ask.

'I don't need to.'

'Her name is Lottie Worthington, her family name is Federenco. Write it down or you'll forget.'

'Believe me, Mrs Parker, if I need to make written notes I will.'

'Okay, I believe you, but please don't forget.'

'Before the police came, what were you doing?'

'Visiting a friend of Lottie's, or rather one of her sister's friends.'

'Why?'

'To talk to her.' I don't know how much to tell this man.

'About what?'

'Kat, Lottie's sister, has disappeared. We thought that Alisiya might know something about her whereabouts.'

'Disappeared?'

'Kat said she was going to England to work, she left Ukraine and that's the last her family heard from her. It's been three months.'

'I see. And did this Alisiya know where Kat is?'

'No, I don't know...there was an argument. Lottie and her were shouting a lot, maybe it was Alisiya who called the police.'

'Have you made enquiries of anyone else?' Charles asks.

'Yes, some men who offer to smuggle girls into England for five thousand pounds each, willing or not. One man who can get student visas for two thousand pounds. Nobody who admits to having dealt with Kat, though. I'm no wiser about her, only confused. I can see why a young girl would want to earn good money in England, but not how anyone could be so desperate as to put herself in the hands of the nasty characters we've met.'

'So you suspect kidnapping?'

'I don't know. Maybe Kat was willing at first but is now imprisoned somewhere.' My heart is sinking at the enormity of the situation. It's as if Kat were a grain of sand dropped into an ocean and I'm only now realising exactly how big that ocean is.

'But you suspect people trafficking, that sort of thing?'

'Yes,' I reply. 'And prostitution, forced prostitution. I've seen it in Salford, young girls from Eastern Europe made to perform degrading acts for men.' I look across at his uncaring expression and almost add the words 'like you'.

'Let me get this straight, Mrs Parker. You suspect that your friend's Ukrainian sister has become a victim of an organised prostitution racket, so you have come over here all alone and tried to put the whole world to rights?'

'It's not quite like that.'

'But it is, Mrs Parker. Even if you find these criminals or worse still, if they find you, what do you expect?'

'Once I know who they are I can report them,' I say.

'To whom? Report a gang of organised criminals to their own police force, or dial 999 when you get home and tell your local constable all about it?'

'Look, there are young girls being abused, raped even. I'm not going to stand idly by and let it continue. I have to try, don't you understand?'

I can feel the prickle behind my eyes and the heat in my cheeks, but I refuse to shed tears in front of this uncaring man.

68

'What happened to your face?' Alex asks.

'It was kicked in by a Ukrainian policeman.'

'Oh.' Alex's face wrinkles. 'Is it as sore as it looks?'

'Worse than it looks, really painful. My ear hurt but this is at least as bad.'

'I can see you're upset.' Alex moves to put his arm around me, to comfort me like an ailing child. I push him away, consumed by shame at my display of weakness, then instantly regret the impulse.

'Leave me alone,' I say. The words are completely empty of any conviction or meaning. After all it's me who turned up disconsolate at his flat, not the other way round.

Alex makes a pot of tea, that weak urine coloured stuff that he drinks without milk. I might as well drink warm water from the tap. Alex and Hector should pal up together, they could have really jolly tea parties.

'You and Hector would get on a treat,' I say.

'Who?'

'The man who's buying GOD Security, you'd like him. He's just like you.' I can't hold back the beginnings of a grin.

'Really?' Alex asks.

'You might actually be twins, you're so alike.' I laugh despite my discomfort. Teasing Alex, even if it's only in my mind, is breaking through my melancholy. This is what I came round here for, I realise. Someone who connects to me deeply. Someone to dispel my gloom, to tell me I'm okay, convince me that the sad death of Lottie's father isn't my fault, to take me away from the grim circumstances that surround me. My culpability hangs heavily on my shoulders. Being with Alex somehow reminds me that I am doing my best, following my heart, not trying to put people at risk. Apart from myself, of course.

'One day I'll introduce you, you'll see what I mean,' I smile. Alex's arms go around me now and I feel myself relax and melt into him.

'When?' Alex whispers.

'Not until I've finished with you. I'm scared that you two might run off together.'

'Hector who?'

'Hector Brighouse.' I feel a tiny shudder as Alex hears the name. 'You know him?'

'Not really,' Alex says. 'I have seen him though, if he's the man I'm thinking of I'll have to watch my diet.'

'Where would you have seen him?'

'Oh, at the office, the occasional meeting. He's the SG chairman isn't he?'

'Meetings with Hector?' I'm feeling very confused. First Peter O'Brian, now Alex: is there no end to Hector Brighouse's circle of influence?

'Police liaison meetings mainly.'

'Why would you be involved in them?' I pull away and look Alex in the eyes.

'Who do you think pays for it all?' Alex smiles. 'SG, the police, everybody, it's all government-funded one way or another, or didn't you know? Security Group operate prisons on our behalf, transport criminals around for the police. We're their biggest customers by far.'

'I do know.' I just didn't think of Alex in meetings with SG and the police.

I hope they never talk about me.

69

'Don't eat anything until the numbness wears off,' my dentist advises as I leave on shaky legs. 'We don't want you eating your own mouth, do we?' he adds pointlessly.

I think all his cheerfulness is entirely false, that he enjoys the prodding and drilling as little as his patients and that very soon he will gas himself in his Porsche. Meanwhile, he's fixed my teeth, or rather dragged them out and replaced them with pretend ones.

By the time I negotiate the awkward entrance to my solicitors and sit down opposite Suriya, a painful throbbing is beginning, even though my lips are still floppy and numb. She appears to be in glorious health, eyes bright, big smile. Life as her must be very good indeed. She pushes across a thick document.

'We need to go through this, thanks for sparing the time to come in.'

'Well, I need this deal to be completed, so I'm not going to hold it up.'

'Can I get you something, you look as if you're suffering?'

'No, I'm fine, let's get on with it.' I know she's being kind, but I don't need her for anything other than sorting out the paperwork.

'Are you sure, can I get you some paracetamol maybe?'

'No thanks. What are these documents? They're an inch thick. What is all this stuff, it's only complicating matters, surely?'

'These are the warranties. I didn't produce them. They come from the other side.'

'Warranties?'

'Yes. Documents that deal with the information you have supplied on the state of the business. You will be confirming that everything is in order, that there's nothing you haven't disclosed.

They give SG the right to withhold or take back money if they're not complied with.'

'I don't understand. Why do we have to do this? What about the due diligence exercise, surely it's up to SG to satisfy themselves they're getting what they're paying for?'

'Yes it is, but this is an additional safeguard for them in case they've missed anything.'

'What if I refuse to sign this?'

'Look, Jenny, there's nothing in these documents that need be of concern to you. They only confirm that what you've told SG is the truth. That there's nothing you're hiding from them. It gives them some comfort in case anything else comes to light, but of course it won't, will it?'

'I hear what you say, but as far as I'm concerned, SG can look at the business and make up their own minds. I'm not underwriting any of their mistakes. If it turns out to be a bad deal for them, I'm not giving them back my money.'

'I'm sure it won't come to that. SG are a public company, they have to do things properly and that includes insisting on warranties. You won't get the deal done at all if you can't agree them.'

'Okay, where do I sign?'

'We need to go through the documents, I have to explain what they mean and we should make changes where we're not happy.'

'It'll take hours, look at them, they're huge. There's no point in going through them, you said so yourself. If I don't sign them I lose the deal, so I'll sign.'

'But there may be some things you don't agree to, remember they produced these documents.'

'Have you read them?' I ask.

'Yes.'

'Then tell me, is there anything unusually onerous about them?'

'No, not really.'

'Fine, I'll sign them. Now please can we get on with making this deal happen, I can't afford any delay.'

I can tell she's disappointed in me, that she expects me to show more interest in the detail. If SG ever decide to use these agreements, I hope they'll find their money long gone and totally inaccessible. I know what I have to do now and can't be putting energy into arguing irrelevant niceties.

My jaw is aching so much I can hardly see. My eyes are screwed up in defence against the pain. All I want to do is go home, curl up and suffer in peace.

As I stagger out of the office, Suriya says, 'Oh by the way, I had a phone call from a solicitor who says you've agreed to sell GOD Security to a company called O'Brian Construction. I told him he must be mistaken, that we were already progressing a deal and that it was almost complete. He seemed quite surprised.'

She shouldn't have told them anything. I look at her face and I see she is oblivious to the implication of what she's done. My face pain is too severe for me to even begin to try to explain to the woman how badly she has let me down.

70

'What's happened to your face?' Tim's wife asks without a trace of concern in her voice. I consider several rude answers then settle for, 'I've had some trouble with my teeth, needed a lot of work doing, bit painful still.'

I can see from her face that she's disappointed. How she would love to hear the truth, how I had my head kicked in by Ukrainian policemen. She'd use it as an excuse to keep Toby from me. But even the most errant of mothers is entitled to visit the dentist once in a while.

Toby goes to her, gives her a hug but looks round at me while he's doing it. We've had a good day, my son and I. There's something settling between us. The tension isn't so high. We both relax more when we're together. I suppose it's me, that Toby has been reacting to my gloomy moods, my desperation, my anger. After my short stay in a Ukrainian prison, I feel better about the situation with Toby, I even find Tim and his wife more amusing than irritating. More pathetic than threatening. Gone are the days when I felt compelled to justify myself to them at every meeting, making up excuses for my slip-shod parenting and haphazard lifestyle. It must be finally getting through to my sub-conscious that I'm no longer married to Tim and that what he thinks of me is irrelevant.

The main thing is that Toby seems to be thriving. He's unaffected by my absence, safe without my constant attention. I am grateful for what Tim is doing, even to the extent that I have some grudging regard for his wife. At least she seems absolutely devoted to Toby, even I can get that.

Alex has helped. Without him I don't think I could have changed. My bitterness would have burned right through and destroyed me. Now things are very different and as long as Alex loves me I'm not afraid. With that thought the fear comes flooding back. Of course he won't love me for ever, nobody ever does that. He could be pretending, but why he should bother is beyond me. He could be run over by a bus, go back to his wife, find someone really pretty and sexy, find someone who has a full complement of ears and teeth. Lots of things can happen. Alex says to live in the now, that there's nothing else that's real. All our past and future is imagination, only now has any meaning.

O'Brian's personal assistant tells me that he's out of the country, holidaying in the Bahamas, and can't be contacted. I can try an email but he's not really got the hang of them yet and rarely remembers to check to see if he's received any. Maybe that's the best news I can possibly have. Maybe his lawyer hasn't told him what Suriya stupidly blabbed. I hesitate to ring Hector to try to speed up the deal in case he begins to feel my desperation. There's also the worrying possibility that his PA will tell me that he's also on holiday in the Bahamas. Then I'll really start to panic.

Alex has bought tickets for a concert tonight at the Lowry. It's some band made up of geriatric musicians from other groups that have either split up or maybe died from old age. He's very excited about it, he keeps referring to the aging participants as legends. I've never seen or heard any of them and, what with my aching teeth and my tiring day with Toby, have no desire to. All I need when I get home is Alex's gentle hands on my body. He can teach me to breathe, he's very good at that and I am close to getting the hang of it. He's even gone to the trouble of booking a table for dinner. I'm very hungry and my sense of dutiful reluctance dissipates in the face of a square meal.

'What do you fancy?' Alex asks as we settle down at a nice table next to glass walls looking out onto the canal side.

'Something soft,' I answer, 'and not too hot, otherwise my teeth hurt, and a lukewarm drink please, no ice in my coke.'

His smile lifts me. When he reacts so positively to my moaning, I get a warm feeling that everything is going to be fine. Even the prospect of O'Brian derailing the deal with SG fades into the realm of unlikelihood.

'I'll mash everything up for you,' Alex says. 'I'll even chew your meat for you if you like.'

'I'm not a baby bird, there's no need to drop pre-digested food down my gullet. My teeth are just a bit sensitive, that's all. I'll manage the pasta perfectly well, thank you.'

'Have you heard from Lottie? What's happening over in Ukraine?'

'Yes, she's emailed me to say she's okay, that the police aren't pressing charges now that I'm not there.

'But she didn't do anything.'

'She was with me when I was fighting with the police. I felt sure she'd be put in prison with me, I was so scared for her. If she had been I'd never have left Ukraine, I still can't believe how that weird man from the Consulate managed to get me out of there.'

'Why do you call him weird?'

'Oh there was something very strange about him, Alex. It was as if he knew a lot more than he was letting on. I'm quite certain he'd already arranged to have me released and flown home before he even met me.'

'At least you should be grateful to him,' Alex laughs. 'Calling him weird isn't very gracious.'

'Oh I'm grateful all right. I'd do anything to get out of that place. Giving him a blow job was the least I could do under the circumstances.'

Alex's eyes widen in surprise for an instant, then his face relaxes again. Too late. I got him with that one. We both know it and giggle together, like naughty five-year-olds.

'Chris is still over there with Lottie for her father's funeral. He sent me an email this morning with an attachment, showing the journeys made by the trailer I tagged.'

'Oh, anything interesting?'

'No, not really. It's been nowhere near Ukraine, I'm beginning to realise that linking it to Kat's disappearance was too much of a long shot.'

221

'Where did the trailer go?' Alex asks.

'Italy, mainly Italy.'

'I'd like to see Chris's email, there might be something we can learn from it.'

'I doubt it. You can have it if you like but I don't think it's any use at all. Doesn't even get as far as Bulgaria, never mind the Ukraine.'

The concert isn't that bad after all, the lead singer is vaguely familiar and has a wonderful blues voice. It's very light-hearted but slick and accomplished. I even insist on Alex buying me a CD from the foyer which I know I'll never play but it makes me feel good just to carry it home with me.

'There,' I open Chris's attachment and leave Alex to look at it while I make some mint tea.

71

'Can you be in London on the 29th?' Suriya's question confuses me for a moment, then I almost drop the phone in excitement.

'Is it all set for then, that's when the deal gets done?'

'Yes, everything's agreed, all the documents are ready to sign.'

'So why do I have to traipse all the way to London?'

'Security Group's lawyers are in London, also they have certain stock market announcements to make and analysts to brief. It does need to happen in London, believe me.'

My heart is racing. Next Wednesday, less than a week until I get my freedom and my money. A prick of concern catches me briefly when I remember that O'Brian is returning from holiday on Monday. He will have two days to stick his oar in, but maybe it's too late for him to do anything to stop me now. Maybe he'll have more pressing things to do with his time than rain on my parade, but I doubt it.

His relationship with Hector is still a worry. Even though it seems that O'Brian hasn't been told about the impending deal, one phone call to his pal might still ruin everything.

'You will be there?' Suriya asks. 'You have to attend in person, the deal can't proceed without you.'

'Of course I'll be there,' I say.

'The meeting's at ten o'clock. I'll be going down the day before and staying the night in a hotel. Would you like me to get my secretary to arrange for us to travel together?'

'No,' I answer quickly. My abruptness is in danger of being rude. 'That's very kind of you, but I'll make my own arrangements.' The prospect of a night away from Alex doesn't attract me one bit.

'If you intend to go down on Wednesday, you'll need to get the 7 a.m. train from Piccadilly. It'll be an early start and a long day.'

'Long day? Surely all I have to do is sign a few papers.'

'I think you'll find that there's much more to do than that. Issues have a habit of cropping up at the last minute, there's always something to resolve.'

I don't like the sound of this. O'Brian is still nagging at me. 'I'll be fine. I'll see you on Wednesday then.'

'The offices are on Bishop's Square. I'll email you directions.'

Although I can't shake off the haunted feeling I have about O'Brian, the prospect of moving out of Salford grips me with greater intensity.

The estate agent's phone rings out for so long I almost give up. The uninterested voice that eventually answers makes me wonder how the most expensive and most life-changing transaction of my whole life ended up in the hands of a young girl like her. I give her the property address, waiting patiently while she taps it into her computer.

'Yes?' she asks.

'I want to increase my offer.'

'The vendors have told us that they want the full asking price of five hundred thousand.'

'Well they're not going to get it. I'm interested in the house because it's empty and I can move in right away. Every day they leave it empty they're losing money. House prices are going nowhere but down, don't they read the papers?'

'We've had a lot of interest in the property.'

'But no offers, apart from mine. How long has it been on the market?'

'Oh,' she hesitates. 'A couple of months, that's all.'

'More like a couple of years. It was with another agent before you.'

'Oh, I wouldn't know about that.'

'Tell them I'll pay them four hundred and fifty thousand, that's my last offer and I want a quick sale.'

'I don't think they'll agree to that,' she says. 'The property is marketed at offers over five hundred, your offer is below.'

'Tell them I'm a cash buyer, they'll not get another chance. In fact give me their number and I'll speak to them myself.'

'Oh no, that's not possible. All negotiations are to be conducted through us, the sole agents.'

'Do you really think that they'll get a better offer than mine?'

'They might.'

'Have they had any other offers at all?'

'I'm not sure.'

'That's a no, then. Look, it's in both our interests for you to make sure they realise that mine is the best offer they are ever going to get.'

'I suppose so.'

'Good, I'll ring tomorrow. Thanks for all your help.'

The truth is I need this house, this particular house. Okay, it's a very nice house with a lovely garden and breathtaking views but there are quite a few homes that match that description, but not so many that are vacant, that I can move into right away. My list is down to one, this one. When I factor in the location in relation to Toby's school it's a five minute walk to his primary school and there's an excellent secondary school ten minutes' walk in the other direction. I'm thinking strategically now, even long term, which is a new experience for me. By being so damned handy, I'm banking on Toby spending more and more time with me. Walking to my house after school, staying over to make the school run easier for Tim. I plan to be nice, accommodating, but not pushy. Toby will come my way, I'm sure of it. Anyway, it sure beats the hell out of the only other option, kidnapping him and trying to smuggle him out of the country to somewhere without extradition arrangements. There's no way I'd ever put my Toby through that, no matter how desperate I got or how bad I felt. The notion of Toby growing up in somewhere like Argentina is absurd, I can't believe I once even considered it.

The price is a problem. By the time I've split the sale proceeds with Doreen and paid the tax I'll hardly have enough to buy the house and I'll not be comfortable until I sell the flat, if I ever do. The most likely prospect is to rent the place out, taking the money in dribs and drabs and hoping against hope for some clean, honest tenants – fat chance of that.

72

It's Alex's idea to spend the whole weekend shopping, cooking, cleaning, washing and preparing before a few hours of partying at my flat. By the time the guests arrive I'm almost completely exhausted and all I want to do is curl up in a corner with Alex until they've eaten and drunk everything and left. He is bright-eyed, enjoying the small yet select number who I can reasonably label as friends of mine. Either he's not got any friends of his own or he's ashamed to show me them. I encouraged him to invite some work colleagues but he hasn't bothered. Instead he seems to be enjoying himself in my world.

It's also Alex's idea to purchase all the food at Selfridge's. He also kindly let me pay. I had to buy a huge amount to insure against the attendance of Mick and Joan. They are here munching away steadily but I have a feeling that they thoughtfully stocked up on fish and chips before they arrived. Either that or Joan is wearing a salt and vinegar au de toilette. It had crossed my mind to buy unsliced loaves, cut them in half and put the contents of a couple of tins of spam between each to give Mick something substantial to eat.

The one non-Selfridge's item is proving very popular. My cheese and pineapple hedgehogs are the object of considerable derision from Alex. I would almost describe him as getting a bit sniffy about them. I forgive him, it's his soft southern upbringing, he doesn't recognise real party food when he sees it. To maintain the general air of sophistication, I did wrap the grapefruit halves in aluminium foil before sticking in the cocktail sticks. I even used real tinned pineapple chunks which blend perfectly with the cubes of processed cheddar. At this rate of depletion, I may have been too susceptible to Alex's gibes and under-estimated the demand by a considerable margin.

I had hoped Chris and Lottie might be back in time and turn up. There's no sign of them, nor any new word regarding their situation. I can't blame either of them if they decide I'm too big a liability in their lives from now on and have decided to keep well away.

Emma comes over with a large glass of coke in her hand and a big smile on her face.

'You're the designated driver then?' I nod towards her drink.

'Oh, I suppose. Best let Ben have a few beers, he's been having a hard time at work lately.'

'Poor lad, it must be hard being a policeman.'

'Not as hard as it is being a policeman's wife.' Her face screws up in exaggerated distaste. My heart sinks with guilt as the thought intrudes that I'm abandoning this delightful woman to the not so tender mercies of SG. Jim Almond is more than fine with the situation and the lads on the ground won't even notice the difference. It's only Emma, my source of positive vibrations, the girl who has single-handedly kept me almost sane.

'Look, Emma, I'm sorry if I'm leaving you in the lurch over this SG takeover. I'll miss being in the office with you, you know I will. It's just that the time has come when I have to do something else. I've never been comfortable running Gary's business, you know that. Forgive me?'

'Don't worry about me,' Emma smiles. 'It's all going to work out fine.' Her eyes twinkle. She raises her glass and pats her stomach. 'I've checked out the SG maternity benefits package and it's much better than ours.'

'Maternity package, do we have one?'

'No we don't. So you see things are working out very well.' My sluggish brain doped with several gin and tonics suddenly catches on to the significance of her gestures.

'A baby!' I hear myself squeal involuntarily, then hug her a little too hard. 'That's so great, I'm really happy for you both.' I look across the room and see Ben and Alex in deep conversation. 'They seem to be getting on well, our two men.'

'Ben gets on very well with anyone, he's wasted as a policeman. I keep telling him he should try to find something else.'

'Maybe Alex can help,' I say.

Emma looks at me with a puzzled frown. 'I can't see how.'

Mick comes over to join us, plate in one fat fist, pint glass in the other, eyes creased in a smile. 'These are nice.' He points his nose at a pile of Selfridge's most expensive canapés, then eats one straight from his plate like a grazing donkey might.

'Joan adores cheese and pineapple on sticks,' he continues, voice hardly affected at all despite his mouth being full. 'She's had a whole one all to herself. Great party, Jenny. Thanks for inviting us.'

'No problem, Mick, wouldn't be the same without you two.' I almost add *who would finish off all the food*, but manage to avoid that level of ungraciousness. Enthusiasm, after all, is something to be encouraged.

'All set for Saturday?' I ask.

'Sure, everyone's well up for it especially now we don't have the worry of those young hoodlums trying to muscle in. Hey, Emma, did you hear what Jenny did to this thug who threatened her with a gun?'

'No.' Emma's eyes widen as she looks at me.

'I'm sure Emma doesn't need to worry herself about our football experiences,' I say in a vain attempt to deflect him.

'She faced up to the guy, Emma, he pulled a gun and pointed it straight at her, and what do you think she did?'

'Ran away, I hope,' Emma replies.

'No, she walks up to the little toe-rag, grabs his gun and he shoots himself in the bollocks – oh sorry, the er…groin.'

'Oh.'

'But that's not the best bit.'

'Really?'

'No, while the little shit – sorry – was in hospital, our Jenny pays him a visit doesn't she?'

'Why?'

'He's going to be looking for revenge isn't he?'

'Yes, I suppose.'

'So our Jenny, she plants his own gun on him, then tips off the police. Now he's safely locked up and out of our way. Brilliant eh?'

'Did you really?' Emma asks.

'Well…yes, I'm not proud of it and don't go telling your Ben about it. We'll all get into trouble.'

'I think you're very brave, Jenny.' Emma frowns and gives me her concerned look. 'But your bravery is getting you into too much trouble, it's about time you stopped trying to fight crime yourself and left it to the people who get paid to do it.'

'I wish it were that simple, Emma. What about Kat, Lottie's sister? She's disappeared. Nobody in the Ukraine cares apart from her mum and the authorities here have absolutely no interest in a young foreigner who might or might not be in this country. Someone has to care in this world, Emma, we all have to do what we can.'

'Yes, but all you do is get yourself hurt, Jenny. All I'm saying is stop putting yourself at risk. Care by all means, help in any way you can, yes, but don't get yourself killed doing it.'

'Okay, I hear you. Thanks, Emma. Maybe I've been a bit headstrong, it's my nature to fly into action, I suppose. I get so angry at the injustice of it all.'

The doorbell rings. Doreen arrives, conspicuously late, with her new man, Fergus. I've not met him before but I've heard quite a lot about him from Doreen.

'This is my friend Fergus.' She blushes violent red as if deeply ashamed to be displaying her affections in public. He's a tall, gangling figure, sandy haired and slender. The complete antithesis of Gary and for that I'm grateful. He has a pleasant enough smile, despite his teeth being rather yellow and very

230

uneven. I'm not one to be criticising other people's teeth these days.

A familiar figure slips quietly into the flat and stands beside Doreen. Her hair is deep purple in colour, half her head shaved, several piercings hang down from her ears and nose. I can't help but be put in mind of the way that cattle are tagged and ringed. Gary's adopted daughter, Carrie, who used to work as my receptionist, looks well enough though. Her smile and hug confirm she has completely forgiven me for biting off her boyfriend's penis.

'It's Wednesday, it should all be put to bed then,' I speak quietly to Doreen.

'So it's all done and dusted, no more sleepless nights for you worrying about us all.'

'Maybe three or four, there are still things that could go wrong.'

'Like what?'

'Like O'Brian for one, he's back on Monday. I only hope he's too late to stop it.'

'Ah he'll not be doing anything of the sort, not unless he wants to have my fingers around his scrawny throat. I've a good mind to give him a ring and tell him so.'

'I'd rather you didn't,' I laughed, despite knowing that she is deadly serious. It's the honesty of the woman, she always says exactly what she's thinking, come what may.

'How are you, Carrie?' I take her to one side. Since the incident with her thuggish ex-boyfriend I've hardly talked to her at all.

'Fine.' She smiles at me. I know that all that outrageous external appearance is camouflage for a shy, uncertain, sensitive girl. 'I'm working in the Trafford Centre now. It's okay, we have some fun.'

'What about your love life, are you seeing anyone?'

'Nobody particular, we just go out as a bunch of friends. I'm a lot more choosy these days.' A hint of a smile hovers on the edge of her lips.

'Doreen looks happy, I've not see her like this before. Her man Fergus looks like he's suiting her.'

'You're not wrong. We can't stop her going on and on about him. She never stops talking about him, it's driving us all mad.'

'Has he moved in with you all?'

Carries eyes widen with shock. I'm not sure if this is a pantomime horror face or the real thing. 'Oh my God, no. My mam wouldn't be having any of that. What would people think of her? There'll be nothing of that sort of thing until they're married. I doubt she would even kiss him without a ring. She's that sort of woman, but you must know that.'

'Yes I do, but sometimes these considerations fly out of the window when love comes along. Do you think she'll marry him?'

'Certain of it. He's already asked her twice. The first time she told him it's too soon after me dad, this time she says she's thinking about it.'

'I'm amazed. I had no idea it was that serious. That's really good for Doreen, isn't it? What do you think of him?'

'He's nice enough I suppose, but he's not like me dad.'

'Nobody's like your dad,' I say, feeling the sadness of Gary's loss still there inside me, as strong as ever.

Emma drags Carrie away to talk about interesting things like clothes and boy bands, I expect. Mick looms over my shoulder.

'Do you know who that tall guy is over there?'

'Yes, he's called Fergus and he's Doreen's fiancé.'

'No, but do you know who he is?'

'I don't get you, Mick, what are you on about?' I consider for a moment that he might be drunk but I doubt I've provided enough alcohol to even get close.

'It's Fergus Lafferty, that's who he is, Jenny.'

'I'm none the wiser, is he famous?'

'Famous, he's the most famous racehorse owner in Ireland. He's also the richest. They say he's worth billions.'

'What, from owning race horses?'

'Don't be daft,' Mick grins. 'Us punters know the only ones who make money from racehorses are the bookies. No, he spends his money on horses, a bit like the rest of us. He's a businessman, property, construction, all sorts of things. Cement, I think. He might even have an airline.'

'Oh.' I look over to Doreen, my eyes adjusting to this new information. I can see what he sees in her, she's a remarkable woman, strong and beautiful. An unkind thought prompts me to ask myself whether she really needs all the worrying I do about her financial wellbeing. I squash it with the answer that she never asks me for anything. When I offered her a share in the proceeds from the sale of GOD Security she originally declined. She's never been anything other than totally honest with me. It really surprises me that she's never mentioned marrying Fergus. Maybe it's because she's the kind of lady who finds discussions of a romantic nature uncomfortable.

Something has changed between us though. The protective feelings I have for her are being released. I know she never asked me to look after her, but if I'm honest with myself, next to Toby it's been my most important preoccupation. Not having Doreen's financial wellbeing on my shoulders is really fundamental. I could for example take O'Brian's offer now. Fifty grand a year would be okay if it were only me. I could take it, but I'm not going to. I'll get that, plus a nice house and still be able to give Doreen the half I promised her. A powerfully selfish idea takes hold, which has me taking all the proceeds, all two million all for me. The greed dissipates as quickly as it comes. It's Gary's business, it's Doreen's money. Getting half is a great deal for me.

Alex sits on the arm of the chair on which I'm slumped. I am totally exhausted, the inevitable result of too much alcohol preceded by too much hard work getting everything ready. Not to mention the strain of trying to stay calm and relaxed. I'm desperate to tell Alex about Fergus, how rich he is. How Doreen's landed on her feet, how I'm off the hook, but she is sitting next to me, telling Emma some long story about forelocks or fetlocks, whichever it is that a horse can bruise to make it limp.

73

Alex is being awkward and evasive. I'm still tired from the weekend's party and I'm getting fed up with his intransigence.

'All I want you to do is go in and look. I'd do it myself if I could, but they'd hardly let me in, would they?'

'It's a horrible drive at this time of the day, we'll hit all the traffic around Manchester. You've got the London trip tomorrow, you're already worn out, you said so yourself. Wait a few days, at least until after you get back.'

'No, if you don't come I'll go myself, I'll find someone else to help me.'

'You're being unreasonable, Jenny. Think about what you're doing.'

'It's her, I know it. Lottie and I went through so much suffering to try to find her. All you have to do is pop your head inside the place and see if it's her.'

'You're basing all this speculation on this internet site that gives one of the girl's names as Ekaterina. The picture has her face blanked out, it could be anyone.'

'It's not much to ask, Alex. She's there tonight. The rota is posted on the website. We have to go now, I might never get another chance.'

'Even if we did go, neither of us knows Kat. We may not recognise her even if she is Lottie's twin.'

'You can ask, for God's sake. Ekaterina Federenco. How many girls of that name are you expecting to find in an East Manchester brothel?' I can see he's running out of arguments. I also get the feeling that he's not really trying to get out of this, only managing my expectations. 'If we go now, we'll be back home by eleven. I'll let you drive.' Alex loves driving the Range Rover. I know he'll fancy blasting round the M60.

The sat nav insists it's here. Alex stops the car in front of a derelict building covered by ragged posters and daubings.

'Does that look like the Evanescence Gentleman's Lounge?' I ask.

'Not really, but this is where the sat nav brought us.'

'There's a woman over there,' I point. 'She's carrying shopping bags, she'll know. Go and ask her.'

I take a quick look at Alex's total lack of mobility and then jump out of the car and confront the woman.

'We're looking for the Evanescence Gentleman's Lounge,' I say.

'Don't know it,' she answers.

'It's a brothel, you know, where men pay to have sex, it's somewhere around here, it must be close.'

She gives me a strange look as if torn between pity and disdain.

'No luck,' I tell Alex. 'There's a pub on the next corner, we can ask in there.'

Alex is less reluctant to enter a pub than accost strange women on the street. I understand this and wait in the car. It doesn't look from the outside like a place that might attract couples looking for a sophisticated evening's entertainment, more like the venue for a knifing or shooting.

He's taking his time, maybe he felt obliged to buy a drink and is making friends with the locals. After a very long ten minutes my phone buzzes. Alex has sent me a text.

THIS IS IT, ROOMS ABOVE, BACK AS SOON AS I CAN. X

My heart leaps with excitement, he's found it. Now all he has to do is get Kat and bring her out to the car.

He went in ages ago, I'm getting worried. It's 10.15. I check the time of Alex's text, 9.35. It seems much longer, hours ago in fact. Sitting here in the passenger seat of the Range Rover I'm getting some unwelcome attention from male punters. One of them knocks on my window. Before he asks, I wave him away but he is reluctant to retreat, face puzzled and a bit upset. I wind the window down a crack and shout, 'Fuck off, I'm waiting for my boyfriend.' Even this doesn't seem to register. He carries on hanging around the car. I slide between the front seats and lie down on the back, protected from view by the black tinted windows.

The longer Alex is, the more I worry. It wouldn't make any sense for me to go in there and look for him. What would I say for a start? *My boyfriend came in here to see a prostitute and now I'm concerned that it's taking too long.* Even if I vary the words, the implication remains the same. All I can do is wait. Patience isn't one of my strongest virtues but I'm determined to stay here impatiently until he returns.

It's been almost an hour now. How long do I give him before I at least text my concern? Another five minutes perhaps? I try to visualise what's going on in there, maybe there's a queue. That could be it. Oh God, my stomach turns over at the images I'm conjuring up in my head. A long line of men moving slowly forward for their turn to…I can't bear to think about it.

ARE YOU OKAY? I text.

Almost immediately the answer comes back, *FINE X.*

HOW LONG?

NEARLY DONE X

This last message gets me so angry I almost scream. I know what he's saying, it's the innuendo that kills me. The thought of Alex in there is horrible. I now know it's all a mistake, that I should never have involved him. I can't believe how stupid I've been. What if he has to perform some sordid sexual act, just to keep his cover intact?

By the time his face appears at the window I'm working myself into a frenzy of despair. Worse than the visions of him with another woman are the images of him being hurt by the vengeful brothel-keepers. I shoot up in relief, click the button to let him in.

'Well? Was it Kat?'

237

'No, sorry. It took a while to get an appointment with her. She turns out to be a forty-year-old housewife from Ardwick. Her name isn't really Ekaterina, it's actually Veronica. She has four kids and a husband. He thinks she sticks sun visors together in a car components factory.'

'Was there a big queue for her?'

'Not really but I had to stay the full twenty minutes or it wouldn't have looked good. You owe me forty pounds by the way.'

'For what?' I almost burst with indignation then see his smile. 'Oh,' I add. 'The twenty minutes, I suppose, did you have a good chat then? Much in common you two? Arranged to see her again, maybe?'

'She told me that all the other women working here are local like her. The management give them the exotic names, it's not because they're foreign.'

'Why does she do it, she's got a husband and kids, how can she bear it?'

'She needs the money.'

'I don't care how much she needs the money, it's not worth it surely.'

'She has a very expensive heroin habit to feed. That's why she does it.'

'Oh. I'm sorry. It's all been a complete waste of time.'

'Maybe not completely. She told me about a rival establishment not far from here with foreign girls, some of them very young, she says.'

'There you are then. We've got to go and check that out.'

'Hang on. It's getting late. You've got to go to London in the morning.'

'Aw, come on. While we're here we might as well take a look. Or are you too tired to take on another prostitute? Worn out already?'

'I really think we should go home, Jenny, I've got work tomorrow as well. We can get the police to check out this other place, let them sort it out.'

'No, they'll not be looking for Kat, only for arrests. Please, Alex. We're here now, let's take a look ourselves.'

The address the pretend Ekaterina gave to Alex is a normal, if uncared for, terrace house. Parking anywhere near in these crowded roads is an impossibility. Alex eventually finds a Range Rover-sized space three streets away.

'Okay, stay here, I'll be back soon.'

'Not a chance, I'm coming with you.'

'Don't be silly, Jenny, it's nearly eleven. You can't be standing around in the street waiting for me. Stay in the car.'

'No, I'll be fine, believe me, it's you I'm worried about.'

I hang back and watch Alex walk up the short path to the front door. It opens, a man's head pokes out, he shakes it, the door closes.

Alex reports, 'They won't let me in.'

I pull out three twenty pound notes from my pocket. 'Wave these at him, tell them Oleg sent you, tell them you're desperate. Be a bit more imaginative.'

As I follow him, he turns and asks, 'Where are you going?'

'While you're getting in the front, I'm going to have a look round the back.'

'Is that wise?' he says.

'Don't worry, I'm only going to take a look through the windows, see if I can see any of the girls. Don't worry about me, I'll meet you back at the car if I get fed up of waiting again.'

As Alex trudges unconvincingly towards the front door, I slip quietly down the alley between the houses, find a tall wooden gate that unlatches easily, then an unlocked back door leading into a cramped kitchen. The worktops, illuminated by a bare bulb, are the same as those in my flat. I've never liked them. There's nobody in the kitchen. I can hear television sounds through the closed door and banging noises from above. A woman's wail keeps time with the thumps. I feel desperate to do something. The voice is distressed; she sounds like she's being brutally raped.

There's a man at the far end of the hallway, holding the door open, presumably talking to Alex. I take the opportunity to open the door on my left and peer quietly into the room. Three girls are sitting around in dressing gowns, I slip in quietly, the girls hardly seem to register my appearance.

'Are any of you Ukrainian?' I ask. A tall blonde girl stands up, her faded pink gown providing inadequate cover for her lanky frame. Her eyes stare at me as if she's looking through me at the wall behind. 'Any of you girls come from the Ukraine?' I ask again.

'You want Ukraine girl?' she asks me in a clipped accent.

'I'm looking for someone, for a friend. I thought she might be here.'

She looks around her, as if searching for something in a darkened room, staring intently at each of the other women in turn. Finally she says, 'Ukraine girl working. Upstairs.'

I become aware of the horrible screams overhead again. I visualise Lottie's precious twin sister being mauled and abused and run out into the hallway, past the man and up the stairs. I can hear sobbing through the first door I come to on the landing at the top of the stairs.

The bedroom door is unsecured. I walk in, see the grotesque sight of flabby buttocks billowing with each copulative thrust. The man's back is peppered with grey hair and completely obscures the object of his salacious attention apart from two thin legs protruding either side of his hips.

I can't see the girl's face, it's buried in the mattress, muffling her obvious distress. I can't help myself, 'Stop hurting her!' I yell. 'Get off her, leave her alone.'

His only response is to increase the intensity of his thrusting. Enraged, I grab him by the hair and try to pull him off her. He stops fucking and flails at me with a thick arm, knocking my hand away and hurting my face. Another blow crashes into my cheek, still tender from the broken teeth. Pain diverts my attention completely. All I can do is slump to the floor, nursing my jaw. The fat man begins shouting, puts his hands under my shoulders and drags me out of the room.

74

I'm lying spread-eagled on the landing. The pain in my face is so bad I can hardly focus my attention on anything else. I hear footsteps on the stairs, hear Alex's voice calling my name. My face is throbbing as if it might explode. When I sit up it gets measurably worse. I try to call out but all I can manage is a weak moaning sound.

'Are you hurt?' Alex asks.

'Yes, my teeth are hurting.'

'You look like you've been attacked, who did this?'

'A fat man in there. He hit me.' Suddenly I'm afraid for Alex instead of myself. He disappears into the bedroom. The door closes behind him. Before I get to my feet he emerges with a girl, still naked, still sobbing. She's thin, almost completely wasted. Her eyes are large and protuberant, dominating her face. This isn't Lottie's sister.

'Let's go,' Alex half drags the girl towards the stairs.

'That's not Kat,' I say.

'No, I can see that, but the poor girl looks like she needs help.'

The fat guy has mercifully pulled on a pair of shorts by the time he comes out of the bedroom.

'What the hell's going on?' he asks. All his belligerence disappears when he looks at Alex.

'What's your name?' Alex asks.

Neither the girl nor the fat guy answers. Loud shouts herald the arrival of two men on the stairs. I can hear noises in the street, car doors being slammed, loud voices.

The lead man on the stairs reaches the top, he's brandishing a knife. Alex lets go of the girl, raises his hands, backs off towards me. The second man with a large piece of wood in his hand makes it six bodies crammed onto the narrow landing. The knife stabs at Alex. He twists away, stumbles against the girl, falls backwards against the wall. I try to push past the fat guy, but he's pressing me against the bedroom door, trying to get away from the knife. The door opens suddenly under our combined weight and I'm deposited on my back. Mercifully the fat guy avoids crushing me by staying on his feet.

I lose sight of Alex, hear yells, blows being dealt, a sudden loud thud that shakes the whole house. I scramble to my feet intent on protecting Alex, scared to the core that I'm too late. The fat man grabs hold of my arm, pulling me back into the bedroom.

'Let go of me!' I shout into his face. His free hand gropes inside my blouse, rips it open, squeezes my left breast hard. His sweaty face plunges towards mine. Leering lips clamp onto my face. I try to hurt him with my knee but I strike only flabby softness.

He's enveloping me, using his bulk to force me down onto the floor. I'm trying to resist while listening for Alex's voice outside, hoping he's okay. My punches are too short to have any effect. My legs are too busy keeping me upright to kick. All I can do is grab his bulbous nose with my teeth and bite hard. Now I have his attention. I can feel the painful surprise in his body. I let go but not before I taste the blood streaming from his face.

His hands rise reflexively in protection. I push him away, extricate myself and run out of the bedroom. There's no sign of Alex. The balustrade is splintered and broken, the girl stands at the top of the stairs. One uniformed policeman appears, then another.

The desk sergeant fills in the forms slowly and painstakingly. All I want is to find Alex or at least know he's safe.

'I've done nothing,' I protest. 'I was only trying to help the poor girl who was being raped by the fat guy.'

His face settles into a world-weary sneer. 'You are accused of assault, actual bodily harm, and there may be other

243

charges once we've made more enquiries. This is a serious incident. There's a man in hospital with serious injuries. This may turn into a murder enquiry.'

'Who's injured? Is it Alex?'

'I don't have any of those details, there are officers at the scene and at the hospital making enquiries.'

'Find him, please?' I ask.

'You say you had a boyfriend present at the house?'

'Yes, Alex Hartley.'

'When you say boyfriend do you mean regular client or is he your pimp?'

'I'm not a prostitute, you stupid man.'

'Really?' He runs his eyes around my body and I realise what he is seeing. I must look a mess, my blouse hanging open, makeup smeared all over my face, hair looking like I've been dragged around the block a time or two. He pulls himself upright and puts down his pen.

'You will be held in custody pending appearance in court in the morning. Meanwhile I suggest you calm down and cooperate with the investigating officers. As I say this may turn into a very serious matter.'

'I can't stay here. I have to find Alex. I have an important meeting in London in the morning, I can't miss that. I want to see my lawyer, call him, get him here.'

The cell is bare but clean and unoccupied, a stark contrast to my Ukraine experience. Alex's welfare is all I can think about. The last time I saw him he was being attacked with a knife, he must be the one in hospital that they're all talking about.

My bag with my phone and my purse are in the Range Rover. Alex has the keys. Even if they let me out I have no way to get to London now. My face aches, my fists are sore from beating on the cell door, my voice is hoarse with shouting. All my energy is gone, all my hope has evaporated. I'm certain that Alex is dying in hospital, alone, without me.

It's my own fault. My stupid obsession with Lottie's sister. How could I ever have believed I could find her on my own? I have to face it, what I'm doing is hardly rational. Everyone is better off without a crazy woman like me. Alex if he survives, Toby, everyone. All I do is bring misery and violence into people's lives. I only ever seem to make things worse. Lottie's father is dead because of me. Now Alex, the man I love, may be dead as well.

75

'This is Mr Ali. He's a solicitor. You have the right to have a solicitor present during your interview.'

'What time is it?' I have no watch, no phone.

'Five-thirty,' the policeman says. 'In the morning,' he adds unnecessarily.

'Where's Alex, what's happened to him?'

The policeman ignores my question. 'Do you want to speak with Mr Ali in private before we record an interview with you?'

'Yes.'

Mr Ali is thin, bespectacled, with tired eyes and agitated hands. 'I have to get to London by ten o'clock. I'm selling my business and if I don't sign the papers it may all fall through. Also I have to find Alex, my partner, he was in the house, they were attacking him. Do you know what happened to him, maybe he's in hospital?'

He looks down at the paperwork on the table. 'You are Jenny Parker?'

'Yes.'

'You're being charged with common assault, the interview is to see what other offences may have been committed. The interview will be recorded and a transcript read out in court. Do you understand?'

'Yes. Never mind about that, can't you get me out of here? I have to find Alex.'

'You're being held overnight, you'll appear at court in the morning, the magistrates will set the terms of your bail then.'

'That's no good. I have to get away now. Can't you do something?'

'I can ask, but it's unlikely to do any good.'

'Then ask and find Alex for me, please.' With a shock I realise his number is on my phone and I haven't committed it to memory. It's 5 a.m. I can't think of anyone else I can ring at this time of night. Anyway, the only two numbers I know off by heart are my own, which used to be Gary's, and Big Mick's of course.

'Can I use your phone?'

Mr Ali looks uncomfortable.

'Ring this number, tell Mick I'm in trouble, where I am, what I need.' I take his pen and write in the margin of his papers.

Two police officers sit down, one of them a pleasant looking young woman, the other an older man. The room is filled with the heavy scent of stale sweat, as if one of the new arrivals has been living in their clothes for several days.

'Do you understand that charges are being brought against you?'

'Yes, of course. Who am I supposed to have assaulted?'

'A man who paid you to have sex with him has complained that you attacked him.'

'That's not true, I am not a prostitute.'

'Then what were you doing in that house?'

'I was investigating reports that a woman was being held there against her will and being forced to have sex.'

'Investigating?'

'Yes. I received information from a woman at another brothel, the Evanescence Club. She told me about the girl, or at least she told Alex about her. It was me who insisted we should find out if it was Kat.'

'Who is Kat? Is that what you call the other girl who was with you in the house?'

'No, it wasn't her. It was all a mistake. The fat man was raping her in the bedroom, she was screaming. I went in to make him stop.'

'So that's when the assault occurred?'

'Yes, he hit me, hurt my face.'

'So you are saying that you didn't assault anyone, it was you who was attacked?'

'Yes, at that time. Later on I had to bite the man on the nose to stop him from raping me.'

247

'When you were arrested you were wearing a short skirt and your blouse was undone. Isn't it obvious to anyone what you were really doing at that house?'

'No. My blouse was ripped when I was fighting, I already told you why I was there.'

'Tell us what happened with the man whose nose you bit?'

'He grabbed me, tried to rape me. He was feeling my breasts, pushing me down. It was all I could do. He was slobbering all over me. His nose was the only thing I could damage. I tried to knee him in the balls, but it didn't have any effect.'

'So you did bite him?'

'Yes, I've already told you that a dozen times. I've also told you he was trying to rape me.'

'That's not really very likely, is it?' The policeman is speaking wearily, in tune with the dead hours of the early morning. 'You are in the bedroom of a brothel wearing very little, he's paid his money, what did you expect him to be doing with you?'

'You bastard,' I jump to my feet. 'Don't you realise what it's like for those poor girls, having smelly perverts rubbing themselves off inside them? You should be ashamed of yourself.'

Mr Ali gently pulls me back to a seated position. 'Mrs Parker would like to enquire about the whereabouts of her partner, Alex Hartley. She's concerned for his safety.'

The two policemen look at each other, the woman nods and then says, 'We have no information that we can help you with.'

My hopes rise as the cell door is opened again but sink again when they announce that they need to interview me one more time. It's been a couple of hours at least since the first one. I have visions of Mick arriving to extricate me and get me down to London.

'Any news of Alex?' I ask Mr Ali, who looks ready for his bed.

'No, nothing. If the police are holding him they're not willing to disclose that to me.'

'What about Mick, did you manage to get in touch with him?'

'Ah yes, I rang the number you gave me but there was no answer. I left a message on the voice mail.'

'Haven't you tried again?'

'I'm sorry, no, I've been busy. There's a lot happening tonight and I have to cover four police stations.'

'What do they want me for now, are they likely to release me?'

'More enquiries, they say. We'll have to ask them what they intend to do about bail.'

It's a different pair, this time both men, one of whom is in plain clothes and much older than the other. They're asking me the same questions. I give them the same answers, but without all the indignation I displayed before. My tiredness has got the better of my bitterness. All I want to do is curl up and sleep.

'I've already told you, the man was trying to rape me. I had to bite him, it was self-defence. It's him you should be locking up, not me.'

'This isn't about your assault charge, Mrs Parker. A man has been killed and you were at the scene when it happened.'

A cold vision of Alex's mangled body, the sound of splintering wood, a man advancing with a knife, all flash through my mind. It's obvious now what happened. Alex must have been stabbed and pushed down the stairwell. He's dead. These men know all about it, all about us, but all they care about is making enquiries. Following the book, obeying procedure. People don't matter to them, my feelings are irrelevant. The distress they're causing is not a consideration to them. I can feel myself sliding off the chair, under the table. My whole body is numb and lifeless. I have no control over my actions. All my hopes have gone with Alex, my being is crushed. My life extinguished.

I'm woken up yet again having only just fallen asleep. Maybe it's part of a process of disorientation to make prisoners more likely to confess. It's more likely to be a reflection of their lack of organisation. I fully expect two new faces in the interview room asking the same things. Instead it's an elderly man on his own. He has an air of familiarity, as if I already know him. In contrast to Mr Ali, he exudes calm assurance and my confidence is inspired.

'Where's Mr Ali?' I ask.

'Oh, he's gone now. Let me introduce myself. I am Edward Knott. Stephen Daly has asked to see if I can be of assistance.'

'So Stephen knows I'm here?'

'Yes. He says not to worry about your London meeting, they'll postpone it until next month, it won't be a problem. His colleague is already down there, so she can explain.'

'No, that's not possible, I can't wait another month, the deal will fall through. Look I'm desperate, can you get me out of here and down to London, it's absolutely vital.'

'Not before you appear in court, I'm afraid.'

'When will that be?'

Edward looks at his wrist watch. 'About two hours, ten o'clock you're scheduled for anyway. It's not likely to be much before twelve though.'

'But my meeting is at ten. Can't you get them to speed up my hearing?'

'The hearing isn't the problem, Mrs Parker. The police are insisting on you being remanded in custody. It's a murder enquiry. You are not only charged with assault, they also think you're implicated in the killing.'

'You mean they'll send me to prison?'

'I'm afraid that's exactly what we are faced with.'

'But I haven't done anything, you've got to make them believe it. Who's dead, do you know if it's Alex?'

Edward consults his notes. 'They have released the name of the victim. A thirty-year-old male, name of Gennady Borodin. No mention here of anyone called Alex.'

My breath sighs out of my lungs. I feel the hurt and tension leaving my body. Alex isn't dead. The knowledge makes me so happy. Prison holds no fears. The deal can fall through if it wants, as long as I have Alex.

'He was there being attacked, surely the police have him here then?'

'Not as far as I know. I can ask.'

'Go and ask, please.'

A female constable stands by the door to keep an eye on me while Edward is gone. When he returns he says, 'No, your friend isn't here.'

I can't understand what's going on. I was sure Alex was dead, otherwise he'd have contacted me by now, surely.

'Where is he, what's he up to?'

76

The longer I go without word of Alex, the more I worry about him. The prospect of being remanded in custody is horrifying enough. The mental image of Alex lying dead somewhere is far worse. Almost as disturbing is my feeling of abandonment. If he isn't incapacitated has he driven home and gone to work, leaving me to manage on my own? The implications of that are too hard to bear. Where the hell is Alex?

The court proceedings are a farce, as per usual. I am forced to stand and face two elderly women and one self-important man who take less than five minutes to decide to accede to every request the police make, despite the best efforts of Edward Knott to convince them that I am neither a prostitute nor a murderer. By now it's almost noon and I'm wondering if Suriya is enjoying tea and biscuits in London and explaining where I am. Worse still, I imagine the reaction Hector Brighouse is having to all his carefully laid plans being put to waste by a tardy female.

I have transformed the prospect of a new house and a new start into another prison term. The last twelve hours have destroyed everything. By the time the justice system is finished with me I'll be back to living in squalor, with no Gary to save me this time.

The van that's taking me to prison has SG markings on it. The driver and his mates are all Hector's employees. I hope this is the final ignominy I'll be subjected to, but I doubt it. The remand centre isn't so bad, at least I get a chance to shower and tidy myself up. The whore image was beginning to fit too well. I regret the moment I crept into that whorehouse kitchen. At the time, I thought I might find Kat, in the event, the only people I found were the fat rapist and the police, and I've lost Alex in the process.

I'm locked up all alone, the cell is modern, clean and airy. The whole establishment belongs to SG. They built it and operate it on behalf of the government. This isn't a business that GOD Security ever had designs on – our employees might feel too much at home.

Despite my desperate mood, the prospect of a few hours' undisturbed sleep is welcome and I resign myself to doing nothing but rest for the foreseeable future. All the thinking, worrying and planning I do now is not going to have any effect or do me any good.

I settle down on the bed and allow my deep weariness to overwhelm me.

The woman disturbing me is stockily built but with a kind face, framed by an enormous quantity of dense hair. 'Wake up, you're needed in the interview room.'

'How long have I been asleep, what time is it?' My head feels thick, I don't feel at all well. I roll over onto my side and retch violently. Spasm after spasm voids my stomach, then continues long after I'm empty. My head feels like it's going to burst with pain. The sour taste of vomit is everywhere. I can feel lumps of sick trapped in my nostrils. The bedclothes and floor are spattered, my tidy room is now disgusting. I wonder if I should try to clean it up, whether there's a mop and bucket I can borrow.

'Come on.' She helps me out of bed, sits me in the chair. She brings me a glass of water and a damp cloth to wipe my face. 'I have a message for you.' She brings out a folded sheet of paper. I open it and see that it's a printed email.

Dear Jenny

Sorry I missed you at the police station. I am not allowed to visit you on remand but I'm with you in spirit. Don't worry I'll do everything I can to sort things out.

Love Alex

My nausea recedes to a distant memory. Alex is alive, well and knows where I am. Now I have hope, now I have something to live for. Suddenly the predicament I find myself in isn't that serious. Biting that man's nose is common assault at worst. Self-defence in truth. A man may have been killed at the house, but I had nothing to do with that. I'll be out of here soon, Alex is waiting for me. Hector can buy the business next month. What the hell am I so concerned about?

I assure the prison officer that I'm okay and she leads me into the interview room. It's the same policemen as last time, the older one in plain clothes and a younger one in uniform.

'We've been making enquiries, Mrs Parker.'

'Yes, good. Now will you let me go?'

'It appears you have previous convictions for money-laundering and assault. You served prison sentences for both offences.'

'It was all a mistake, self-defence, I was attacked by my cellmate.'

'That's as maybe. It's not what the record shows though. What we want to ask you about is your role in this chain of brothels, how you launder the money, what you do with it?'

'Don't be ridiculous.'

'We see you own a security business, is that the vehicle for your money-laundering activities?'

I can feel the blood in my face, the betrayal of my unconscious reaction. I lose the power of speech, they're wrong about the brothels, they are dead right about the money-laundering. If they believe that's what's happening they will surely keep digging until they find out everything, the caravan sites, O'Brian, false payroll entries, everything.

I've gone from despair to hope and now I've been cast down more deeply than ever before. It's all gone. The business, the deal, the money and worst of all Alex, Toby and my freedom. I am going to get a very long sentence when they convict me this time.

77

Stephen Bailey is sitting calmly in the visiting room explaining that Edward Knott is the best man to deal with the case. Edward is quietly listening, apparently unaffected by Stephen's effusive praise and whole-hearted recommendations.

'To be honest, Stephen, I'm not seeing any of that on my side. All that happens is that my situation goes from bad to worse. I might as well have stuck with Mr Ali for all the good it's done.' Even my outburst has no visible effect on the unflappable Mr Knott.

'There was never any prospect of getting you out on bail, not with such a serious charge over your head.'

'Maybe not, but now look at me. They're going to go through GOD Security with a fine-tooth comb and get enough to put me away for ten years.'

'I can hardly lay that at Mr Knott's door, Jenny, all that's come about because of your previous conviction. How serious are their allegations?'

'Serious enough if you must know.'

'You must tell us only what you think we need to know in order for us to defend you properly,' Edward speaks for the first time. 'There's no merit in widespread admissions of guilt or unfounded protestations of innocence. Let's examine what they have to build their case, then we deal with that.'

'All that they have is suspicion that I'm up to no good, laundering money through GOD Security.'

'Do they know the source of this black money?'

'They're assuming it's related to the brothel they found me in.'

'And that of course has nothing at all to do with you. As I recall you were there on a mission of mercy, looking for some poor Ukrainian girl forced into sexual slavery.'

The way he puts things is really helping me to drag myself out of the melancholic resignation I've been wallowing in. 'That's right, if they follow that lead they'll get nowhere.'

'Fine, let's see what they do. In the meantime I'll work on the assault charge. I've a feeling that's not going anywhere, their plaintiff is not going to be a good witness for them, being twice your size and yet complaining that you assaulted him and left him injured and incapacitated. If we get one or two female magistrates that sort of allegation isn't going to hold water and the police know it.'

'What about the murder?'

'Again good news on that front. The current theory is that the dead man fell over the banisters and onto his own knife, at least that's what the witnesses appear to be saying. You are not implicated at all so we should have you out of here within a couple of days.'

'What about the new allegations?'

'They're a different matter, but I can't see them getting you remanded. Even if they do charge you with something, I'm certain we can get bail.'

'And then what?' The prospect of getting out of here before they give me a psychopathic room-mate is attractive, but I have my doubts about how long my freedom might last. What the hell do I say to Alex? Oh sorry I've been up to my usual tricks, see you in a few years?

'Then, as I say, we see what case they have. Just because there might be evidence for them to find it's by no means certain that they'll be clever enough to discover it. Even if they do, courts can take a lot of convincing, particularly when the case is highly technical, as many of those involving complex financial transactions inevitably are. If it were obvious how the money was being laundered it wouldn't be a very effective method, would it?'

I'm not sure I share Edward's optimism, but I much prefer him to my previous legal team who urged me to confess everything and expect a lenient sentence. They were wrong. Maybe Edward is wrong too. Perhaps the criminal justice system has it in for me.

78

'What happened to you? Where were you when I needed you?'

Alex picks me up outside the prison, looking bright and cheerful. The Range Rover really suits him, maybe I should give it to him as a farewell present.

'Hang on a minute, let's get out of the car park first. How are you feeling?'

'Glad to be out of there, glad to see you, worried I'll be sent back, dying for the loo. How about you?'

'Happy to see you. You don't look as bad as I expected.' He smiles. 'Maybe prison suits you.'

'After my experience in the Ukraine, this was more like a Travelodge.'

'Oh,' Alex's nose wrinkles, 'I didn't realise it would be that bad.'

Suddenly Alex's presence makes the world worth living in. He has a way of making me feel alive and full of hope. All it takes is a few words from him. He stops at a pub so that I can use the toilet; when I emerge, he's waiting with a gin and tonic for me.

'So where were you all the time I was getting arrested and put in prison?'

'I'll explain everything later. First of all, tell me about what happened to you and why they've kept you there until now?'

'First they accused me of assault. They gave up on that one and changed it to murder.'

'The man who fell down the stairs?'

'Yes, I suppose so. I explained to them that all I did was bite a man's nose when he tried to rape me.'

'And now?'

'They've dropped the assault charge, but now I'm accused of money-laundering.'

'Oh, why's that?'

'They think I'm the mastermind behind the sexual exploitation business, that I'm the one who legitimises all the money.'

'But you're not, so that's not going to be a problem is it?'

'Yes it is. When they investigate GOD Security they will find things.'

'What things?'

'Money things, the kind of things they're looking for.'

'Oh.'

'Oh, indeed. I couldn't tell you. Anyway, I'd stopped doing it by the time I got to trust you enough to tell you. I found out where the money was coming from and put a stop to it. So that's me, what about you?'

Alex looks a bit weary, I suppose he's been worried about me. That feels comforting. I don't want him to be oblivious to my distress.

I prompt him, 'Last time I saw you there were two men coming up the stairs to get you.'

'Oh yes, those guys.'

'Well, what happened?'

' I didn't expect you to be sneaking in the back door, when I saw you creeping up the stairs I couldn't believe my eyes. I never thought you'd be that daft..'

'Thanks.'

'You're welcome. The man blocking the doorway wouldn't let me in. I tried money but he was having none of it, he kept telling me it was a private party. I kept begging him, especially with you already inside. In the end, he shoved me outside and slammed the door on me.'

'Whilst you were standing on the doorstep I was upstairs being attacked. You should have bashed the door down, why didn't you?'

'I realised you must have got in the back way, so that's what I did. I got to you as quickly as I could.'

'The two guys, what happened with them?'

'Well, I saw you disappear inside the bedroom and thought you'd be safer in there. I decided to calm things down, talk with the men and get you safely away. Unfortunately they were a bit upset and refused to listen to reason.'

'There was one with a knife, Alex, weren't you scared?'

'Terrified, but I had no time to do anything about it. Fortunately for me, the guy with the knife was a bit clumsy. He tripped over and fell downstairs.'

'Through the banisters?'

'Yes, he was a big guy; they gave way under his weight when he fell against them. I tried to get to you but I couldn't because the guy with the stick started hitting me. Look.' Alex undoes his shirt and reveals an angry-looking bruise on his left shoulder. 'See what he did? I thought he'd broken my shoulder it hurt so much.'

I have some sympathy for him but not much, after all I was the one in the bedroom being molested by that naked ball of flab. All Alex got was a smack on the arm.

'It looks okay now,' I say, hearing my own off-handedness but letting my resentment reveal itself.

'It's still sore.' Alex looks at me, holds my eyes with his. 'I couldn't get to you. The man was intent on beating me to death. I fought my way into the other bedroom and climbed out of the window. He came after me, chased me into the garden, so I kept running, over fences, out into the next street. I thought I might run back to the car but he caught up with me and I had to fight with him. By the time I got rid of him and ran back to the house, the police had taken you away. They nearly took me as well, just for asking questions.'

'Why didn't you come to the police station?'

'I did, but they wouldn't let me see you. They even refused to give you a message. It was only when you got to the remand centre that they let me email you.'

'I was so scared you had been killed.' My eyes brim with the memory of dark feelings of desperation.

'I nearly was.' Alex jumps up, leads me back to the car. I should feel less abandoned, not as neglected, now I've heard Alex's story. There should be a warm comfortable feeling now we're back safely together, but I don't feel it at all. The prospect of prosecution, the fear of imprisonment, the disappointment of losing the deal are all minor in comparison to the sadness I am sinking into. All my instincts tell me that Alex isn't telling me everything and this is worrying me more than everything else put together.

79

'Who?' I voiced my irritation at being disturbed by my mobile phone. Stupidly I left it on when what I need is a good sleep, here in my own bed. Despite all my cravings for his comforting touch I am too weary and upset even for Alex's company. Now I've got this strange female voice dragging me out of my soporific state.

'Kayleigh,' she repeats, as if in explanation.

'What do you want?'

'I have some good news for you.' I nearly end the call at this over-ambitious boast, nobody ever has any news I'd consider good. She's trying to sell me something, I wonder how she got my number.

'I'm not really interested.' My finger hovers over the red button.

'Your offer has been accepted,' she adds.

'What offer?'

'The offer you made on 27 Rawlinson Park Lane, it's been accepted. All we need now is the name of your solicitors so that we can issue the contract documentation. If you don't have a solicitor we'd be happy to arrange one for you.'

'I do have a solicitor.' I give her Stephen's details, then ring him to tell him he's buying me a house.

'I don't think that's wise under the circumstances,' he says.

'But I need to have this particular house, it's near Toby's school, it's perfect for me. I'll have the proceeds from the sale to buy it with, what's the problem?'

'I've been talking to Edward. In most cases like yours, the police get a restraint order over your assets. It means that they freeze your bank accounts, including company ones. You won't be able to access any money at all.'

'But I've not even been charged, never mind convicted. Surely they have to convict me before they take all my assets?'

'No they don't. Under the Proceeds of Crime Act, all they need is enough grounds for suspicion. They don't even have to go to court, the restraint order is issued by a judge without any opportunity for us to make representation. Once it's issued, you won't even be able to pay my fees.'

'That's crazy, how do you get paid then?'

'I don't, Jenny. There's the problem. You'll have to rely on Legal Aid and I don't do that sort of work. The rates are much too low for a practice like mine.'

'What about Edward?'

'He's the same. I'm sorry, Jenny, but if a restraint order is issued, I won't be able to help you any more.'

'But it's not been issued yet, or has it?'

'No, but Edward thinks it's inevitable.'

'So I should take a thick wedge of cash and hide it somewhere?'

'I can't advise you to do that, Jenny. You'll have to consider your own position. All I can say is forewarned is forearmed.'

'Thanks. In the meantime can you please buy this house for me. I might not have any money to pay for it, but I can't let it go because of these charges hanging over me. I can only carry on as usual, can't I?'

'I'll need a couple of thousand pounds up front, just in case. You do understand don't you, Jenny, I have to protect myself.'

For an instant I consider telling him to shove his advice but for once I manage to restrain myself. 'I'll make a bank transfer today. I'll also include some advance fees for Edward, at least I can have him acting for me until that money runs out.'

'Good idea,' Stephen says. 'I'll let him know.'

80

There's a bad smell in the flat when I awake again. It's the stink of decomposition and I track its source to the bin in the kitchen. Alex has invited himself for Sunday lunch and I'm not in the mood for either a roast dinner or Alex today. All that longing for him, all that worrying and now I'm not sure I can face up to a proper reunion. I was very weary on the drive back from the remand centre, but not so tired I couldn't tell I was being fobbed off. There's something not quite right about Alex's story, or maybe it's the way he told it to me. Nothing big, no large discrepancy, only a vague uneasiness when I cast my mind back to the events of Tuesday evening.

Alex said that the man with the knife fell through the banisters and into the stairwell. Okay, the rails were broken, it certainly looked like someone had crashed through them. But where was the body? The police took me down the stairs and out to their van, I didn't have to walk over a dead body. There was no time surely for an ambulance to pick him up and leave before the police took me in.

As I walk out of the building to deposit the bin bag in the wheelie bin, a man is crossing the road towards me. He's thirtyish, wearing an olive green body-warmer and a surprised look. When he sees me he turns round and walks away as if shocked or scared to see me. I watch as he clambers into a blue transit van.

'The police are watching the flat,' I say as soon as Alex picks up his phone.

'Oh. I suppose they could be there for any reason.'

'No, they're watching me.'

'How do you know, Jenny?'

'I could see the look on the man's face, he recognised me, then ran away back to his blue van.'

'Are you sure it's the police?'

'Who else could it be?'

'I don't know. I'll watch out for the van when I come round.'

'You do that and you could pop to Marks & Spencer's for something to eat. I'm too tired to shop, or cook for that matter. Get something nice, something we can pop in the oven, oh and some of those croquette potatoes, I like them.

'Okay. Do you have any preferences?'

'No. Oh, not pies. Don't get pies. At least not for me. You can have one if you want. I need something a bit more wholesome, maybe some nice fish.'

'Salmon?'

'No, not salmon, I'm fed up of salmon, it's all I seem to eat these days. I've read that salmon farms in Scotland are polluting everywhere. Get something else. Anything at all, you choose. Use your imagination.'

'How about beef?'

'That's not exactly fish is it?'

'No, but it's what I fancy.'

'Please yourself, then. Beef it is. As long as it's free range, organic and from happy cows.'

'Of course, I'll make sure of it. Anything else you need?'

'Oh yes, I've nothing much in. Be a love and get me some essentials, that would be great.'

'What do you need?'

'Oh the usual, get everything and something nice for afters, some chocolate.'

'What sort?'

'Anything, surprise me.'

'Okay.'

Alex sounds confused, I can't believe he makes such a fuss out of a simple thing like going to the shop for some food.

'How much is that costing then?'

'What, the food?' Alex is decanting his purchases onto baking trays.

'No, the police surveillance unit outside. Two men and a van at least, on a Sunday, presumably round the clock, or what would be the point. Plus the others.'

'What others?'

'There must be others, round the back, down the road. It would be too easy for me to slip away otherwise.'

'I don't know, I'm not even sure they are police.'

'You should know. Didn't you tell me you're the one who pays for it all? It's your government department that foots the bill.'

There's a joke in there somewhere, but I'm not feeling at all humorous today.

'Don't start me off on the complexities of local government finances and the relationship between DCLG and the Home Office. It's Sunday, my day off, and I want to spend it with you having fun.'

'I'm not much fun. They're going to take all my money and lock me up in prison. Those men outside are there to make sure that I can't do a runner before they get the restraint order in place. Face it, I'm finished. You might as well spend your Sunday looking for another girlfriend, you'd be better off.'

Alex walks slowly over, arms ready to hold and comfort me. I push him away. 'If you're here you might as well get on with the cooking, I'm starving. They don't feed you anything decent in prison.'

Croquette potatoes doused liberally with gravy and garnished with thick slices of roast beef do wonders for my physical state, but little to ease the anguish when I look across at Alex.

'So when are you going to tell me?' I ask, fixing him with my most serious look.

'Tell you what?'

'What really happened at that house. Where you really were when I needed you. That sort of thing.'

'Everything I've told you is the truth, Jenny.'

'But you've not told me everything, have you? It's the bits you left out that matter to me.'

'I've been meaning to tell you but it's…complicated. I don't want you to get the wrong idea about me.'

'What, that you're not a liar or a cheat – that's the wrong idea is it?'

'Yes it is; I'm not. There you go, you see, I knew you'd react badly whatever I say.'

'So you have been lying all along. I knew it.'

'No, I haven't. Listen, Jenny. I've not told you everything, I admit that. I'll tell you now if you'll listen to me.'

I shove my plate aside and put my hands flat on the dining table. 'Go ahead, I'm listening.'

'It starts with my job. I've never told you much about it, have I?'

'No, you always said I'd be bored.'

'You probably would but that's less likely when I start my new one in October.'

'Why?'

'I'll no longer be seconded to DCLG then. From October I'm back at the Home Office.'

'Back? But I though you always looked after local government finance.'

'Not always, previously I was at the Cabinet Office in London, you know, working directly for the prime minister. Before that I was at the Home Office.'

'Home Office, that's the police isn't it? You never said you were a policeman.'

A shiver of distress catches my breath. My mind tries to adjust to Alex as the vengeful establishment, privy to my innermost thoughts. I really am doomed. I feel desperate sorrow at his subterfuge.

267

'Not a policeman, never a policeman. Policemen work for police authorities, local establishments. I've always worked for central government.

'So if you're not a policeman, what are you?'

'Strictly speaking I'm classed as a civil servant. That'll not change, even when I take up my new position.'

'Which is?'

'I'm going to be working for the National Crime Agency.'

'I don't get it. How can you move from local government to that, it makes no sense.'

'I've been involved all along in the NCA, first as a policy advisor in the Cabinet Office and now seconded to DCLG to implement the new financial arrangements between government and police authorities. Now that they're in place, I'm joining the NCA.'

'Oh.' The implications of all this are too immense to sink in. All I'm left with is the idea that Alex is saying goodbye. I can't see him being able to continue his relationship with me, particularly in view of my impending charges.

'So I won't be seeing you again, I suppose.'

Alex chews at his bottom lip. 'You never know what might happen. If things stay as they are I don't see why not. If the NCA picks up the case against you, that could be very awkward, but I doubt they will.'

'What do you mean?'

The doorbell rings. There's someone trying to get in to my flat. Alex leaves the table to investigate. I see him pause in front of the CCTV monitor then he shouts, 'Shit! Get down, under the table.'

I do nothing of the sort, instead I join him at the screen, looking at our visitors. Two men, one with a hand gun, the other brandishing a machine gun.

Alex is already talking on his phone, giving our address, telling them what's going on. The men outside appear agitated, now they're knocking and ringing more than waiting.

'Keep quiet,' Alex says. 'Pretend we aren't in, maybe they'll give up and go away.'

'No chance.' I point at the screen. 'That's the man from the van, they've been watching us, they know we're in here.'

The knocking turns to kicking. I watch as the man with the AK47 takes a short run and hits the door hard with his shoulder. This seems to hurt. He raises his weapon and fires. The sound of the gunshots is deafening. My body is reacting as if already hit. I can hardly prevent myself collapsing onto the floor in shock.

The man firing into the door suddenly twists and falls and the gun swings round. His partner tries to dodge but the stream of bullets rips into him. The noise stops. I can see two bodies lying on the floor at the top of the stairs. Alex's arms draw me to him. I settle into their protection as I continue to stare at the screen.

It takes twenty minutes for the police to arrive. In that time, one of the men manages to crawl out of sight of the cameras. The other stayed where he lay. Now the flat is filled with men wearing black body protection and grim faces. We're showing them the CCTV recording, I'm trying to understand what happened.

'Why did he shoot his mate?' I ask nobody in particular.

'Look at that, an AK47 in Salford on a Sunday afternoon, that's something I hoped I would never see.'

'It's your door, where did you get a door like that?'

'I had a break-in, they fitted a new security door.'

'What? The landlord gave you a door like that?'

'No, it was my guys fitted it.'

'That's a hell of a door, that is. That's all I can say. Normally one sharp kick is enough. Look at this.'

The policeman stops the video and backs it up a few seconds. 'That's where he's hit with his own bullet bouncing off your door.'

The way this policeman is talking I begin to wonder if they're going to prosecute me for killing the man with my door. There's probably a Health and Safety rule somewhere that requires me to have a notice prominently displayed, warning against ricochets. Something like 'WARNING BULLET PROOF DOOR, FIRE WITH CAUTION'. It wouldn't surprise me.

81

'Can you think of anyone who might want to harm you?' The policeman stands with his pen poised over his notebook. Now that the SWAT team has dispersed and the bodies cleared away normality returns in the form of repeated inane questions.

'It's your job to find out who they are and stop them. What kind of police force are you, allowing armed gunmen to wander the streets?' I'm not well, the shock is getting through to me now the adrenalin has gone. I'm back to being needy and tired. Desperate and vulnerable. If it weren't for Jim Almond and his magic door, I'd be dead. Alex is hovering uncertain, uncomfortable.

'They were outside in a blue van waiting for the right moment. The van should be full of clues.'

'Why didn't you report this van and these men?'

'Because I presumed that they were the police, no point in ringing up the police to tell them they're sitting outside my flat, they would already know.'

'Not necessarily,' he admits. 'But in this case it would have been wise to check with us. What made you think you were under police observation?'

'I'm under investigation, you should check with your colleagues. I went looking for a young girl who has gone missing. They arrested me, put me in prison and are now threatening to prosecute me for running a brothel. You lot have much to answer for.'

'Can you think of anyone who might have been responsible for this attack?'

I look across the flat to where Alex is in deep conversation with another policeman. 'I don't know who those men were. That's your job to find out, maybe you have a list of armed gangs that work around here?'

When they eventually stop asking questions it's only so that I can pick up a few things under supervision. I don't see why the inside of my flat is designated a crime scene. The men never got inside. That's the whole point, if they had I'd be dead. I'm not even permitted to scrape my cold croquettes into the bin, it all has to be preserved exactly, frozen in time to when the firing occurred.

We were questioned separately. Alex is back at his place waiting for me. He suggests that I leave the Range Rover and get a taxi as a security precaution. Whatever I do I doubt I'm any more secure at Alex's flat than I am here. At least my front door is Kalashnikov-resistant. One of the policemen who interviewed me suggested that I book into a hotel for a few nights. All he could offer me in terms of protection was an emergency phone number that would get me instant attention. When I asked him how that might work in practice he had no good answer. The general consensus seems to be that because the two gunmen are incapacitated I'm safe. My worry is that these were contract killers and there may be more where they came from. My opinion seems to carry little weight with the police.

I cram as much as I can into a suitcase and carry it to the waiting taxi.

'Where to?' he asks.

'Manchester Airport,' I tell him.

Alex worries me. I don't know what to say to him. There's this involvement of his in the National Crime Agency that he kept so quiet. It's difficult to see any future for us because of that. There's also the realisation that I'm not good for him. I've nearly got him killed twice already, third time lucky they say. If I go to him now it might turn out fatal for both of us. At first I think about flying off somewhere but they took my passport as part of my bail conditions. Then I remember that there's lots of armed police and very strict security measures at the airport. It's

272

possibly the worst place for a Kalashnikov-carrying murderer to do his work. Even if they do shoot me there, I'm betting they've got less chance of getting away than anywhere else. Being near the airport might not make me completely safe, but it's the best I can think of at the moment.

Bewley's Hotel is a vast, featureless place, crowded with travellers and businessmen and as near to the terminals as I can be. I suppose I should still be cowering in my modest bedroom but a whole day and night up there watching crap telly is all I can stand. The busy sprawl of the lounge and bar area makes me feel less isolated, even if I am a bit more accessible. I'd rather take my chances here, sitting in a crowded bar, than cowering alone upstairs.

Alex keeps himself foremost in my thoughts. Should I answer his texts? Tell him where I am? Invite him to join me, explain what I'm doing and how I'm feeling? Ask him what the hell did he think I would do when I found out he's a policeman?

The bell chimes again as my phone announces yet another text from him. I can't keep quiet, the poor man must be worried sick. I slowly form the words, I'M FINE, TALK TOMORROW X, then press the send button.

There's hardly a pause before the answer dings back. WHERE ARE YOU X. I feel an almost overwhelming need to tell him, then I can sit here and see if he comes to me. A very young waiter brings me another gin and tonic, distracts my line of thought. He sounds foreign, I wonder where he's from. When I think about it, most of the staff here seem to be from Eastern Europe. Maybe this lad is from the Ukraine, maybe he knows Kat. Perhaps she's actually serving drinks in a hotel somewhere, making a living, unmolested, not in any danger at all. I want to ask him how he got here, why he came, whether his family know where he is. But I don't. Because his answers can't help me at all. I know how ready I am to believe that the human cargo delivered to Trafford Trailers is destined for clean, honest work in shops, restaurants and hotels. The problem is I've seen things that tell me different.

'I'm waiting for my boyfriend,' I tell the man who sits down opposite me. Unlike two previous contestants, this one doesn't instantly stand up and move away.

'Then you might be better to do that somewhere a little less conspicuous, Mrs Parker.'

His voice triggers instant recognition and puts me back to the fear and hopelessness I experienced in the Ukraine. I look up and see the man for the first time. If it weren't for the voice I would have found him only vaguely familiar. Here, out of context, he could have quietly sat next to me all evening and I doubt I would have placed him. Without that unmistakable tone of superiority and condescension I might never have realised that Charles Smith, the man who got me out of Ukraine, is now accosting me in Manchester.

'Oh, it's you,' I say. The effects of the drinks in the day combine to make me worse than speechless. As I look at him I'm getting a good feeling through the surprise, as if I'm grateful he's here.

'On your way back to the Ukraine, I suppose?'

'No, not at all. I'm looking for you, actually. Now I've found you, I rather need you to listen very carefully to what I have to say.'

Visions of being extradited and being sent back to prison over there run through my head. I tighten with panic, fear begins to grip me yet again. I swallow the rest of my drink, savouring the bitter sweetness.

'I'd like another drink before we talk,' I say.

'There's not actually any time for socialising, I'm afraid. It's not safe here. We need to go somewhere a touch more secure.'

'I've got a room. We can go there.'

Mr Smith's face takes on a stern expression. He reaches over the table to gently touch my shoulder as I start to rise.

274

'I don't understand,' I say. 'Is this about that policeman in the Ukraine, are they wanting me back?'

His eyes are looking behind and beyond me. 'No, nothing of the sort. It's our current predicament I'm concerned about. I must say, Mrs Parker, you do seem to have the knack of making yourself unpopular wherever you go. Now don't look round, as they say, but I spy a person with evil intent towards you heading this way.'

I feel compelled to turn and look, to jump to my feet, to run for my life. Instead I watch Mr Smith, take my lead from his body language, wait for his instructions. He's on the edge of his seat, feet firmly planted, body upright and poised. A man passes my shoulder, I feel him look down at me, sense his reaction, then watch as he turns back towards the reception area.

'He's calling his colleagues. They'll no doubt be upstairs looking for you in your room. We really need to move quickly as soon as they appear.'

'They can't do anything to me in a public place, I'm safe here, aren't I? Can't you call the police, have them arrested?'

'No time for the police, by the time they get here it'll be far too late. These people won't mind killing everyone else here to get to you, if they need to. Okay now, hold my hand, don't let go.'

Mr Smith leads me casually to the bar. I can feel the danger behind me as if it were incandescent heat. He half drags me behind the bar. I watch the barman's look of surprise, his mouth opens in complaint, but we push past and through a door into a scruffy stock room. Smith opens an emergency door and we emerge into the cool evening air. There are crates of bottles stacked around the doorway, empties on their way out, full ones on their way in. One of these explodes, showering liquid and glass onto the side of my face. I have no time to discover whether the liquid running down my neck is blood or lemonade before Mr Smith yanks my arm violently, drags me across a flower bed and deposits me in tall bushes.

275

Something smacks into the tree above my head. I wriggle further into the foliage, aware of the wet earth caking my knees and the prospect of yet another ruined skirt.

'They're shooting at us.' I find myself automatically whispering now I'm in a hiding place. 'Can't you do something?'

'I suppose you want me to return fire,' Mr Smith hisses.

'Yes.'

'Not a wise move, I'm afraid. The gunman is concealed, maybe half a mile away, there are hundreds of civilians around and it will in any case reveal our exact position to him. Best we keep still for the moment. When his friends emerge, the sniper may stop firing in case he hits his colleagues.'

'But you do have a gun?' My hopes rise with a vision of Mr Smith calmly shooting our pursuers and saving my skin.

'I'd need something rather large and powerful if it were to be of any use, I'm afraid. My apologies if I seem inadequately equipped for the job in hand.'

My heart sinks again. I'm lying in the mud, pinned down by a sniper, waiting for armed thugs to come out and finish the job. Mr Smith is muttering to himself again, he's been keeping a running commentary going ever since we ran behind the bar. Another shot hits the trees. This time it's a long way above my head and well away to the side. Even so I flinch and cower, wanting to dig myself into the ground.

They should have followed us out by now, unless the barman decided he'd had enough traffic for the one evening and made a stand. They surely were closer behind us than this. Maybe they're scared of getting shot, waiting inside, trying to get a message to whoever it is that has the rifle. When they do come out I'm certainly going to die, there's no other outcome possible. I've nowhere to run to, nowhere left to hide. I send one last text to Alex.

SORRY I LOVE YOU. TELL TOBY I LOVE HIM X

82

The moment I send the text, I start regretting it. Here I am, trying to hide myself from deadly danger, the last thing I need is the distracting buzz that announces Alex's almost immediate reply. It may be the very last message I get.

The two men emerging cautiously from the back door of the bar are blatantly carrying handguns and the noise of my phone draws their attention instantly towards my clump of bushes.

I try to keep perfectly still, blend into the gloom. I'm torn between putting my head down to make my white face less obvious and keeping my eyes on the men. The temptation is too great, I watch through splayed fingers, my equivalent of a polar bear hiding its nose. My eyes are fixed on the open door, the cascade of yellow glitter strewn about, the lights blazing brightly through the windows of the hotel.

One man stays by the door, the other, tall and wearing a leather jacket, begins to walk slowly towards me. My breathing stops completely, I'm frozen in position. It's obvious from the way he's walking that he isn't sure of my exact location but he's on a course that will bring him very close to me. Charles seems to be adopting the same plan as I am, he's so still I can hardly register he's there at all.

The man in the leather jacket is almost upon me, he's about to start poking around in the bushes above my head. There's a sudden shout, 'Armed police, drop your weapons.' Two policemen are standing at the far corner of the building, machine guns pointed at the man in the doorway. The gunman nearest to me drops to his knees and continues to peer into the foliage. He's so close now, I can see his eyes.

My phone dings to remind me I've still got an unread text message. The sound jolts me as if I've received an electric shock. The eyes fasten onto me, the gun comes forward almost into my face.

'Oh shit,' Charles Smith's voice is followed by two deafening bangs almost simultaneously exploding in my ear. The man's expression changes from determination to surprise as he flops down onto the grass.

83

More shots. I feel bullets hitting the trees close by, then silence. Charles is muttering to himself again. I poke my head up to see two policemen dressed entirely in black standing over the other assassin slumped in the doorway.

Charles stops muttering, stands up, arms outstretched, gun held aloft. Then he walks slowly towards the policemen. I stay where I am, watching, too scared to move, not sure it's all over, still feeling in mortal danger.

Charles hands the gun to a policeman who takes out his own pistol, gives it to Charles then puts the discharged weapon in his own holster. When he comes back for me, Charles has to lift me to my feet, I'm almost too weak to stand, my legs are as numb as the rest of me.

'You said you didn't have a gun,' I say.

'Not really supposed to have one, thought I might be allowed an exception in this case. Having to fire the damn thing is a bit of a paperwork nightmare. Hopefully, I can sort out the mess with the help of that nice firearms officer over there. He is authorised to discharge a handgun so we might be able to come to some arrangement.'

The evening gloom is descending into darkness. There have been no shots for a long time, or what seems a long time. Mr Smith is still muttering sporadically. I can't make out what he's saying, nor can I hear any replies he might be getting.

'Ah, jolly good.' Mr Smith breaks silence. 'We can relax a little now. It seems our sniper has been apprehended. They found him on the top floor of Terminal 3 car park. The police are here now, evacuating the hotel. We should be making ourselves scarce.'

As he walks, I notice that he's taller than I expect him to be. Had I been asked to describe the man I met in the Ukraine, I would have used the words small, wimpish, academic, unremarkable as well as weird and snobbish. Now I can see that he's none of these things and I'm left confused at being so mistaken.

He leads me around the side of the hotel, into the car park, where we encounter two more uniformed policemen. Mr Smith waves some form of identification in their faces and they allow our passage. The same procedure works for the policeman on the barrier as we exit in Mr Smith's rather swish red Jaguar.

'I need to let Alex know I'm safe.' I look across at Mr Smith's calm features. 'I am safe, aren't I?'

'I'd rather appreciate it if you would turn off your mobile phone, you never know who might be tracking you, you understand. If you could remove the battery that would be even better.'

'It's an iPhone, it's all sealed up,' I tell him.

'Then pop the little SIM card out. There's a tiny hole in the top, use this to poke it.' He hands me a pin that he takes from the lapel of his jacket. I prod about until the SIM pops up and show it to him. He takes it from me and puts it in his pocket.

'Is that how you found me?' I ask.

'Oh yes, very useful things, mobile phones, if you're looking for someone. People use them to find out where their children are, husbands can keep an eye on their wives and vice versa. Marvellous. You also used your credit card to pay for your room, that's another useful piece of information.'

'Is that how they knew where I was?'

'Probably. Or you may have been followed. As I say, people aren't hard to find if you know how.'

'What about Alex, he'll be worried.'

'Don't fret. Mr Hartley is being kept fully informed regarding your situation.'

'You know Alex?'

'Not personally but I believe he has worked in our department previously.'

'What department is that?' I'm pretty sure I already know.

'Security Services.'

So Alex is a spy. I'm not surprised, there's been something not quite right about his job all along. First he says one thing and then another. All that business of DCLG and then he tells me he's in police meetings. Has he been spying on me? I can't believe that my Alex would do that. There's no way he'd betray me, my trust, my love, everything.

'I can see you're a little perplexed,' Smith continues.

He's right about that, I'm puzzled and almost frantic with it.

'I'll explain something about your Mr Hartley that might assist. He can be best described as a mandarin, or a mandarin in the making if I'm to be strictly accurate. Very soon he will be running this glorious realm of ours and, if I may make so bold, doing a pretty good job of it.'

'Mandarin?'

'I beg your pardon, mandarin is a rather opaque term. Let's say Head of Government Department instead, shall we.'

'So Alex is going to be a politician and run the country?'

'No.' Smith's face creases into a wide grin. He seems to find my question very amusing. 'Certainly not. Mr Hartley is a civil servant, part of the permanent establishment. Politicians come and go, the smooth operation of government can hardly be entrusted to such a temporary and transient population.'

'But you said he was a spy, so he must still be one, mustn't he?'

'Certainly not, and anyway Mr Hartley was engaged in a strategic role rather than an operational one. He was responsible for the concept of the National Crime Agency, an organisation he helped set up from the Cabinet Office. Now he's implementing the changeover to the new regime, a job which I wouldn't wish on my worst enemy. However if he somehow manages to pull it off without civil war, riots and a general strike, it will do his career no harm at all.'

'So he's not a spy?'

'Far from it.'

'Or a politician?'

'Certainly not.'

'Oh.' I'm grateful to Mr Smith but I can't understand why Alex has kept all this from me. Or perhaps he's been telling me about his job all along and I've not really listened. Everything Mr Smith tells me is vaguely familiar, worryingly so. Most likely my own lack of interest in anything other than my own business is what's made me so ignorant. It's a big relief though. My mind is teeming with instances where Alex's behaviour seemed odd. Now I think back, it's no wonder he's interested in finding Kat, dealing with traffickers, using tracking devices. He's already worked in that sort of environment and now he has the likes of Hector Brighouse in police committees to deal with. None of it is to do with me. He's not spying on me. He's looking after me, supporting me, protecting me. He probably even loves me. The sadness at having to give him up when I go to prison is even greater now that I can trust him again – that's if I survive long enough to be convicted.

The apartment I'm left hiding in is pleasant enough, part of a big house, set back from Mauldeth Road. A young man who introduces himself as Tariq pops in twice a day to check on me and run any errands I need him to. His shopping skills are not great, half of the list I give him is generally unobtainable. I suspect he uses the Tesco Metro rather than a proper shop. Fresh vegetables seem to be considered exotic items. I've put kale on the list for three days running and my wish remains unfulfilled. It may be the shop but I suspect the motley collection of tins and frozen packets are the product of Tariq's idea of what's good for me.

My suitcase from the hotel arrived on day two, at least avoiding the difficult problem of clothes shopping. There's been no sign of Charles Smith since he left me here and suggested that, although I am free to go as I please, it would be prudent to stay indoors until it's safe. The concept of it becoming safe is an appealing one, it would be nice to think that there were no more gunmen after my blood.

Tariq's idea of fish, frozen cod in batter suitable for microwave cooking, is warmed up and on my plate, together with boiled frozen peas and a generous portion of instant mash. I am hungry but not yet starving. The peas are quite nice but the slab of fish is unappetising and inedible.

I've kept the TV on all the time for company and to distract me from reality. There's been only a brief mention of the attempt to assassinate me at Bewley's Hotel on the local news. It describes only a precautionary evacuation following suspected terrorist activity. There's not been any mention of a sniper firing or a woman cowering in the bushes.

I've been thinking about Alex and how I misjudged him. It's so easy for me to dismiss the possibility that he loves me. I've never felt worthy of anyone's love, that's why I can't trust him. All this chasing around inviting danger is my way of punishing myself. When I get into trouble, it's all I deserve. I need to be held in the thrall of quiz shows and soap operas to avoid confronting myself about this. Who is driving me to destruction? Why am I constantly throwing my life away? All I know is I've done it very efficiently. There seems no way back to salvation for me now unless I can be with Alex.

'Push, push harder then.'

'I'm pushing as hard as I can, Jenny.'

'Try bashing it with your shoulder.'

'Ouch, that hurts.'

'I think you've loosened it, try again.'

The door to my Salford Quays apartment is sticking again. This time I'm inside, trying to admit Alex. Three more solid thumps and it springs open, revealing Alex red-faced and displeased. I put my arms around his waist and hang on tight. I feel his hands on my back, warm and comforting, reminding me of what I'm missing.

'You'll have to get that fixed,' Alex says.

'I think it's the weather, it's been very damp lately.' I don't want Alex's attention on my door, I need it on me.

'I don't suppose you've considered the possibility that it might have something to do with the bullet holes?'

'Okay, you're right, it has crossed my mind.' There are five deep indentations, made when the Kalashnikov was fired at my door. The force of them must have been enough to distort the whole thing. One of the bullets bounced off and put paid to the two men intent on murdering me. My special door saved both our lives. It deserves a little consideration and sympathy now that it doesn't function properly.

'I'll have it replaced but only after I move out.'

'It's not a great advert for selling the flat,' Alex says.

'I don't much care at the moment, to be honest. They've got me hidden away at a safe house in Didsbury. A secret location where nobody can ever find me.'

'Should you have come back here?' Alex asks.

'I needed to see you. I told them I needed to collect some things, that I was desperate. They said they'd come back for me in an hour, but for all I know they could be hanging around on the staircase.'

'I didn't notice anyone when I came up.'

I tighten my grip on him. 'I'll forgive you if you forgive me,' I say.

'There's nothing to forgive.'

'Oh yes there is.'

'It's okay, I forgive you then, but I don't know what for.' Alex draws back and gives me one of his careful looks.

'You don't get away that easily, Alex Hartley. First you've got to say you're sorry and promise to be truthful in the future.'

'I've always told you the truth, Jenny.'

'No you haven't. You've been deceiving me, it's caused me so much pain and worry. Say you're sorry.'

'I'm sorry, Jenny, for causing you distress, that wasn't my intention.'

'I know it wasn't. If it were, I'd not have let you in.'

'You hardly let me in,' Alex smiles, 'I had to bash down your door.'

'Yes, but with my permission.'

'I still don't get it, Jenny. When do you think I've deceived you?'

'All the time you pretended not to be a policeman.'

'But I'm not a policeman.'

'There you go again, yes you are. You're in the National Crime Agency, you admitted it yourself.'

'That doesn't make me a policeman, Jenny.'

'Of course it does, what else could it make you?'

'I'm an administrator.'

'Hah – pull the other one, you're a policeman. You used to be a spy, now you're a policeman. Admit it.'

'Look Jenny, if I worked for the National Health Service would you expect me to be able to cure your diseases, perform surgery?'

'Not unless you were a doctor.'

'And not everyone who works for the NHS is a doctor. There're nurses, cleaners, orderlies, receptionists, lots of different jobs and administrators, managers, accountants. It's the same in the NCA. We have some policemen, but not all of us are.'

'You'd make a good policeman, though,' I laugh.

'Why's that?'

'You're ever so good at bashing down doors. Maybe you should do that for a living instead of being a mandarin orange.'

'What are you talking about?' he laughs.

'That's what Charles called you. It doesn't sound very appealing.' I grimace at the joke that appeared entirely of its own volition.

'There you see, even your hero Charles knows I'm an administrator. You should listen to him.' Alex looks relaxed and welcoming now.

'Did you miss me while I've been hidden away?' I ask.

'Yes, of course I did.'

'What did you do for sex without me?'

Alex's face twists. 'I masturbated vigorously and often.'

'Aha. But did you think of me while you were doing it?'

'Most of the time I did.'

'Which bit of me were you thinking about?'

'Your inquisitiveness was what generally got me going.'

'No, not a characteristic, I mean a body part, which one did you visualise?'

'All of them. I started at the top of your head and worked my imagination slowly downwards. By the time I'd reached the tip of your big toe I was ready to burst.'

I flop backwards onto the settee and wiggle my toes in the air. 'Here they are in all their erotic glory. You can start with them this time as a special treat.'

Alex is sitting on the side of the bed, feet firmly planted on the floor to bear my weight. His hands hold my thighs, controlling my movements. Because my legs are flat on the bed I can't push myself up, I have to rely on him to move his penis in and out. He's all smoothness and gentleness. His hands encourage deep, slow breaths and all I want is to hold my breath, clench my thighs, ride him to quick release. I need him to abandon his calm, to lose himself in mechanical passion, to fuck me hard and quickly.

I need the tension in my abdomen to be gone in one flare of instant gratification. Instead, I have Alex exhorting me to breathe, inviting me to feel into his touch, guiding my awareness. Now he's slowly sliding himself into me, driving me half crazed with lust. There's no alternative but to let it happen Alex's way. I let my urgency subside with my deep breathing, feel the exquisite longing, let it go, breathe it away, then feel it return with greater intensity. Breathing in fullness and pleasure, breathing out, spreading the glorious energy up my spine and into my head.

We're rocking gently together, he pushes deeper, touches my very core and retreats, leaving me tingling and longing for a return. The waves are beginning to envelop me. I'm no longer able to breathe with them, to spread them away from my genitals. I am being overwhelmed, taken over. My head can't contain the white hot explosions that are shooting through my insides. For a few shuddering moments I'm transported into a helpless, screaming abandonment. As the waves of exquisite pleasure subside I find myself collapsing, sobbing into Alex's shoulder, breathless and spent. Then I feel him move gently inside me again, a tiny spark of urgency ignites and the waves of pleasure begin to lap against me. My exhaustion subsides, the beautiful process begins again. When it's over, I lie back and hear the persistent knocking for the first time. I wonder how long they've been waiting to take me back to the safe house.

'Oh I beg your pardon, Mrs Parker, please do carry on. I don't want to interrupt your meal.'

Mr Smith appears at the kitchen door, continues his entrance and sits down at the table. I push away my plate.

'You can have it if you're hungry.'

'That's very kind, but I couldn't possibly eat a thing.' He looks down his nose at the mess on my plate.

'Have you got them?'

'I'm sorry, got who?'

'The ones who were trying to kill me.'

'Of course, my apologies. We've been questioning some of the unfriendlies we apprehended at Bewley's Hotel, at least the ones we identified. We also have the sniper in custody, so that's a positive thing.'

'So I'm okay now? It's safe for me to go home now?'

'Not exactly. We can't be sure that there aren't others out there who have been engaged for the exact same purpose.'

'Those men, they're only the hired help, aren't they?'

'Yes, you're right. Apprehending them doesn't necessarily help your situation.'

'So I'm stuck here for ever, eating frozen food and watching daytime television?'

'Oh dear, Mrs Parker, we can't let that dreadful fate befall a brave lady like yourself. We do have a proposal that might do the trick, though it rather depends on your willingness to participate.'

'It sounds like I've not got much in the way of choice. What do I have to do?'

'In a nutshell, work for us. Become a valued addition to the service, assist in the protection of your country. How does that sound?'

'It sounds simple but I don't see how that can possibly help me. Why should working for the Security Service protect me? I can hardly go around announcing the fact to anyone that might have a grudge.'

'Of course you can't, but it doesn't work like that. If you agree to our terms and conditions, as it were, our job will be to protect you, as one of our own.'

'So you'll be following me around?'

'Not exactly, but we will be well placed to keep an eye out for you. It's more a case of altered status. Most organisations wouldn't take your contract if you were under our protection. It's a matter of economic viability for them. If they start killing our people, they know that our response is going to be very bad for business.'

'What do I have to do, move to London, turn up at your office every day?'

'Nothing so formal. You will be more of an associate than an employee. You'll go about your normal business, apart from the occasional task that we might give you.'

'Do I get paid?'

'Certainly not, though certain expenses might be claimed providing the correct forms are completed and prior authorisation is obtained.'

'What if I don't like the job, what if I refuse to do it?'

'Then, Mrs Parker, there will be no hard feelings at all. We both go our separate ways, tear up our unwritten agreement, if that were possible. Naturally you would no longer be a member of our team.'

'So you would no longer protect me?'

'Obviously we are committed to continue to protect you in exactly the same way we try to protect every citizen of this fine country. Our resources are limited, however, as you are fully aware.'

'So I'd be on my own and at the mercy of hit men again?'

'Only insofar as our special interest in you would no longer be maintained.'

'I get it, Mr Smith, I don't have any choice at all, do I?'

Mr Smith sits silently, hands placed flat on the table, face relaxed.

'I won't be much use to you if they send me to prison though, I can't do any of your tasks in there, can I?'

'I don't think that will be a problem, Mrs Parker. Although there's no guarantee, the police do tend to lose interest in you if it's clear that your continued freedom is a matter of national security.'

This makes my heart leap with hope. All this talk seems academic if I'm being prosecuted but now, if they drop the charges, it suddenly all makes sense. They have me completely under their control, though. Unless I do everything they say I'll either be killed or sent to prison. As long as I co-operate, I've got a chance.

'So where do I sign?'

Mr Smith smiles. 'No signature required, it's all about trust.'

'Will I be working for you, will you be my contact?'

'We may see each other from time to time. You will be part of a team run by a man we refer to as the Brigadier.'

'Brigadier?'

'Yes, he was until very recently the Head of the Territorial Army, a remarkable man, enormous field experience, very capable. You'll get on well with him. He's very happy to have you.'

'When do I get to meet him?'

'That depends on whether you decide to turn up this time.'

'I don't get you.'

'Sorry for being opaque, my poor attempt at humour. You're selling your company to him, his name is Hector Brighouse.'

'Hector? A Brigadier? But he runs Security Group.'

291

'Ah, the wonders of the Territorial Army system. That's the way it works, everyone in the territorials has a day job, even the big cheeses like Hector. It's strictly for part time soldiers, though still deadly serious for all that.'

'I had no idea.'

'Why would you? Anyway, he asked me to get you thinking about your first task. There are two names on this piece of paper, both represent a major threat to our national interests. You will be helping him to bring them down.'

Smith gives me a sealed white envelope with my name neatly typed on the front.

'Before I agree to help you, there's one thing I have to have in return.'

'Apart from our protection?'

'Yes, I'm absolutely adamant about this. I need you to help me find Lottie's sister, Kat. And I need you to put a stop to the traffickers who are trying to kill me.'

'That's two things.' Charles smiles, one of his more annoying ones.

'It might only be one, but okay, two things if you're going to be picky.'

'I'm sure we can arrange something once you're fully on board. In the meantime I suggest you have a think about how you're going to help us.'

I wait until he's gone before I open the envelope. The two names inside are:

PETER O'BRIAN

FERGUS LAFFERTY.

The End